pu1

THE MURDER OF GONZAGO

THE MURDER
OF GONZAGO

R. T. Raichev

Constable • London

Constable & Robinson Ltd
55–56 Russell Square
London WC1B 4HP
www.constablerobinson.com

First published in the UK by Constable,
an imprint of Constable & Robinson, 2012

First US edition published by SohoConstable,
an imprint of Soho Press, 2012

Soho Press, Inc.
853 Broadway
New York, NY 10003
www.sohopress.com

A copy of the British Library Cataloguing in Publication
Data is available from the British Library

UK ISBN: 978-1-78033-101-0

US ISBN: 978-1-61695-086-6
US Library of Congress number: 2011038392

Printed and bound in Great Britain

1 3 5 7 9 10 8 6 4 2

MIX
Paper from
responsible sources
FSC
www.fsc.org   FSC® C018575

For Imogen
'Tis the sharpness of her mind that gives the
edge to my pains!
In appreciation and with much love.

Contents

'All is not well;
I doubt some foul play.'
Hamlet, Act I scene ii

'One mustn't refuse the unusual, if it is offered to one.'
Agatha Christie, *Passenger to Frankfurt*

Prologue

Death in a Hot Climate

Three minutes passed before they realized he was dead and another two before it was established how he had died, though any suspicious observer might have argued that at least one of the five people in the room had been aware of both facts all along.

'Don't go near him,' Dr Sylvester-Sale said, removing the cardboard crown from his head.

'Stop filming. I am talking to you, Augustine. Get the bloody camera out of the way at once!' As Clarissa Remnant raised her hand, her bracelet in the shape of a coiled serpent glinted ominously.

'But – how is that possible?' Basil Hunter said. 'Are you – are you sure, SS?'

'Positive.'

'Why are you still filming, Augustine? Are you out of your mind? Didn't you hear what I said?' Clarissa Remnant's eyes flashed. Her crown was still on her head.

'We must turn the music off,' Louise Hunter said. 'We really must.'

But nobody did. The scratchy LP continued to revolve on the ancient wind-up gramophone with its huge brass horn, and 'The Bilbao Song' was followed by 'Le Roi d'Aquitaine'.

The door opened and a middle-aged woman in glasses entered the room. 'It's so hot – I am afraid I felt faint – I don't think the air-conditioning system is working properly, is it?' She sounded breathless.

She stood peering at the body on the couch. 'Is Lord Remnant unwell?'

'He is dead,' Basil Hunter said.

'Would one of you take the camera from Augustine? The man is a complete idiot, or else he's doing it on purpose!' There was something terrifying about Clarissa's white make-up and lips the colour of old blood.

'*Dead?* But how dreadful,' Hortense Tilling whispered.

'The little beast,' Dr Sylvester-Sale said. He was looking in the direction of the french windows. 'He did it after all. He said he would – and he did.'

'I don't think you should jump to conclusions, Syl,' Clarissa said.

It was perhaps unfortunate that it was to Hortense Tilling, Clarissa's aunt, that Augustine handed the camera.

'Oh dear. Is this the right way to hold it? It's not upside down, is it? I'm terribly sorry but I'm hopeless with cameras,' Hortense moaned. 'Perfectly hopeless.'

Having been very pale, her face was flushed now. She was frightened but also excited. Her thoughts were confused. Dead – Lord Remnant was no more – it wasn't dreadful at all – one always said things one didn't mean – the beast was dead – destroyed at last – *questo è il fin di chi fa mal* – this is the end of evildoers – there should be singing and dancing in the streets – the death of those who do evil is always the same as their lives!

Don Giovanni was her favourite opera.

'I have no idea how this thing works,' she said. 'No idea at all.'

'It doesn't matter how it works. Really, Aunt Hortense! *Just turn the bloody thing off.*' Clarissa Remnant sounded at the end of her tether.

'We must call an ambulance,' Louise Hunter said.

'I don't think that would be much use,' Clarissa said.

'The police – we *must* call the police. It would be wrong if we didn't call the police. We'd be breaking the law.'

'Shut up, Louise,' Clarissa said. 'Just shut up.'

The next moment she turned and left the room.

Renée Glover was the only one who hadn't uttered a word. Clarissa wasn't going to call the police. Of course not. Clarissa would come up with a plan. Basil Hunter would go along with anything Clarissa said, of that Renée had no doubt. So would Syl. Old Hortense was still struggling with the camera. Louise Hunter seemed larger than ever and she had an outraged expression on her face. Renée tried to catch Dr Sylvester-Sale's eye and failed. They'd agreed to be careful, but surely they could look at each other when Clarissa was not about?

The silk curtains were drawn across the french windows and they stirred slightly. Was that the evening breeze – or was someone standing there?

Renée walked up to the curtains and pulled them apart sharply. She didn't believe the killer would be outside.

Behind the net curtains the windows gaped wide open.

Renée Glover walked out through the french windows and glanced round the terrace. No one. The warm Caribbean night closed in on her. The stars shone with fierce brilliancy – was that Canopus? The full moon above the palm trees had a purplish tinge. Only an hour previously she had stood on this very spot, admiring the crimson-streaked sunset and listening to the surf and the mournful cries of seagulls . . .

All was quiet now. There was not a breath of wind, just a wonderful balminess in the air. The only sound was that of the insects, a kind of low, steady hiss produced by the rubbing together of thousands of gossamer wings. A moth brushed lightly against her face.

She gazed into the night, at the great avenue of spreading palms thick with shadows, at the harbour lights in the distance. Odd, that she was not at all afraid. Suddenly she heard a tiny splashing noise close by, then another. Stephan? He liked sitting beside the pool, dropping in pebbles.

Her nostrils twitched as they caught a whiff of something she thought was familiar. *Very* familiar. But it belonged to a different place – it belonged to London – to Belgrave Square—

Moonlight lay in knife-shaped patterns on the terrace. She took a step to the left and stumbled over something—

A monstrous head with preternaturally long ears leered up at her.

The head was made of papier-mâché. A gleaming object lay beside it. *Two* gleaming objects. Renée glanced over her shoulder, then stooping, she quickly picked up the smaller of the two objects and put it in her pocket.

It had taken her exactly three seconds to realize what the smaller object was and to whom it belonged. Had she been right about the smell then?

A moment later the others joined her on the terrace. Someone gasped—

Renée Glover's expression didn't change. She prided herself on being able to exercise perfect control over her emotions.

1

Before the Funeral

In St John's Wood Lady Grylls was talking to her butler.

She was not wild about going to Roderick Remnant's funeral, she wasn't in any way *obliged*, she was merely a cousin twice removed, but there was nothing better to do at the moment, so would Provost have the goodness to get her hat out? Her *funeral* hat, she added, not her wedding one. The two hats were strangely similar and no one would notice, so perhaps it didn't really matter, though of course one liked to do the right thing.

And could she have another glass of sherry? She didn't think the hat needed cleaning, or dusting, for that matter. She had worn it only the other week, for Caroline Heppenstall's funeral. Caroline had been a mere seventy-two. These days Lady Grylls went to more funerals and memorial services than weddings. Most of her friends' grandchildren were already married and some of the *great*-grandchildren too, now wasn't that extraordinary? Made one feel positively ancient.

'But don't misunderstand me, Provost, I am not in the least depressed. Not a bit of it. I am now quite used to funerals. Well, I'll be eighty-two this year, so that's perhaps how it should be. How many funerals do you think I have attended so far?'

'This year, m'lady?'

'No. In my entire life.'

'I couldn't say, m'lady.'

'Come on. Have a guess.'

'A thousand, m'lady? Two thousand?'

'Don't be silly, Provost. Twenty-eight. One day I sat down and calculated. My doctor keeps telling me I need to exercise the old cerebellum, otherwise it will simply stop functioning. I may have omitted one or two, mind.' She took a sip of sherry. 'I will go to Roderick's funeral, but I don't think I will attend his memorial service. *If* there is a memorial service. I cannot imagine anything in Roderick's life that deserves to be celebrated as such. I have an idea he won't be much mourned.'

'Perhaps not, m'lady, but it will be some time before Lord Remnant is forgotten.'

'Roderick's personality may have been more forcefully colourful than those of the bland and timid masses, but one does tend to forget people the moment they stop coming to dinner, Provost. Certain people one even forgets *during* dinner. It's most disconcerting. You look across the table and you wonder, who the hell *is* that? You don't think I am suffering from Old Timer's, do you?'

'Old Timer's, m'lady?'

'That's what Mary Gaunt calls it, awfully funny. You know what I mean – the brain-melting disease. I seem to have forgotten its name, which is a bad enough sign.'

'I don't think you are suffering from Alzheimer's, m'lady,' Provost said.

Lady Grylls took another sip of sherry. She had known Roderick Remnant's first wife, the tragic Deirdre, rather well. Deirdre had been at school with one of Lady Grylls's younger cousins. Lady Grylls didn't care much for Roderick Remnant's *second* wife, who was the widow now. She had been younger than him, though no spring chicken, on the wrong side of forty, or so Lady Grylls believed, though forty-five was considered 'young' these days. 'What was her name now?'

'Clarissa, m'lady. Née Vuillaumy.'

Lady Grylls cupped her ear. '*Villainy*? How terribly interesting. Suggestive, wouldn't you say? Clarissa is apparently one of those women who don't improve with age, only learn new ways of misbehaving themselves. She has a son, but he is not Roderick's son.'

'Lady Remnant has a son from a previous marriage, m'lady. The young man's name is Stephan Farrar.'

'Stephan, that's right. I understand he takes drugs. Same as your boy used to do, only worse, much worse, I think. Gerard Fenwick is Roderick's only brother. I used to be great chums with Felicity Fenwick's mama. Gerard will be – what?'

'The thirteenth earl. According to Debrett's.'

'It seems to me you know too much about the aristocracy, Provost, it's positively unhealthy. You need to get yourself a girlfriend. Gerard writes, or tries to. Everybody nowadays seems terribly keen on becoming a writer. Can't understand it myself. My niece-in-law writes detective stories, though she says her advances are staggeringly small. Felicity dabbles in interior decorating and sells furniture, I believe.'

'The new Lady Remnant has a shop in South Kensington, m'lady.'

'The extraordinary things you know, Provost. You should be on *Mastermind*. The Fenwicks are frightfully nice. As it happens, Hugh's got his eye on Felicity's Damascus chest, so it's a small world. I have an idea neither Felicity nor Gerard cares for Roderick's island. What *was* the island called? There was a TV documentary about it. Somewhere in the Caribbean.'

'The Grenadin Island. One of the Valance group. Previously known as the St Philippe group.'

'What fun that documentary was. I believe we watched it together, Provost, didn't we? It made Roderick look quite mad. That high-pitched giggle! Those snow-white pyjamas! Never took them off. Had *fifteen pairs*, he said. Boasted about it. Would *you* boast about it if you had fifteen pairs of snow-white pyjamas, Provost?'

'No, m'lady.'

'The way he strutted about, fanning himself! He looked a bit like Alec Guinness playing Lawrence of the Caribbean in an Ealing comedy.'

'It was not the most flattering of representations, m'lady.'

'Far from it. Well, Roderick had only himself to blame, though I don't think he was the sort of man who blamed himself for anything. The camera made a big thing of his outsize sombrero, his temper tantrums and his fan. How did he explain the fan now?'

'Lord Remnant said that in another existence he must have been a geisha, m'lady.'

'*The Grenadier of Grenadin*. That's what the documentary was called, I believe? No doubt a reference to the fact that Roderick had been in the Guards as a young man. But why did they call it a *meta*-documentary? Have you any idea?'

'I am afraid I haven't, m'lady.'

'I must say Roderick behaved terribly badly. At one point the camera showed him waving money at what was said to be a transvestite prostitute. He then kicked the documentary director in the shin and hit him on the head with his fan! Remember, Provost?'

'I do remember, m'lady.'

'That poor chap! It looked as though he was going to cry. Roderick said he had many abilities including irritability. That was terribly funny, though of course one could see what an impossible character he was.'

'Lord Remnant gave every appearance of enjoying himself. He talked about his profligate lifestyle with considerable relish.'

Lord Remnant had boasted of spending forty million pounds on buying and developing property and throwing parties. He had admitted to blowing ten thousand on a special kind of tent which had been hand-made in Ceylon and delivered to Grenadin by helicopter.

'Back in the seventies those parties were considered the epitome of glitz and glamour, Provost. Or what in the seventies passed for glitz and glamour. Roderick became known as the Jet Set Monarch. He was always photographed wearing a crown . . . I believe he was interested in witchcraft as well?'

'Lord Remnant dabbled in voodoo or hoodoo, m'lady. Apparently he attempted to resurrect the dead.'

'His idea of a party trick, I suppose. Well, it seems to be the right part of the world for that sort of thing.'

Provost cleared his throat. 'Lord Remnant and his family were said to be under a curse, m'lady. It has been claimed that he built La Sorcière on top of a piece of West Indian holy ground, which he should never have done.'

'The curse, yes. It all comes back to me now. Well, I don't know. It's true that Remnants have had all sorts of problems. Roderick never had any children. Poor wretched Deirdre became a kleptomaniac following her menopause, then she hanged herself most inexplicably. They say Clarissa has had as many lovers as there are Chinamen in China. I am sure you know all about Clarissa's lovers, Provost?'

'I am afraid not, m'lady,' Provost said after a little pause.

'The stepson is a drug fiend and he's got a screw loose. Roderick has now died at the comparatively young age of sixty-eight and the title has passed to his younger brother who is a compulsive scribbler, though he can't get anything published.'

'Most distinguished families are said to have a curse. The Sassoons, the Tennants, the Kennedys, the Grimaldis—'

'Sometimes, Provost, I wonder if a curse is not just a handy way of excusing generations of self-indulgence and general bad behaviour.'

'Certain members of the Royal Family used to be regular visitors at La Sorcière, but then they suddenly and for no apparent reason stopped going.'

'Is that to be blamed on the curse as well?' Lady Grylls appeared amused. 'You don't have to speak of the Royal Family in such hushed tones, Provost. Ridiculous. I don't suppose you still pray for the Royal Family, do you? You do? Goodness. Remnant parties were the stuff of legend. One had to be terribly amusing or good-looking or fascinating or outrageous to get an invitation to a Remnant party. Not any longer, it seems. Still, they appear to have been getting up to all sorts of silly things. The latest craze – there was something about it in the *Mail*. What was it? Miltonesque litanies?'

'Shakespearean capers, my lady.'

'Sounds like the kind of thing that would drive me mad. Who was the ugly character in Shakespeare who lived on an island?'

'Caliban, m'lady.'

'Are you sure, Provost? I thought the Caliban was a somewhat extreme Afghan nationalist movement.'

'That's the Taliban, m'lady.'

'I wonder if the stepson will be at the funeral. The stepson is subject to sudden and intense disorientation, or so they say. His head, apparently, poses great problems for the medical brains of Harley Street. They keep sending him to some terribly expensive place, but then he comes back and the whole thing starts all over again. He hates his stepfather. *Hated*, one should say. I understand he threatened to kill him on a great number of occasions.'

2

Conversation Piece

'Do correct me if I am wrong, my dear, but you seem to be enhaloing the name La Sorcière with a whole new morbid aura,' said the former Gerard Fenwick, now the thirteenth Earl Remnant.

'I am certain they are all involved in some way, the whole Sorcière set. Clarissa and Glover and Miss Tilling and Dr Sylvester-Sale,' Felicity Fenwick said. '*And* the Hunters. The Sorcière Six, as the press may well dub them one day. On the analogy of the Tapas Seven.'

'Can't imagine the Hunters being involved in anything.'

'They all had a guilty air about them. They looked conspiratorial. They kept exchanging furtive glances. Don't tell me you didn't notice.'

'I'm afraid I didn't.' The new Lord Remnant crossed over to the drinks trolley and poured himself a whisky. 'No one is at their best at funerals. I thought they looked subdued and terribly pale and pinched, but then didn't we all?'

'You couldn't look pale even if you tried.'

It was the kind of cutting remark that made Gerard Fenwick wonder about the state of their marriage. Better pretend he hadn't heard.

He raised the whisky glass to his lips. 'That was an embarrassing little scene, wasn't it? Never imagined

Tradewell was an emotional chap. Falling to his knees – praying in that booming voice, with his hands clasped above his head. *Sobbing.*'

'I am sure Tradewell was crying for himself. His fate is a bit uncertain now.'

'Tradewell's an oxymoron. *An emotional butler.* But you may be right. Don't suppose Clarissa cares much for Tradewell. I know he "goes" with the house, but we may not need him either.'

'We don't *have* to live at Remnant, do we?'

'We'll be expected to put in an appearance every now and then. *Noblesse oblige* and all that sort of rot.'

Gerard Fenwick stood beside the window, nursing his drink, gazing at the sky, which was a gash of crimson and orange. His thoughts turned to Renée Glover. The way she had smiled at him – *such* a sweet smile. Renée was genuinely interested in his writing . . .

Felicity said, 'No second thoughts about starting the – what is it you wanted to call it? Dilettanti Drag?'

'Dilettanti Droug. Was that meant to be funny? It will be a small but rather exclusive press,' he said stiffly. She doesn't understand me, he thought. She doesn't understand me at all.

'Oh yes. *Droug* is Russian for "fiend", I keep forgetting.'

'It's Russian for "friend". There is a difference, you know.' Felicity was doing it on purpose, he was convinced of it. She was trying to get at him. 'No, no second thoughts, my dear. No reason why I should have changed my mind, is there?'

'Clarissa says she'll move to La Sorcière permanently. Grenadin clearly agrees with her.'

'Clearly. It doesn't agree with me. Thank God we only got invited once. So hot – and all those mosquitoes! I don't suppose we were their sort of people. We don't seem to scintillate.'

'I wouldn't have said the Hunters scintillated exactly. Louise Hunter is so fat. The Hunters lack – what is it they lack? A significant *something.*'

'Charm? Unity? An edge?'

'That's it. No edge.' Felicity nodded. 'I have known beach balls with more edge to them than the Hunters.'

'I believe they are frightfully mismatched. Louise is dire, I agree, but I don't think there's anything really wrong with Hunter.'

'I don't suppose I could ever like Louise Hunter, not even if she were to save me from drowning or death by fire.'

'I feel sorry for Hunter. He is a first-class farmer. I wouldn't be able to do half the jobs he does. He *understands* cattle . . . When was it we saw my brother on the box? Was it last year or the year before?'

'Last year – you mean that ghastly documentary, don't you?'

'Yes. It was ghastly, wasn't it? Roderick's teeth didn't seem to fit and he never for a moment took off that ludicrous hat. He seemed peculiarly rejuvenated, didn't you think?'

'People always look different on the box,' Felicity said dismissively. 'Would you get me a Scotch, Gerard? With plenty of soda.' Kicking off her shoes, she sat on the sofa. 'I am chilled to the bone. Hate funerals. The trawl from Remnant Regis to the crematorium was unbearable. It's a miracle I survived.'

'I know exactly what you mean. I feel as stiff as a varnished eel myself.'

'And that vicar, how he droned on! I didn't feel a flicker of spiritual devotion, not a flicker, only a vague kind of annoyance. I can't imagine your brother being in heaven now playing the harp – can you?'

'I don't think the vicar said anything about a harp, did he? It would have been unscriptural.'

'I *hate* the idea of an afterlife. The shocking insecurity of it all – the spectacular lack of privacy – bumping into people you'd hoped never to see again or wondering why so-and-so was not there! It would be my idea of hell.'

'Plenty of soda, did you say? Wise girl. Here you are, my dear.' He handed her a glass. I am not sure I like having drinks with my wife, he thought. I used to, but I no longer do. And she is wrong if she expects me to start discussing my religious beliefs with her. 'Chin-chin, my dear.'

'Chin-chin . . . The moment the coffin disappeared into the furnace, the Sorcière Six all looked immensely relieved. Why *did* they look so relieved?'

'Scotch and soda is my favourite drink,' he said. 'No question about it. Next to frozen Daiquiris.'

'Clarissa was wearing all her pearls and all her diamonds, which was certainly *de trop*, and *such* a theatrical little hat. To start with, her face was a studied Madonna Dolorosa, but then it began to crumple—'

'You don't think Clarissa loved Roderick?'

'Don't be ridiculous.'

'Clarissa is the voguish vamp type. In profile she brings to mind Madame Sarkozy.'

'Clarissa is so overloaded with sex, it sparkles. She reminds me of one of those golden striped things that roam the jungle . . . It's perfectly obvious she's had an affair with the doctor, which he has now ended.' Felicity put down her glass. 'What do we know about your brother's death, Gerard? How exactly did he die?'

'You know perfectly well how he died. They told us how he died. He had a heart attack. They were having a fancy-dress party or something, it was terribly hot and it all proved too much for him.'

'I believe there's more to it. *Much* more.'

'One good thing about funerals,' Gerard said, 'is that they bring people together and rekindle old friendships. It was good to see Nellie, wasn't it? She's getting on, but seems completely *compos*. Doesn't drool or dribble or lurch about. Got rid of Chalfont and bought a house in St John's Wood. The very best of decisions. That's what all of us should do.'

14

'I'd hate living in St John's Wood . . . Nellie's nephew is a detective.'

'Don't think Peverel is a detective.'

'No, not Peverel. Hugh.'

'Hugh Payne? I thought Hugh Payne was in the army.'

'He isn't a real detective, but one of those amateur ones. I've heard some incredible stories. He may be interested in buying the Damascus chest, Nellie says. He's seen it in my catalogue. She is bringing him over to look at it tomorrow.'

'That's splendid, absolutely splendid. I'm afraid I'll be off at some unearthly hour, so I'm bound to miss them. Good lord, it's starting to rain again . . . Rain falling limply in intermittent showers.' He whistled what sounded vaguely like 'The Rain in Spain' between his teeth.

She gazed across at him in an exasperated fashion. 'Aren't you the tiniest bit curious about the sinister secret of La Sorcière, Gerard?'

'I do believe, my dear, that if you ever went to Plato's cave and were asked about a Form or an Ideal, you wouldn't talk about Love or Truth or Beauty, but about the sinister secret of La Sorcière. Why, you make it sound as though they all killed my brother and hushed it up!'

'Perhaps they did. In fact I am sure they did. They looked conspiratorial.'

'Renée Glover seemed as self-possessed as ever. Her manner was perfectly amicable. She said hello and I am so sorry about your brother and she actually smiled at me.'

'It is *me* Glover hates, not you. It was I who dismissed her. Glover adores you. She worships the ground you walk on.' Until a year ago Renée Glover had worked as Felicity's secretary. 'What she did was inexcusable. Outrageous. Poking her nose into my private affairs. Reading my letters.'

'I am sure you were mistaken, my dear.'

15

'I was *not* mistaken. Oh, I know perfectly well you have a soft spot for her, Gerard. All those cosy little chats in your study. You don't think I am blind, do you?'

'No, not at all, my dear. One couldn't imagine anyone more eagle-eyed than you. Sometimes you even . . .'

'Sometimes I even what, Gerard? See things that are not there? Is that what you were going to say?'

Gerard put on his oblique expression. 'No, no, not at all.' Felicity's getting difficult, he thought, fed up with having to change the topic. 'Such a blessing, never to have been fond of one's brother. Thank God he arrived in a hermetically sealed coffin and now of course he is in an urn. We are terribly lucky, you know. In Greece and countries like that relatives are expected to kiss the loved one's corpse as it lies in the coffin, by way of a final adieu.'

'You should have given that poached egg a wide berth at breakfast,' Felicity said sullenly. 'You're coming out in spots.'

'This is not an allergy. It's a nervous thing.'

She said she didn't believe he had any nerves. 'Did you hear about Stephan? Apparently he's been taken back in.'

'He should never have been allowed out.' Gerard Fenwick stole a glance at his watch and said he needed to go to his study. 'Sorry, my dear, but I am, as they say, being possessed by the Muse, which is also known as the divine *furor*. It would be unwise to ignore the call. The Muse is capricious and wilful and notoriously unpredictable. I may never get another visit.'

'What are you going to do in your study?'

'I am going to write.'

'You are going to *write*?'

'Well, yes. You know perfectly well that's something I do. Do you have to sound so amazed?' He paused with his hand on the door handle. 'I am divided between writing an essay on the subject of funeral cortèges and a bitter-sweet

16

story of a chap who realizes he is in love with his wife's former secretary.'

'Oh, that's been done *so* many times. I think you should write a murder mystery about a suspicious death that takes place on a tropical island.'

'Murder is something I know nothing about,' he said. He frowned down at his right hand, at the red blotch, which he knew perfectly well was a mosquito bite. 'I suppose I could write a one-act comedy about a distinguished middle-aged couple having a desultory and somewhat pointless kind of conversation. One of those fictions that are rooted in reality. *L'art égale la vie*. It would be fun, I think.'

3

Why Not Say What Happened?

The moment her eyes fell on the Revd Duckworth's clerical collar, a miasma of oppressive gloom descended on Hortense Tilling, not unlike the onslaught of sudden fever. She felt a shudder run through her. This is absurd, she thought. I have seen his collar hundreds of times.

'Dear lady, there is an odd look about your eyes, which I cannot read,' he said playfully.

'I've only just come back, Ducky.'

'Back? My dear Hortense, you are the most travelled person I have ever known! Back from what distant shores this time, pray?'

'Back from Hertfordshire. Remnant Regis.'

'Ah – Lord Remnant's final journey. A melancholy occasion. Coronary thrombosis, I believe you said? *Suddenly at his residence* – they still write that, I've noticed. *Cherished husband.* I never cease to be amazed at the resilience of certain clichés. *We all feel blessed to have known him* . . . There is safety in clichés, I suppose . . . You will give me some tea, Hortense, won't you?'

'Of course I will, Ducky . . . The cup that cheereth,' she murmured ruefully as she left the room.

They had known each other a number of years. He was a widower, she had never married. Both were in their mid-sixties. He invariably addressed her as 'dear lady'. She called him 'Ducky'. At one time Hortense had imagined the Revd Duckworth was steeling himself to propose to her.

In the kitchen, as she occupied herself with the tea, she suddenly felt on the verge of tears. I cannot live with so much doubt and fear and with so much intensity, she thought. I *must* talk – otherwise I will burst.

It took her a couple of moments to compose herself.

She re-entered the drawing room and put the tea-tray on the table.

The Revd Duckworth beamed at her. '*Towards a clergyman, common benevolence expresses itself largely through the medium of a cup of tea*. I have no idea if this is a quotation or whether I just made it up.'

'Sounds like something out of Trollope,' she said. 'Trollope teems with clergymen, doesn't he? All those bishops and archdeacons and prelates swimming in satins and port.'

It would help her if she talked. It would blow away the clinging cobwebs of her low and anxious mood. I don't have to tell him the *whole* truth, she thought, I cannot possibly tell him what happened exactly, but I will certainly tell him about the bribe.

'Who's that?' He was peering at one of the photographs on the wall. He was an old fool but she was fond of him. '*Such* an innocent face. Something of the lost angel about it. Brings to mind one of our most accomplished choirboys.'

'That's Stephan. Clarissa's son.'

'Your great-nephew. Of course. Was he at the funeral?'

'No. He is not at all well.'

'A most impressionable young person, I believe you said? Easily led astray? Short attention span? Undesirable friends?'

'It's much worse than that, Ducky. I've *told* you.' She spoke a little impatiently.

'Was it—? Not—?'

'*Yes*. He started quite young, at thirteen, I believe. I am afraid they can do very little about it. Poor Clarissa is out of her mind with worry . . . A mother's heart—' Hortense broke off. She took a deep breath. 'I find myself blaming God.'

'One mustn't blame God.'

'I do blame God. I am afraid in my very personal hierarchy God does *not* occupy a front seat. What I actually most believe in is the imponderable perception of God. It is my idea that God is aware of everything but is holding back, doing very little.'

'Dear lady!'

'I am convinced that God leaves us to get on with whatever cards we have been dealt, then sits back and watches us make a spectacle of ourselves . . . I don't suppose you encounter such heretical thoughts often, do you? Now, tell me honestly, do you?'

'As a matter of fact I do. More often than you imagine. I myself am not exempt. You'd never believe this, Hortense, but sometimes I question my suitability for the cloth. I catch myself wishing I were a chat-show host, a wedding singer or a champion snooker player.'

'*Vouchsafe, O Lord, to keep us this day from being found out.* That's not in the Bible, Ducky, is it?'

'No.' He looked at her. 'I have always regarded you as a woman of strong nerve and sanguine temperament, but today you seem far from your usual self. I imagine you found the funeral unsettling?'

'I did, yes. Very much so. Extremely unsettling. Not a single tear was shed for Lord Remnant. I couldn't describe anyone among Lord Remnant's nearest and dearest as an "inconsolable wreck" . . . I don't think he was "cherished" by anyone . . . Heretics roast in hell, don't they?'

'That is the accepted theory. Ultimately, that is. *Not* if they undergo a change of heart while they still have the chance and ask God's forgiveness.' The Revd Duckworth took a sip of tea.

'Should one fall on one's knees when one asks forgiveness?'

'Kneeling focuses the mind wonderfully well, though I find getting up increasingly difficult. I hope that didn't sound too flippant? I must say the Battenberg cake looks terribly tempting . . . Earthly appetites are *so* difficult to suppress . . . May I? I shall restrict myself to a single slice . . . This is scrumptious, absolutely scrumptious,' he said, munching.

A haunted and troubled look had settled upon her features. She clasped her hands before her. 'Tell me, Ducky, honestly and truly, do you believe I am capable of committing a crime? No, I am serious – do you?'

'Honestly and truly? No, I don't. You are the last person I would associate with crime, though of course it very much depends on what you define as "crime".'

'I'd be extremely grateful if you tried to picture the following scenario. Something terrible is perpetrated, an act of the utmost wickedness. There are witnesses but they have been forced to keep their mouths shut. In fact the witnesses have accepted hush money. The witnesses have been too weak to refuse the bribe. Or too greedy.'

'Are you by any chance talking about people you know?'

'No, of course not. The whole situation is entirely hypothetical. I sometimes like to imagine that I am faced with a moral dilemma and I try to provide a solution for it. People often need money rather badly, don't they? I don't mean only for bills, debts and overdrafts. People have extravagant tastes. Most of mankind craves opulence and splendour. The majority of people are self-indulgent.'

'That indeed is so,' he agreed. 'I must confess to a peculiar taste for sudden and isolated luxuries. I am particularly susceptible to a certain rather exclusive type of macaroon one can get *only* at Fortnum's.'

'This is a matter of life and death, Ducky. So they – these people – accept the hush money, they allow themselves to be bribed, but as a result some of them lose their peace of mind. They are unable to sleep. They feel as though they might explode. They feel alienated from their surroundings. Nothing seems to make sense any more. They start popping pills—' Hortense broke off. 'I am sure I am putting things rather badly, but I hope you get the picture? The point, Ducky, is that the victim *deserved to die*.'

The Revd Duckworth blinked. 'Is there – was there – a victim?'

Hortense Tilling's gently wrinkled face was quite flushed now. 'The victim didn't possess a single redeeming feature. The *Don Giovanni* aria got it all wrong!'

'What aria?'

'La nobiltà ha dipinta negli occhi l'onestà.'

'The nobility – um – has honour painted in their eyes?'

'Honesty. The nobility has honesty painted in their eyes. Well, Ducky, this particular nobleman was far from honest. He was devious. He led a life of decadence and depravity. He was arrogant, egocentric and cruel. He talked of selling his soul to the Devil!'

'I can't help the feeling,' the Revd Duckworth said slowly, 'that you are talking of someone you know.'

'He *enjoyed* upsetting people. He liked to say hurtful things, awful things. He had an extremely nasty sense of humour. He was an unregenerate bully. He was a mental sadist.' She had started talking very fast. 'He got kicks out of seeing people in tears – especially women. He had a thing about women. *Not* a nice thing. He treated women very badly indeed. Both wittingly *and* unwittingly.'

'Dear me!'

'One particularly outrageous act he committed unwittingly. However, it is my conviction that even if he *had* realized the enormity of what he was about to do, he would still have done it. He was that kind of man, yes. Therefore he deserved to die.'

'Who's this person? A nobleman, did you say? My dear Hortense, you are not by any chance talking about—'

'No!' She reached out and covered his mouth with her hand. 'Not another word, Ducky! No, don't speak! Please, no! No more questions. *Toute verité n'est pas bonne à dire.* But one thing I will say. *The murder was entirely justified.* This particular murderer does *not* deserve punishment. I assure you this particular murderer did the right thing.'

Tears had sprung in her eyes. She sniffed. She glanced up, at Stephan Farrar's photograph.

How terrible not to be able to tell the truth!

4

Insomnia

So that's that, Louise Hunter thought. It's all over. No one will ever know now. What a relief. Thank God for cremations. Obliteration of all the vital evidence. Of *all* evidence. Reduced to cinders, ashes, amen. Unless someone broke down and confessed, the truth would never be known.

I can't believe we agreed to it, she thought.

They had let Clarissa persuade them. Basil hadn't hesitated a moment. He'd said yes to her proposition at once. Yes, yes and yes again. Basil was in thrall to Clarissa.

Louise had dreaded hearing a voice calling the proceedings to a halt, commanding the coffin be pulled back and opened. Some plain-clothes policeman showing his badge and asking them all to leave the crematorium and stand outside while they checked Lord Remnant's body.

Augustine had been the only servant there when Lord Remnant had been killed, but he might have told the other two – what were those two noisy black women called? Caresse and Sandra Dee. Both of them seemed to be married to Augustine. The three of them seemed to live together. Trios like that appeared to be common enough on the island of Grenadin. A legacy from the long years of slavery, no doubt.

Lord Remnant's body had been taken away very fast. Basil and Dr Sylvester-Sale had carried him to his bedroom upstairs. Augustine had been talking about 'the Master having a fit'. It had taken him some time to realize his master was dead, or that was the impression he had given. He had then broken down and cried like a child.

Louise was relieved to be back in England, but at the moment her mind was enshrouded in profound depression. She looked out of the window – at the dreary grey skies that presaged rain. Basil had insisted on taking the dogs out. He said he needed fresh air. The real reason, of course, was that he didn't want to be with her.

The night before, she had decided to sleep with her feet away from the wardrobe since she had become convinced that the late Lord Remnant would emerge from the wardrobe, stretch out his hands and drag her in – back into hell, with him. She'd got it into her head that the wardrobe was in fact the gateway to hell.

The thought of those pale limp hands, last glimpsed crossed over the dead body, closing round her ankles made her shudder. According to some legend or other, male Remnants rarely found peace in death and tended to come back . . .

She had slept badly. She had had the most appalling nightmares, through which she had tossed and turned and sweated in horror; nightmares exploding with strange flaring lights and fires and the terrible cries of people being burnt alive. She had woken up hearing herself scream, and as she had come to her senses, she heard someone laugh, a triumphant kind of laugh. She was certain it had been Lord Remnant.

She and Basil had had separate bedrooms for quite some time now. She wondered if her irrational fantasies might have something to do with her husband's refusal to share a bed with her . . .

Louise sat at her dressing table. The mirror showed a moon-shaped face surrounded by carefully arranged auburn hair – formless features – emotional gold-brown eyes. Her expression managed to be at once neutral and unrestrained. She lacked allure. Perhaps she should dye her hair blonde and start doing it differently – over the ears, in sibylline coils? No – her face was too puffy. She had a double chin. How she hated herself!

She had too many curves and protuberances. She should lose weight. She should take up skipping, or perhaps she should stop eating altogether. She felt a hot tear roll down her cheek. Inconsequentially, she remembered reading somewhere that cures for melancholy included ballroom dancing and scourging.

For some reason she couldn't get Lord Remnant's hands out of her head. There was something about Lord Remnant's hands that troubled her . . .

The day Lord Remnant had died, 25 February, had become a watershed in her and Basil's lives, a line of demarcation, or a point in time, rather, before which the world seemed to glow with a patina of innocence and clarity, contentment and health. Since then everything had turned murky and tortured and incomprehensible, bearing nothing but portents of greater darkness to come.

Louise had been to London the day before. It hadn't been her day for London, but there was something she needed to do. A couple of things, actually. It would have been unwise to go to a local post office. Her lips twitched into a smile. She could be quite clever when she put her mind to it!

Lord Remnant's hands – why did she keep thinking about Lord Remnant's hands? As though she didn't have enough on her mind! Well, they were the hands of a nobleman. Clean, well-tended, meticulously manicured, *smooth*. She couldn't say what it was about them that filled her with such unease.

In some dim corridor of her mind the nebulous importance of the hands grew and grew . . .

* * * *

Dr Sylvester-Sale was on the telephone, talking in his low, well-modulated voice.

'I couldn't call you because I didn't have my mobile with me. I'd left it at home. These things happen. I am really sorry. No, I am not lying. You're not crying, Clarissa, are you? Oh God.'

'You could have stayed with me. I needed you. The moment you disappeared, I felt unsafe. The ground shook under my feet. I can't live without you, Syl. No sanctuary left, I kept thinking. *No sanctuary.*'

'I couldn't stay with you. You know I couldn't.'

'Why couldn't you? Why?'

'It would have caused comment.'

'So what? I don't care! Do you? Do you?'

'As a matter of fact, I do, Clarissa. We agreed that we needed to be careful, didn't we? Better to play it safe for a while . . . What was that? No, I am not going to "abandon" you, you silly girl.' He glanced at his watch.

'You intend to go off with one of your adoring lady patients, why don't you admit it? You have a mistress. I am sure you have a mistress. She's with you now, isn't she? Some clever young girl. You like clever young girls.'

'Now, listen carefully, Clarissa – take one of the sachets I gave you. It will calm you down at once. It's getting rather late, so hop into bed. No, I am not trying to poison you. I am not trying to get rid of you. Do be sensible.'

'Please, Syl – can you – can you come *now*? I need to see you. I must see you.'

'I am sorry but that would be quite impossible.'

'We must talk. About us. About the future.'

'We are talking now.'

'I can't live without you.'

'Apparently people kept ringing while I was away, leaving messages. I am under a lot of pressure. Hell of a lot to do.' Heaven give me strength, he thought. 'My secretary has been finding it incredibly difficult to cope. Devil of a backlog . . . No, I don't feel greater sympathy for my secretary than for you. No, I am *not* having an affair with my secretary. Do try to understand – no, you can't come to see me. I won't open the door,' he said desperately. 'No, Clarissa. *No*. Out of the question.'

'You are trying to get rid of me. You said once that I was given to emotional extremism.'

'I never said that.'

'You did! You would like nothing better than to be shot of my leech-like devotion, why don't you admit it?'

'For God's sake, Clarissa, pull yourself together . . . What was that about Stephan?' Sylvester-Sale held the receiver closer to his ear. 'No, he needs to stay there,' he said firmly.

'He is dreadfully unhappy. He hates the food. He hardly eats *anything*. He wants to know when he can come home. He keeps asking, "When can I come home, Mummy?" He sounds desperate. When will they release him? When will he be able to come home?'

'I don't know. It all depends how well he responds to treatment. They know what they are doing, I assure you. Sans Souci is one of the best places, if not the best.'

'Sans Souci costs squillions. It's incredibly expensive. Incredibly. For a loony bin.'

'Sans Souci is *not* a loony bin.'

'It's more expensive than the Taj Mahal . . . More expensive than the Empire State Building . . . More expensive than Windsor Castle . . . And *so* much more expensive than the Kremlin.' She giggled.

'I hope you haven't been drinking, Clarissa.'

'I am having a little drinkie.'

'You are a bad girl,' he said wearily. 'You promised you were not going to touch the stuff.'

'I am in pain – in deep searing pain. I miss you terribly, Syl. I can't live without you. If you leave me, I'll kill myself. I am going to take an overdose.'

'The Sans Souci staff are extremely efficient. The best specialists in the land,' he said. 'The rooms are airy and tastefully decorated. They have a *cordon bleu* chef—'

'Life without you is not worth living.'

'They know *exactly* what should be done for Stephan. Stephan will be all right, so there is absolutely no call for you to worry.'

'What if he talks about what happened? You know he lacks any instinct for self-preservation. What if he tells everybody about it? He can't be trusted to control his tongue . . . I mean the murder, Syl. What else could I possibly mean? What if he starts saying it was he who killed his stepfather?'

'No one will take it seriously.' Sylvester-Sale spoke reassuringly. 'They are used to the wildest talk at these places . . . Sorry? Who's accusing you? What bloody nonsense is that? You have had – an anonymous letter?'

He is going to leave her. He told me so last night. Clarissa never meant anything to him. He was bored, that was the only reason he started the affair. Also because he hated her husband. It was a form of revenge. He admitted he had made a mistake. It is me he loves. He told me I made his life worth living.

Clarissa is cunning like a fox, seductive like a she-cat and cold like a snake. She is obsessed with Syl. How she kept staring at him! She seems to have thrown all caution to the winds. That old boy at the funeral, Sir Gyles Napier, said Clarissa had been the sweetest girl when he first met her twenty years ago. Innocence personified. Sugar and spice and all things nice. Is that possible?

What's that in my pocket? God, why do I keep carrying it about? No one saw me pick it up . . . The Remnant coat of arms and his initials are on it . . . Couldn't be more damning!

He's always been nice to me. *Exceptionally* nice. Always so kind and encouraging.

If I had been a different sort of person, I could have started blackmailing him . . .

What was he doing standing on the terrace outside the french windows at the time of the murder? What was he doing in Grenadin?

5

Travels With My Aunt

Lady Grylls and Major Payne were on their way to the Fenwicks' house in Belgrave Square, where they were expected by Felicity Fenwick, or Lady Remnant, as she had now become.

'I hate driving in London,' Payne murmured.

'Isn't the mayor any good? I understand he is in fact a Turk – or was it an amateur cyclist? Some of my sources are far from reliable, mind. He is *both*? How extraordinary. What do mayors *do*? I am sure we could do without mayors. What are mayors *for*?'

'I really have no idea, darling.'

'Places like London practically run themselves, don't they? Which is as it should be, given the high prices of *everything*. In my humble opinion, Hughie, mayors are surplus to requirements.'

'You may be right, darling. But you were telling me about the Remnants – about the strange etymology of their family name?'

'It was originally de Ruminant – de Revenant, according to some sources, which doesn't seem terribly likely but it is interesting, nevertheless, given that dead and buried male Remnants have a trick of coming back and causing mischief.'

'Coming back as revenants?'

'Yes. Dead male Remnants frequently fail to find peace and they tend to return in the shape of malignant ghosts. There's a legend about it. That's why they had Roderick cremated, I suspect, though of course they'd never admit it, to prevent him from walking out of his grave. They clearly didn't want to be left with a tenantless grave,' Lady Grylls concluded.

'Something whispers to me that the late Lord Remnant wasn't a terribly nice man.'

'He wasn't at all nice. *The Grenadier of Grenadin* made that abundantly clear. He was far from popular with those poor locals. He had an awful lot of people evicted, you see, and he had their houses demolished. His explanation to the camera was that he was averse to sharing. He said he couldn't help his overdeveloped sense of privacy.'

'I wouldn't call that a particularly satisfactory explanation.'

'Neither would I. Roderick boasted of building a golf course and an English bar. That cost him a pretty penny, he pointed out. But the locals failed to appreciate his efforts and they bombarded him with death threats, though he insisted he didn't let that bother him one little bit. The camera showed him shrugging and yawning in an exaggeratedly unconcerned manner.'

'Death threats, eh?' Payne gave his aunt a sidelong glance. 'What did Lord Remnant die of exactly?'

'Heart attack or stroke or something. You don't suppose one should suspect anything more sinister, do you? *Tenantless Graves*. That would make a good title for one of Antonia's novels, you know.'

'I don't think Antonia's ever written a novel to match a title.'

'Would I be right in saying the appeal of Antonia's books lies not in appeasing the reader's appetite for sensation or emotion but in satisfying curiosity?'

'You would be. Jolly well put, darling.'

'What's Antonia up to these days?'

'Not much. Writing as usual. Or thinking about it. Or talking about it.'

'You don't mind?'

'No, not at all. It's all great fun. She's giving one of her rare interviews to some magazine this morning.' Payne glanced at his watch. 'In about an hour or so. Poor Antonia. She hates giving interviews.'

'Poor Antonia. I am not sure I'd ever want to be a writer. I am being urged to write my memoirs, did I say? I was told I belonged to a vanishing breed and that whatever I wrote would sell like hot cakes . . . I rather doubt that . . . Do you think I could write about Corinne Coreille?* After all, the whole extraordinary episode took place at Chalfont.'

'I don't see why not. But you were telling me about the Remnants.'

'The Remnants, yes. There's a website devoted to the Remnant family, Provost tells me. Last night Provost got on the computer and ferreted out an awful lot of the most fascinating facts. No more fervent aficionado of the aristocracy than he exists among London's millions.' Lady Grylls shook her head. 'Did you know you could get both *Debrett's* and the *Landed Gentry* "online"? All at the click of a button!'

'The internet has a lot to answer for,' Payne said sternly.

'There was something profoundly dubious about the early Remnants,' Lady Grylls went on. 'They thrived on patronage and blackmail and depended on largesse rather than industry for their richer hours. They worked exclusively at their pleasure and liked nothing better than striking attitudes. Remnants were single-minded and incredibly devious. They were liars and looters. They lacked self-awareness.'

* See *The Death of Corinne.*

'Mad?'

'Oh, indubitably. But they were always methodical and always enterprising. Shakespeare's said to have come up with one of his most famous phrases as a result of his association with a Remnant. Can't remember which one it was now. Madness comes into it.'

'Method in his madness?' Payne suggested.

'That's it. Yes. Remnants were notorious for coming up with loony schemes, which they somehow managed to make work. They were flamboyant and reckless. They were awfully keen on theatricals. During the reign of Elizabeth I, a Remnant maintained a private band of actors at Newstead, which was the scene not only of dramatics but of debauches as well.'

'Tenantless graves. That's *Hamlet*, I think,' said Payne.

'Is it? I'd be grateful if you concentrated on the road, Hughie. You are a bloody marvellous driver and I love it when you drive like a fiend, but I am sure we'll have a fatal accident if you insist on taking your eyes off the road. How dreadful, if we got trapped inside the car and they had to cut us out of the wreckage. Like the sardines in the French song.'

'What French song?'

'*Marinés, argentés, leurs petits corps décapités.*'

'I don't believe there is such a song. Too macabre.'

'It goes back to the early days of the French Revolution, I think. Mayfair wouldn't be such a bad place to die,' Lady Grylls went on in a reflective voice, 'if one absolutely had to. It would be better than most places, in fact. All these lovely houses and wonderfully tended gardens, with the Ritz just round the corner.'

'I believe I've got the *Hamlet* quotation,' said Payne. '*The graves stood tenantless and the sheeted dead Did squeak and gibber in the Roman streets.*'

'Romans saw no virtue in moderation and very little in virtue. Nor for that matter did Remnants. Roderick's great-grandfather, the ninth earl, was sent to a French military academy, but apparently he preferred to mount his campaigns in wanton female company. He frequented *les maisons de tolérance*.'

'Not brothels?'

'I am afraid so. The ninth earl was not famous for his self-control. His own sisters as well as his young and pretty aunt were said not to have been exempt from his gallantry, though perhaps "gallantry" is not the right word— Why are we stopping?

'Journey's end, darling.' Payne was taking off his driving gloves.

'So glad we've arrived in one piece,' said Lady Grylls. 'Belgrave Square looks perfectly splendid after the rain.'

6

Riddles in Mayfair

A maid opened the door and let Lady Grylls and Major Payne in. As they walked across the hall, Payne paused to glance at the photographs in silver frames.

The drawing room, with its high ceiling and Adam chimneypiece, was furnished with restrained good taste. Half a dozen early-nineteenth-century paintings of dogs hung on sashes against walnut panelling that had been glazed in three shades of pistachio green. The moment they entered, the carriage clock on the mantelshelf chimed eleven.

Felicity Remnant, a placid-looking woman in hound's-tooth tweeds and two strings of pearls, rose from the sofa. She had a preoccupied air about her. She seemed unable to tear her eyes from the frozen black-and-white image on the TV screen.

Putting the remote control on the low coffee table, she turned to her visitors.

'So good of you to come.' She and Lady Grylls exchanged kisses. 'Gerard is sorry he can't be here, but he's had to go to Remnant. Meetings with solicitors and all sorts of other people. As you can well imagine, my brother-in-law's death has pitched us into a wholly new life with a lot of incredibly tedious responsibilities. It's complete madness.'

'Felicity, my dear, I don't think you have met Hugh, have you? Hugh is my favourite nephew. The only one of my living relatives who understands me.'

Payne gave a little bow. 'Lady Remnant. How do you do?'

'How do you do? I have heard an awful lot about you, Hugh, and I must say I am intrigued.'

'So good of you to let me look at your Damascus chest.'

'I understand you are renowned for your stratospheric IQ and uncanny gift for divining guilty secrets. Can you really do the Sherlock Holmes trick of guessing facts about people in a seemingly legerdemain manner?'

'I believe I can.'

'Frequently with spectacular success, or so I have heard?'

'Usually with spectacular success. Usually rather than frequently,' said Payne in a meditative voice. 'I wouldn't call it a trick but a knack. And it isn't exactly guessing, it's deducing.'

'How terribly tantalizing. I wonder if you could deduce anything about me?'

'You'd like me to tell you things about yourself which no one but you could possibly know?'

'Yes, please.'

'Wouldn't you think it presumptuous of me?'

'Not a bit of it.'

'You may find what I am going to say annoying.'

'I am sure I won't,' she reassured him.

Major Payne's eyes narrowed. 'Well, you have been careful to cultivate a perfectly plausible patina of respectability and an instantly recognizable type of Englishness. You speak and dress and do your hair the way your mother and grandmother spoke and dressed and did theirs, but underneath lurks a highly unconventional woman.'

Lady Grylls beamed. 'Isn't he wonderful?'

'In what way unconventional?' Felicity asked.

'Once you were something of a wild girl. You had a passion for rock-and-roll. You are a dab hand with a gun. You have a quirky sense of humour. You used to have a tattoo, which you sported pretty prominently.' Payne drew his forefinger across his jaw. 'You have a Lithuanian maid and you smoke Cuban cigars.'

'Not Trichinopoly ones?' Felicity's brows went up ironically.

'No. Cuban. As a child, you were scared of pom-pom dahlias. Your second boyfriend was a strategy analyst at a government-sponsored institution called Stonehenge Madagascar.'

'I suppose you recognized Goda's accent, but how on earth did you know about the gun?'

'Who or what is Trichinopoly?' Lady Grylls asked.

'Place in southern India. Location of a famous battle . . . A silver-framed photograph in the hall shows you and your husband wearing combat gear and handling guns in a most expert manner.'

'You are certainly good at noticing things. But you can't be sure that's my husband. It may be my lover. Or my dentist. I may have been entertaining my dentist, so there.'

'No,' Payne said firmly. 'It's your husband Gerard Fenwick, who is now the thirteenth Earl Remnant. I believe I was introduced to him once. I never forget a face. It was at a dinner at the Military Club, I think, or perhaps Brooks's. Can't remember which one exactly.'

'Gentlemen's clubs are all the same,' she said acidly. 'How did you know about the rock-and-roll?'

Payne pointed to a shelf above the TV set. 'Those videotapes. Glastonbury 1971, 1972 and 1973. They can't possibly be your son's – I understand he is still at school – too young. Besides, it is all DVDs nowadays. Or are you going to tell me they belong to your husband?'

Felicity looked a little annoyed. 'Perhaps they do.'

'No, they don't,' Lady Grylls wheezed. 'They are all yours, my dear. I remember your mama being frightfully worried about you when you were eighteen. About the shiny black leather you used to wrap yourself in! There were pictures of you in *Tatler*, I remember. Sorry. Shouldn't butt in. This is Hugh's show.'

'You have had a small tattoo removed from just above your wrist. The scar is infinitesimal, practically invisible to untrained eyes. I believe you had the operation done about twenty-five years ago. Was that when you first got married?'

'It was. I didn't want my mother-in-law to have a fit. My mother-in-law was the most disapproving woman who ever lived.' Felicity's expression did not change. 'OK. You are right about my wild youth. I was something of what is known as a "rock chick". But you are wrong about the cigars. It is my husband who smokes cigars. That's why the house reeks of them.'

'There is fresh cigar smoke in this room. You have tried to get rid of it by opening the window, but you haven't been entirely successful. Besides,' Payne went on, 'there is a bit of a cigar leaf stuck to the thumb of your right hand.'

'Is there? Oh yes, how tiresome. Very well. I help myself to Gerard's cigars every now and then. I don't think he notices. That's my one guilty secret.'

'Only one?' Lady Grylls laughed.

Felicity frowned. 'What about my quirky sense of humour? And what about the pom-pom dahlias? However did you deduce that?'

'You have created a persona that is *too* good to be entirely true. It is clear you get a kick out of misleading the world. Then there are the dogs in those pictures.' Payne pointed. 'They seem to have been chosen for no other reason than their exceptional ugliness. I don't think you care for dogs much, do you?'

'I detest dogs. What about that nonsense about my second boyfriend working at Stonehenge Madagascar? I don't believe such a place exists. And I never had a second boyfriend.'

'I said that to impress my aunt,' Payne admitted.

'Hughie!' Lady Grylls cried in an outraged manner.

'And I suppose it was your aunt who told you about my childhood phobias?'

'I did.' Lady Grylls nodded. 'Your mama was terribly worried, you know. Thank God you grew out of it.'

Felicity turned to Payne. 'Do you have any idea at all in which story Sherlock Holmes makes the following deduction: "You have had five husbands and the man you now have is not your husband." I assume you know the "canon" inside out?'

'I believe I do,' Payne said, 'but that's not Sherlock Holmes. It is Jesus speaking to the Samaritan woman.'

'I must say, Nellie, your nephew is quite something.'

'He is my favourite nephew,' Lady Grylls said as though that explained it all.

'I have the feeling of having passed a test,' Payne said.

'Perhaps you have. Would you like some coffee? You are not in too terrible a hurry, I hope?'

'We'd love some coffee. I hope it is not decaffeinated? At my time of life, I can't tolerate any manner of dietary deprivation. Are you all right, my dear?' Lady Grylls peered at Felicity Remnant. 'You are not ill, are you? You strike me as a bit preoccupied.'

'Something awfully peculiar happened this morning. And how curious that you should be here now. I have an idea Hugh might be able to help me.' Felicity's eyes rested thoughtfully on Major Payne. 'But let's have coffee first. No, it is not decaffeinated. It is Davidoff Supreme Reserve.'

'It isn't a well-known fact but American police have their own coffee brand,' Payne said. 'Gun Barrel. I read about it in the *Telegraph*.'

'I won't be a jiffy. Do take a look at the Damascus chest, Hugh. It's over there.' Felicity pointed. 'I hope it comes up to your expectations.'

7

Through a Glass, Darkly

It was a chest of drawers of exceptional workmanship. Standing beside it, Major Payne ran his hand across its surface. 'Mid-nineteenth century. Made in Damascus. Typical of the region. Outstanding quality. Inlaid with mother-of-pearl, ivory and silver wire.'

'It actually changes colour in the light. Can you see it? Or is it my eyes?' Lady Grylls pushed her glasses up her nose.

'It does change colour in the light, you are absolutely right, darling. It would look marvellous against a salmon-coloured background.'

'It gives the impression of *exuding* light. It's got a fairyland quality about it.'

'They usually have secret drawers, chests like this . . . One needs to press one of these small marquetry insets – *comme ça.*' Payne demonstrated and imagined he heard an old spring being triggered somewhere. A little panel shot out.

'Goodness – there *is* a secret drawer! Are you ever wrong, Hughie?'

'No, not often.' He opened the secret drawer.

'What's that piece of paper? A secret message! What does it say, quick!'

Payne unfolded it. 'Doesn't seem to be much. Um. Headed paper. *The Grand Jewel Hotel, Marrakesh – I accept. You are right. All I need to do is shave off my whiskers and go bald! But we need to meet, so I can get the details right. Q.'*

'Who is Q?'

'Not Quiller-Couch, for sure. And I can't imagine the Queen writing cryptic notes. Besides, she signs herself ER. It may be James Bond's Q. Marrakesh suggests foreign intrigue.'

'Extraordinary. Why *does* Q want to go bald? What's this all about?'

'Haven't the foggiest, darling. I don't suppose we are meant to be reading this. Terrible manners.'

'Felicity need never know,' Lady Grylls said as she watched her nephew fold up the note and return it to the tiny drawer.

Their hostess reappeared, accompanied by the maid Goda, a languid-looking girl with pale straw-like hair and wide-set mournful eyes of lymphatic blue. She was pushing a trolley with a large coffee pot, three Meissen porcelain cups, a cake and a stand with sandwiches.

'That will be all, Goda. Thank you very much.'

Lady Grylls exclaimed, 'My dear – a feast! Romantic passion, overweening ambition and fabulous wealth all pale into insignificance beside such mouth-watering elevenses . . . That was a clean, nice-looking gel,' she said after the maid had left the room.

'Goda is Lithuanian, as Hugh correctly guessed. We try to move with the times. She came staggeringly cheap. I got her on the black market, *not* through an agency. I seem to have contacts in the most unlikely places. There is always some risk involved, but I like taking risks.'

'You're not afraid she may skedaddle with the spoons?' Lady Grylls raised her cup of coffee to her lips.

'No, not really. I don't believe she will. She has turned out to be the best maid I've ever had. Pure gold.'

'Entrap the alien at the proper time,' murmured Payne.

'That was old Kipling's shockingly non-PC advice to our island race.'

'The gel is very quiet,' Lady Grylls observed. 'She's not one of those unfortunate semi-mutes, is she?'

'No. She's shy. She doesn't speak English terribly well,' Felicity said. 'Her accent is marked but not particularly tiresome. I give her English lessons. One hour every evening.'

'I suppose you take it out of her salary?' Lady Grylls bit into an egg-and-cress sandwich. 'No? Jolly generous of you, my dear. Well, I taught my butler the rules of vingt-et-un. I also did it for free.'

'Does Goda ever keep you waiting?' Payne asked.

'No, never. Why? She is most punctual. Oh. Is that a joke?'

'Yes. A somewhat feeble one, I fear.' The two ladies continued to look puzzled. '*Waiting for Goda.*'

The conversation then turned to the Damascus chest. Felicity explained that it had been the property of her late brother-in-law, but Clarissa had asked Felicity to take it off her hands. 'Clarissa believed the chest was haunted. She warned me there was a noise coming from inside. She described it as a *crump, crump, crump* kind of noise. She kept hearing it, she said. A ghostly kind of munching.'

'Did *you* hear it?'

'Oh yes. *Crump, crump, crump.* Exactly as she'd described it. It was particularly bad at night. Gerard said he couldn't bear it. It really got on our nerves, so I took the chest to a shop in Kensington Gore. I explained about the noise.'

'I bet they thought you were prey to aural illusions,' Lady Grylls said.

'Well, they heard it too, so they agreed to investigate and to reline the drawers, as they seemed to have been gnawed by some sort of creature. A couple of days later they called me and showed me a jar containing what looked like a cross between a worm and a slug. The thing was large, white, obese and obscene beyond belief!'

'How perfectly ghastly.' Lady Grylls took a sip of coffee.

'They found it inside the chest wall, they said. Heaven knows how long it had been there, but it had managed to eat all the surrounding wood of the drawers. To cut a long story short, the creature was handed over to the Natural History Museum where it now stands, pickled for posterity, while the chest was repaired and returned to me. It is perfectly all right now. No more monsters.'

'It's definitely got a presence about it,' Lady Grylls said.

'I've had the chest back for six months now and it's as quiet as the grave,' Felicity said.

'It is magnificent. I would be delighted to have it,' Payne said. 'If you are still willing to sell it.'

'Oh yes, I am. Clarissa insists the creature was in fact a reincarnated Remnant who came to haunt her. She is convinced it was one of Roderick's late uncles, who was repulsively white and quite fat.'

'My dear, what is that you've been watching?' Lady Grylls gestured towards the frozen image on the TV screen. 'It all looks terribly melodramatic. Is that man dead or dying? They strike me as familiar somehow – that woman with the wild hair – the dashing chap – where *have* I seen these actors before?'

'They are not actors,' Felicity Remnant said. 'Look carefully, Nellie.'

Lady Grylls pushed her glasses up her nose. 'I have an idea I saw them at the crematorium yesterday, but I am sure I am imagining it. I get more and more muddled these days.'

'You did see them at the crematorium yesterday.'

'What in heaven's name do you mean, Felicity?'

Their hostess seemed to have come to a decision. 'I received a package early this morning. It came in a Jiffy bag. As a matter of fact, it was addressed to Gerard. I had an odd feeling about it, so I opened it. It contained a videotape, which had no label – no writing of any kind – nothing to indicate what it was. An old battered videotape. I put it on – and I had the shock of my life.'

Major Payne finished his coffee. Realization had dawned on him. 'You don't mean that the man lying on the chaise longue is the late Lord Remnant?'

'That's my brother-in-law, yes. My brother-in-law's death has been captured "on camera", as I believe the expression is. I'd like you to see it.' Felicity picked up the remote control. She looked at Major Payne. 'I may need your advice.'

8

The Murder of Gonzago (1)

The image was black and white and not very clear. An intermittent jerking movement suggested the recording had been made with a hand-held camera. There was no sound.

A man was seen sitting at a dressing table, in front of a mirror. He was almost bald and his eyes had sinister dark circles round them. He gave a knowing wink at the camera and proceeded to put on a wig, a pair of caterpillar eyebrows, a beard, and, finally, a crown. Then, giving every impression of it being an afterthought, he put on a false nose. As he did so, he stuck out his tongue at the camera.

'My brother-in-law is quite impossible. Was.' Felicity paused the video.

'In that documentary he said he could be himself only when he was somebody else,' Lady Grylls said.

'It seems Roderick didn't want to do that documentary to start with, but then suddenly changed his mind,' Felicity said. 'Gerard couldn't recognize him at first; he hadn't seen him for so long, you see. Roderick seemed to have become more manic and he kept losing his temper.'

'That's what happens if one spends too much time in the sun,' Lady Grylls said.

'Apparently he used to pay regular visits to a local witch doctor,' said Felicity. 'He was in the habit of taking all sorts of highly dubious potions and powders and things, though they did seem to have had the desired rejuvenating effect. The rumour among the locals was that he'd actually sold his soul to the Devil.'

Lady Grylls gave a reminiscent laugh. 'He sang "Chattanooga Choo Choo" in duet with his estate agent, but got excessively cross when the poor fellow deigned to walk ahead of him and he tried to punch him on the nose. How he screamed at him. He clearly considered it *lèse-majesté*. You and he didn't get on frightfully well, did you, my dear?'

'Not frightfully well, no. My brother-in-law was an acquired taste and that's putting it mildly. Well, since he chose to spend most of his time in Grenadin, we hardly ever laid eyes on him.'

'When was the last time you saw him?'

'About ten years ago. We were invited to Grenadin, but it wasn't a particularly auspicious occasion. Poor Gerard suffered the most awful mosquito bites. My brother-in-law boasted of having become a crack shot. He was terribly eager to do a William Tell. He asked me to stand in the garden with an apple on my head. He claimed he could fell it with a single shot.'

'Did you agree to it?' Payne asked.

'Of course not.'

'That's how Paul Bowles killed his wife . . . Similar sort of set-up.'

'You haven't seen the documentary, Hughie, have you? Oh, but you *must*,' Lady Grylls said. 'For some reason they kept referring to it as a *meta*-documentary.'

'Did they?'

'You look as though you know what that means. I believe Provost recorded it when it was on the box, so I'll give you the video. Do remind me.' Lady Grylls turned to their hostess. 'Let's see what happens next, my dear, shall we?'

As Felicity pressed Play, the scene changed to a room of a striking art deco design. They saw an arch hung with a shimmering, transparent curtain and double doors made of what Payne imagined was onyx and silver. The enormous torchieres with serpentine curves had been derived, as Payne was to learn later, from Poelzig's expressionistic columns designed for the foyer of Max Reinhardt's Grosses Schauspielhaus in 1919.

The room was spacious and accented with circular and semicircular lines and arches placed within arches. The windows were curved like goldfish bowls, there was a rounded fireplace and clustered flowerlike lighting fixtures hung from the ceiling. The camera focused on a chaise longue covered in what looked like camellia blossoms.

'La Sorcière. Roderick's house on his island,' Felicity explained.

A couple of feet behind the chaise longue were french windows with net curtains over them. A middle-aged woman went up to the windows and drew the silk curtains across. She had silver hair, dramatically mascara'd eyes and star-shaped earrings; she was clad in a long dress. At one point she produced a pair of glasses and put them on her nose.

The camera swirled round and several other people came into view. A man and a woman wearing cardboard helmets raised their hands to their foreheads in a military salute. A young woman with long dark hair parted in the middle and a white diaphanous dress curtsied.

Lady Grylls shook her forefinger at the TV screen. 'I know these people! I've seen them. They were at the funeral yesterday! The very same!'

'Clarissa's aunt. The Hunters,' Felicity said.

'Who is the pretty girl?' Payne asked.

'What pretty girl? Do you mean Glover? Her name is Renée Glover.' Felicity pursed her lips. 'You think she is pretty?'

'Well, yes.'

'What are they supposed to be?' Lady Grylls asked.

'Characters out of Shakespeare. That, apparently, was the craze at La Sorcière at the time of Roderick's death.'

'Of course. There was something about it in the *Mail*.'

Major Payne stroked his jaw with his forefinger. 'I imagine Silver Hair is meant to be either Titania or Gertrude, the Helmets Rosencrantz and Guildenstern. Miss Glover is Ophelia – or maybe Cordelia.'

A man and a woman were walking at a stately pace towards the chaise longue. They were wearing crowns and richly embroidered robes and were holding hands.

'The King and the Queen,' Lady Grylls murmured. 'Though which king and which queen? Shakespeare is full of kings and queens. I think Roderick is the King . . . Is Clarissa the Queen?'

Felicity said in a flat voice, 'That's my sister-in-law, yes.'

Lord Remnant was heavily bearded and moustachioed; his long hair reached down to his shoulders. His caterpillar eyebrows slanted slightly upwards. Clarissa's face was white, her lips very dark; she brought to mind some sinister Vampyra – all she needed were fangs, Payne reflected. Her eyes were excessively made up.

The King drew the Queen to himself, brought his heavily bearded face close to hers and kissed her, first on the forehead, then on the cheeks and finally on the lips. The Queen in return stroked the King's hair.

'Jolly uncommon for royalty to look so ostentatiously in love, but maybe they did in the old days,' Lady Grylls observed. 'Or maybe they are not meant to be British?'

The King yawned and rubbed his eyes. The Queen pointed to the chaise longue.

54

'*My darling. Do take a nap,*' Lady Grylls said in a funny voice.

The King nodded. He took off his crown and placed it on a little round table. He then reclined on the chaise longue. He lay on his side, folded his arms and shut his eyes. The camera followed the Queen as she tiptoed in an exaggerated manner out of the arched doorway.

Once more the screen went black, then the sleeping figure of the King was seen again, but he was no longer alone. Another man had entered the frame. He was young and handsome and sported a black moustache with waxed-up ends. His head was covered in romantic curls.

In his right hand the man held a tall glass painted black and decorated with what looked like a skull and crossbones. He glanced furtively to the left, and to the right. His eyes then fixed on the crown and he contemplated it for a moment or two.

'I think I know what this is supposed to be,' Payne said.

The man stooped over and held the black glass to the King's ear. For a moment only the man's back could be seen and the recumbent form was hidden from view.

'What's he doing?' Lady Grylls leant forward.

'Pouring poison into the King's ear.'

'Really? This rings a bell . . . *Hamlet*?'

'Yes. *The Murder of Gonzago*. The play within the play.'

The King's body was seen jerking spasmodically upwards. The King's eyes looked as though they were about to come out of their orbits. His mouth opened in a silent scream. Then he slumped back and lay still.

'Ruin seize thee, ruthless King!' Lady Grylls made the sign of the cross.

The Queen re-entered. She glanced at the King, then at the Poisoner who made a slashing gesture across his throat and smiled. The Queen's hand went up to her mouth, then she smiled too. She crossed over to the Poisoner and the two embraced. The Poisoner then picked up the crown and placed it on his head. He and the Queen kissed again, then arm in arm they walked up and down the room. They waved royal waves.

'How terribly interesting. The King is dead, long live the King. Who *is* the new King?' Lady Grylls asked.

'Chap called Sylvester-Sale,' Felicity Remnant said. 'Dr Sylvester-Sale.'

'Look! I have an idea they are no longer acting,' Lady Grylls said.

Dr Sylvester-Sale and Clarissa Remnant were shown gazing across at Lord Remnant's body. Lord Remnant's hand was hanging limply, the fingers touching the floor. Dr Sylvester-Sale went up to the chaise longue and bent over the body. Something in his manner suggested none of this was scripted.

'No, they are no longer acting,' said Felicity.

The doctor lifted Lord Remnant's hand and held it by the wrist, checking the pulse. He then turned round and held up his hand; he was stopping the others from getting close. He said something. Louise Hunter was seen covering her mouth with her hand. Clarissa shook her head as though in disbelief.

'Is Roderick dead? I mean *really* dead – *is* that how he died?'

'It looks like it,' Felicity said expressionlessly.

'Heart attack? That's what it said in *The Times*.'

Dr Sylvester-Sale was seen bending over the body, once more concealing it from view. He rose and said something which made Clarissa's mouth open in a show of incredulity. Clarissa turned towards the camera. She looked cross. She waved her hands. The camera lingered on the bracelet on Clarissa's right wrist.

Clarissa gesticulated peremptorily. The camera swirled round. Hortense Tilling was seen entering the room. She looked flustered. Basil Hunter's expression was a mixture of dismay and disbelief. Louise Hunter looked outraged. Renée Glover's face remained blank.

Clarissa was seen speaking to the cameraman again. There was a movement. The cameraman seemed to be walking towards Hortense Tilling, who looked at once frightened and excited. The camera jerked up and down. They saw the ceiling with its ornate plasterwork and crystal chandelier.

There was a momentary blackout and when the image reappeared, it was upside down.

'What *is* going on?' Lady Grylls asked.

'The camera has changed hands. I think it's Clarissa's aunt who's got hold of it,' said Payne. 'Um. I believe she has been asked to turn it off but she doesn't seem to know how.'

'Oh, how tiresome! It's impossible to work out what they are doing now. No chance of turning the box over and watching it upside down, is there, my dear?'

'Better not,' Felicity Remnant said.

'This is making me feel seasick. No, can't watch it.' Lady Grylls turned her head and rested her gaze on a picture of a particularly repulsive pug. 'Can someone tell me what's happening?'

'Miss Glover is walking towards the french windows.' Payne paused. 'The Hunters have taken off their helmets. Dr Sylvester-Sale is scowling. Now he is putting the black glass with the skull into his pocket. It looks like an automatic gesture. There is a tall black man with them. He has the puzzled expression of a child. The original cameraman, I imagine.'

Lady Grylls spoke. 'Roderick is not moving? He is not rising?'

'No.'

'So he is dead, *really* dead?'

'I believe so. His death seems to have been captured on camera. Yes. Mrs Hunter is now walking towards the french window. She looks *enormous*—' Payne broke off. 'Oh. The

57

screen's gone black. It's all over. The aunt seems to have managed to switch the camera off at last.'

Felicity tugged at her pearls. 'What I am interested in ascertaining is the exact cause of my brother-in-law's death.'

9

Behold, Here's Poison

Lady Grylls frowned. 'He had a heart attack, didn't he? That's what the *Times* obituary said. Goodness, my dear, you look as though you doubt the *Times* obituary! You think there is something fishy about his death?'

'As a matter of fact I do. I have the unshakable conviction that there is something very wrong indeed.'

'*Something is rotten in the state of Denmark,*' Payne quoted.

'I believe they all know what happened. The Hunters, Clarissa's aunt, Dr Sylvester-Sale, Glover. I couldn't help noticing that when the coffin disappeared into the furnace, they seemed incredibly relieved.'

'You think Roderick might have been murdered like the character he played in the dumbshow staged at Hamlet's request? What was it all about, Hughie?' Lady Grylls turned towards her nephew. 'All that Gonzago business. What was the reason for it?'

'Well, Hamlet suspects his uncle Claudius of having killed his, Hamlet's, father, in order to replace him on the throne and marry his, Hamlet's, mother, after whom Claudius has been lusting.'

'Oh yes. The evil uncle. It was the ghost who told Hamlet, wasn't it? The ghost of Hamlet's father. Remember Olivier's Hamlet? I had a big crush on him, you know – so tantalizingly indecisive and blond. I had quite a thing about indecisive blond men at one time.'

'Claudius pours poison into his brother's ear as the King lies sleeping in the garden. Well, Hamlet needs proof, so he gets a troupe of itinerant actors to stage a play that shows Gonzago being killed in precisely the same manner. Claudius is in the audience and he gets up and leaves abruptly, which Hamlet – who's been watching his uncle closely – interprets as a guilty reaction.'

'How awfully ingenious. I don't suppose such a person as Gonzago ever existed, did he?'

'He did exist. The murder of Gonzago is believed to have been a reference to a real sixteenth-century murder. A Luigi Gonzaga murdered the Duke of Urbino. It seems to be generally accepted by Shakespearean scholars that Shakespeare's plot was founded on an Italian original. The dumb players have been identified as a *commedia dell'arte* troupe. Well, Italians of noble birth did poison each other. They were Machiavels at heart, poisoners like the Borgias, and libertines like the Venetians.'

Lady Grylls nodded. 'Broadening the intellectual basis of *any* discussion is something my nephew excels at. How he does it I have no idea, but he makes it look so terribly easy!'

Payne gave a self-deprecating smile. 'My forehead positively bulges with useless information.'

'Going back to what you were saying, my dear.' Lady Grylls addressed their hostess. 'Do you actually suspect your brother-in-law was poisoned?'

'I don't know if he was poisoned,' Felicity said, 'but I don't believe he died of natural causes. Well, since he's been cremated, we'll probably never know how exactly he died.'

'*Must* be the doctor. The doctor seems implicated, wouldn't you agree? It was the doctor who bent over the divan and held a glass to Roderick's ear.'

'That's what his part required him to do, darling. He was playing the regicide,' Payne reminded his aunt.

'It all fits in perfectly. Doctors know about poisons. Doctors are used to death. They take it in their stride. And this Sylvester-Sale had a good motive for wishing Roderick out of the way. He was having an affair with Clarissa – who is now a terribly rich widow. The doctor is a libertine, as you said.'

'I never said Sylvester-Sale was a libertine. I said Venetians were.'

'He is dark and handsome, therefore it is not inconceivable that he should have Venetian blood. He might have had a Venetian grandmother. We saw him bend over Roderick with the glass of poison in his hand. All terribly straightforward and simple. He killed Roderick while pretending to be killing him. That was the cleverness of it. It is only in murder mysteries,' Lady Grylls concluded, 'that things are never straightforward and simple.'

'Why did I choose to write murder mysteries? I don't really know. It's so difficult to explain.' Antonia frowned. 'I always wanted to be a writer and that seemed to be the only type of story I was drawn to writing. As it happens, detective stories were my favourite form of reading in my adolescence. Most people grow out of detective stories but I didn't seem to.'

'Did you only read murder mysteries of the classical kind?

'Mostly. I liked the idea of suspicion falling on all the characters, even on the most unlikely. It seemed to suit my sceptical and somewhat paranoid imagination.'

The owlish young man cleared his throat. 'I believe you were involved in a real-life crime – about the time you were writing your first detective novel – is that correct?'

'I was,' Antonia admitted. At once she wished she had held her tongue.

How could her interviewer know about it? As far as she was concerned, no one but she and Hugh knew about the murders at Twiston.** That murderer, as it happened, had got away with it. Could the murderer have confessed and been arrested without her knowing about it? No – it would have been in all the papers. Could the murderer have *confided* in someone? Antonia thought it highly unlikely, but then one never knew.

'Did your involvement in a real-life murder have any effect on your development as a detective story writer?'

'I am not sure. It may have done. I believe it served to cure the writer's block from which I happened to be suffering at the time.'

'Do you agree with the assertion that the whodunnit is an extremely artificial form and that it obeys rules as rigid and ridiculous as those of North Korean formation dancing?'

Antonia gave a little shrug and said she knew next to nothing about North Korean formation dancing. 'Isn't all fiction artificial? What is fiction but the selection of the writer's internal compulsions, preoccupations, passions, fears and external experiences distilled in a form which he or she hopes will satisfy the reader's expectations?'

'Do you read much modern crime fiction?'

'No, not much.'

'Are you familiar with the names of Martina Cole and Dreda Say Mitchell?'

'I am not . . . Should I be?'

'Do your books conform in any way to Henry James's definition of the purpose of a novel? *To help the human heart to know itself.* Or do you write exclusively for entertainment purposes?'

'I write exclusively for entertainment purposes,' Antonia said in a firm voice.

'Do you ever try to enlist the reader's support for views and theories of your own?'

* See *The Hunt for Sonya Dufrette.*

'No, I don't. Sometimes my characters express opinions of books or authors which happen to be my own. On the whole, I am careful to keep my views as inconspicuous as possible.'

'Do you exercise complete control over your characters?'

'Complete and absolute. I like playing God to the page,' Antonia said gravely. She tried to keep a straight face. She had started to enjoy herself.

'Do you regard plotting as the most fascinating aspect of detective story writing?'

'I suppose I do. But I also like to balance setting, characterization and plot, so that all three are interrelated and contribute to the whole. The kind of story I write,' Antonia went on, 'might have been written in the 1930s or early 40s, though I do make some concessions to modernity.'

'Mobile phones and the internet play an active part in your novels, don't they?'

'They do . . . No, I must admit I know very little about police procedure, forensic medicine or the intricacies of the law. I write extremely old-fashioned detective stories . . . "Propulsively readable"? Who said that? Really? Are you sure?' Antonia smiled. Must tell Hugh, she thought. 'I had no idea . . . My detectives depend exclusively on their capacity for noticing things. My detectives are obsessively observant.'

'How important is setting to you?'

'Important enough. Though I try not to overdo it. Some writers tend to overdo the setting. Settings establish atmosphere and they can also influence the plot and the characters. Settings can enhance the horror of murder, sometimes by creating a contrast between the outward peace of the scene and the turbulence of human emotions.'

'How would you describe your books?'

'Do I have to? OK. I'd describe them as unpretentious celebrations of reason and order. Oh, and of logic as well. Logic is very important.'

'E. M. Forster once wrote something like, The husband died, then the wife died is a story. The husband died and the wife died of grief is a plot. The wife died for no apparent reason is a mystery, a higher form. Can you improve on that? Can you come up with a definition of a murder mystery?'

Antonia scrunched up her face. 'How about, The wife died and everyone thought it was of grief until – um – until they discovered the bullet hole in the back of her head?'

'But if he did do it,' Lady Grylls said, 'there *must* have been a cover-up. You are absolutely right, my dear. They must have agreed to keep mum. All six of them, which is not as extraordinary as it may appear. Conspiracies are said to be a part of everyday life. Perhaps they were bribed by Clarissa to form one of those spectacular pacts of silence?'

'Yes. That's what I think,' said Felicity. 'They all had a conspiratorial air about them at the crematorium. They looked guilty as hell. Gerard pooh-poohed it. He says I imagined it.'

Lady Grylls shook her head resolutely. 'You aren't the fanciful sort. So let's see what happens. The dashing doctor poisons Roderick and of course he is only too eager to sign the death certificate. Clarissa bribes everybody into keeping mum. The official version presented to the authorities will be that Roderick died of a heart attack. That is how it is to appear in *The Times*.'

'There have to be *two* doctors' signatures on the death certificate,' Payne pointed out.

Lady Grylls waved her hand. 'They managed to rope in another doctor. Couldn't have been difficult, persuading a local chap to sign on the dotted line and so on, given that Clarissa now owns the island.'

'I doubt somehow that Dr Sylvester-Sale killed Roderick by pouring poison into his ear,' Felicity said.

'Why not?'

'In front of everybody else? Using a highly theatrical black glass decorated with a skull and crossbones? *On camera*?'

'Perhaps they were all in on it from the start and the dashing doctor was their appointed executioner,' said Lady Grylls. 'Maybe they all hated Roderick so much, they put their heads together and came up with the idea of getting rid of him? Like in *Julius Caesar* or – or on that stranded Orient Express.'

Felicity Remnant conceded that it was an intriguing theory – but would they have filmed the killing?

'I don't see why not. People do the oddest things,' Lady Grylls said. 'Years ago I used to play bridge with a woman – her husband was in the diplomatic corps – our man in Vaduz, I believe – and she would do anything to avoid bidding diamonds.'

'That must have been somewhat limiting. Did you ever find out why?'

'I did, my dear, yes, eventually. She was rather coy about it at first, but in the end it turned out she stuttered very badly on the letter d.'

'I don't believe my brother-in-law was *meant* to die on camera. It was obvious that it just – happened. Clarissa seemed to want the camera switched off at once. She looked extremely agitated. What do you think, Hugh? You are very quiet.'

'The doctor couldn't have poured poison into Lord Remnant's ear since the glass was empty,' said Payne. 'There was nothing in it. He only *pretended* to be pouring.'

'How can you be sure the glass was empty?' Lady Grylls said.

'Well, he was holding it upside down.'

'*Upside down*? Are you sure, Hughie? I never noticed!'

'I didn't notice either,' Felicity Remnant admitted.

'It's the kind of thing I tend to notice. You see, I am one of those obsessively observant people. I seem to possess what is known as "sensitivity to visual impressions".' Payne spoke in apologetic tones. 'Let's play that bit again, shall we? I'll show you. Lady Remnant, would you be so good as to rewind? There it is – stop. Look. *Look*.'

There was a pause.

'Goodness, yes. How extraordinary,' Lady Grylls said. 'You are perfectly right, Hughie. *Yes*. It happens very fast. He's holding the glass upside down and then he realizes it looks silly and turns it over quickly and handles it properly! The glass is empty, that's as plain as the nose on your face . . . Does that mean Roderick wasn't killed after all?'

'If he was killed, it was done in some other way.'

Felicity said, 'The anonymously sent videotape showing the precise moment of my brother-in-law's death suggests that there was something wrong about it, wouldn't you say?'

Payne nodded. 'Yes. I believe it does. Though it isn't immediately clear from watching it *how* Lord Remnant died. The tape was sent to Lord Remnant's brother, the present Earl Remnant . . . The sender is most likely to be one of the people who was there when Lord Remnant died. Some poor soul tormented by a guilty conscience or – or someone intent on stirring up *miching mallecho*.'

'I'd be grateful if you spoke plain English, Hughie.'

'Mischief, darling. Trouble. *Miching mallecho* is the phrase Hamlet uses . . . Did the tape sender mean to plant a suspicion or suggest a line of inquiry? Does the recording perhaps contain something which we should have seen but didn't?'

'I thought we saw everything there was to be seen,' said Lady Grylls.

'The bit where Lord Remnant dies – I'd like to see it again. If Lady Remnant doesn't mind. It may be my imagination, but—' He broke off.

'You saw something? What is it? Out with it!' Lady Grylls cried.

'I want to see that bit again . . . If I am right,' said Payne, 'you will see it too.'

10

Maid in Waiting

The phone rang and Clarissa's heart jumped inside her. She wanted to answer it because she thought it might be Syl, whom she loved with a love that was passionate, single-minded and overpowering, but she also feared it might be the call she dreaded. When she eventually did pick up the receiver, she discovered it was somebody from the *Sunday Telegraph*.

A journalist. A man. He said they wanted to do a feature on Remnant Castle – would Lady Remnant be good enough to show them around and give them an interview? The feature would appear in the *Telegraph* magazine. It was a friendly enough voice.

Clarissa said no, impossible, out of the question; her husband had been dead only ten days, they must know that, surely? Couldn't they be more sensitive? Her husband's ashes were still warm in the urn, she was terribly upset, she was ill, she had been sleeping badly, everything was at sixes and sevens, she was receiving no one, couldn't they leave her alone?

'Perhaps you could call again when my brother-in-law takes over. You may find him more welcoming. He may even suggest writing the piece himself!' She slammed down the receiver.

Her brother-in-law had hinted he might sell the place. She was not at all surprised. That was what she had always wanted to do herself. Gerard needed the money for some crackpot idea of his. Another futile writing venture, she imagined.

The day was cold and grey. She felt oppressed by the mists that invariably rose around Remnant. She felt cut off, isolated. The central heating wasn't working properly and there was no one who could do anything about it. She had got rid of the servants – she had followed the instructions to the letter. *No servants and no visitors.*

Her eyelids fluttered – closed.

She dozed off.

She had a dream.

They were back at La Sorcière and her husband lay on the chaise longue and he was bleeding profusely from a wound in the back of his head. There was blood everywhere, on the floor, on the walls, even on the ceiling, the whole room glistened with it. Then the french windows burst open and someone dressed in white and wearing the Bottom head sauntered in, calling out breezily, 'Anyone for tennis?' A man. Only instead of a tennis racquet, he held a gun – and his voice was very much like her husband's voice—

She woke up.

She rose to her feet. She felt sick. She couldn't bear sitting another moment in the barn-like drawing room with its crimson-clad walls, hung in 1895 and now faded to a shade of raspberry fool, huge crystal chandeliers that brought to mind inverted fountains, Ming vases, Remnant portraits painted by the likes of Gainsborough, Reynolds, de Lázló, Sargent and Lucian Freud.

Mr Quin. She was expecting a call from Mr Quin. Mr Quin had her in his power. She needed to obey Mr Quin's orders. She shut her eyes. I pray and hope I die before I go mad, she thought.

It was only midday, but it was getting darker by the minute. Twilight at noon. How she hated England! She longed to go back to the Caribbean. That morning she had woken up filled with the depressing foreknowledge that it would be another day of unmitigated misery . . .

She intended to turn on every single chandelier and she was going to light all the candles. Her instructions hadn't included having to keep Remnant sunk in gloom. Thank God for small mercies. She laughed shrilly and at once felt the ache in her throat that preceded tears.

As she walked across the drawing room and opened the door she tried to divide her thoughts into manageable portions and make sense of the events of the last ten days.

She might have been the abbess of a nunnery heading for a private audience with the Pope. Her face was free of make-up and her short fair hair was entirely concealed by a black chiffon scarf; her black dress was loose and long, though her slender ankles were clad in black silk and she wore vaguely erotic black high-heeled shoes.

She was also wearing enormous round black sunglasses, which was odd of her, she knew, one didn't wear sunglasses *indoors*, especially not in *England*, but they dramatized her lightly bronzed face, which was an effect she rather liked. But her carefully cultivated Grenadin tan had started to fade and she needed to do something about it. The moment I stop caring how I look will be the absolute unconditional end, she thought. She paused to light a cigarette and dropped the match on the floor.

Not so long ago there had been an insolent air of authority about Clarissa, of confidence, of arrogance even, also of carelessness and insouciance; she had managed to display the negligent drop-dead chic with which a mannequin swishes down a catwalk.

No more. She was aware that she was walking rather stiffly, stagily, self-consciously; she might have had a bit part in some amateur production. She almost expected the director to shout and halt her and order her to start again, to walk away and do it again, properly . . .

Catching sight of her reflection in one of the murky mottled mirrors made her shudder. She took off her dark glasses. The Bride of Frankenstein, she mouthed. She had lost a lot of weight. She looked preternaturally ethereal; thinner than ever before! Beneath the fading tan she was as pale as an ivory opium pipe. Well, she had hardly eaten a thing for heaven knew how long. She had been subsisting on the odd bowl of soup and cups of strong Arabica roast, which, she suspected, accounted for the panic attacks she had been having.

Syl had said once she looked a bit like Marilyn Monroe. She was miming 'I Wanna Be Loved By You', in front of the mirror. She put the dark glasses back on.

She had been taking a range of drugs, including lithium and Sarafem, for her anxiety and depression. What she really felt like doing was smoking a reefer, but at the thought of Stephan feeling suicidal at Sans Souci, she decided against it. No. No drugs.

'I am the twelfth countess of this thousand-year-old place,' she said aloud. For some reason the sound of her cracked voice made her feel marginally better. She went on speaking to an imaginary audience. 'Remnant Castle contains fifty-eight rooms and eleven intricately carved staircases. It's a classic example of opulent and gilded decay.'

The distance between the main dining room and the nearest kitchen was a hundred metres. The roof, on the other hand, covered an acre and not once in living memory had it been completely watertight. She could hear a dripping sound now from somewhere. The corridor walls were covered in satin and gold and hung with faded tapestries of mythical birds. She passed by ornate mirrors and perfectly pointless consoles, little couches and marble tables and a lot of pictures in gilded frames.

Remnant Castle had once been an Augustinian priory, consecrated in 937 and dedicated to some saint or other. It had become the property of her husband's family at the Dissolution of Monasteries in the 1530s. The earliest part of the building dated from between the third and fifth centuries.

The daughter of minor gentry, she had been brought up in an elegant enough Georgian townhouse in Upton-upon-Severn, but it hadn't exactly prepared her for the transplant to this monstrosity of a mansion, which spoke eloquently of times more spacious than the present and sported thirty-five chimneys on its roof.

She spoke again. 'In one of the cellars there is a semicircular protuberance in the wall that cannot be accounted for by any ordinary architectural rule. Here, it is said, many years ago a blaspheming monk was walled up alive, and sometimes, in the depths of the night, his ghost can be heard moaning and tearing at the walls of his prison.'

What was that? Something scurried, slithered and squeaked inside the wainscoting. No, not the monk – rats? Were they trying to gnaw their way out? That would be the final straw – armies of rats rampaging at Remnant! She had seen a dead rat once in the corridor outside her bedroom, lying on its back, its pink paws disconcertingly bringing to mind the hands of a human child.

Clarissa suddenly recalled the time she had been pregnant with Stephan. How he had moved inside her – kicking – wriggling like a fish. She had felt an incomparable joy unlike anything she had known before – or since. Tears welled up in her eyes. My baby, she whispered. My baby, I miss you so.

She must tell Tradewell to set traps or call the exterminator, before it was too late. No, she couldn't. She kept forgetting she had dispensed with her butler.

Clarissa had started walking fast – faster and faster – she nearly broke into a run. She forced herself to stop.

She wondered if she was in a state of hypomania. Syl had warned her about it.

Passing by a bronze statue representing Actaeon set upon by hounds, she was filled with terrible pity. 'You poor wretched thing, I know *exactly* how you feel,' she murmured. She took out her mobile phone. It was on. Didn't need recharging either.

He had said he would phone her. It wouldn't do to miss his call. It would make him cross. She dreaded hearing his voice. Oh, how she dreaded it.

This is all a little bit too much, she thought. The truth is I can't cope. I am scared. I am edging towards the abyss. I am on the verge of collapse. I have got myself involved in murder and deception of the most bizarre kind.

11

Laughter in the Dark

The weather was damp, the air filled with the reek of rotting leaves. Basil Hunter couldn't say he was enjoying his desolate ramble, but he had been quite unable to stand the familiar atmosphere of solid, unchanging monotony that reigned in his house. He had found it difficult to breathe.

At one point the sight of Louise reclining in the window seat, looking like a bloated Buddha, or Jabba the Hutt, breathing like a suction pump, gazing at him yearningly, had caused his intense annoyance to mount into furious rage. He had decided to go out, to prevent a conflagration.

Things seemed the same, yet they would never be the same. In a peculiar way Lord Remnant's violent death had triggered something in his mind, something he had never suspected was there . . .

He discovered he was walking in the direction of Remnant Regis and soon enough he saw the castle rising in the mist, not unlike some crouching primeval monster with spikes on its back – that was what the chimneys made it look like.

Set in a kind of valley, next to a grey-watered artificial lake, Remnant Castle was surrounded by oaks, beeches and chestnuts of great size and strange growth. Long untrimmed branches dangled to the ground and creaked whenever the wind blew. There was a park on the other side, but it was invisible from where he stood. The lake was enshrouded in mists in most seasons, diaphanous and delicate in summer, thick and blighting in winter.

He raised his binoculars to his eyes. Somebody was turning on the lights at Remnant. How was Clarissa coping? When he had spoken to her at the crematorium, he had offered his services. She had allowed him to hold her hand in his for at least half a minute. He would have held it longer, but Louise had been hovering in the background, making impatient noises, sighing heavily, damn her. Clarissa had thanked him and said she would call him if she needed anything. She had sounded as though she meant it. She had looked him straight in the eye.

He wanted to see her. He *longed* to hear her voice. He could walk up to her front door and present himself. No, not yet. He shouldn't act on an impulse. He was not the sort of man who took foolish and unnecessary risks – with one notable exception . . .

The Hunters lived at Clarenden Farm, set among acres and acres of land less than a quarter of a mile from Remnant Castle. They had been neighbours of the Remnants for quite a bit, though he'd never imagined they'd become anything like friends. He had been surprised when Clarissa had asked them for drinks, then to dinner, then to tea, then for drinks again; and had finally issued the invitation for a visit to their very own island.

Why had they been invited? They were not exactly Clarissa's sort of people. Not as some kind of camouflage for Clarissa's affair with the doctor, surely? That was what Louise had suggested. Louise was a nasty cat. He never ceased to marvel at the fascinating depths of his wife's inexhaustible banality. Louise had gone out of her way to poison his mind against Clarissa. Louise was jealous. Terribly jealous. Well, there was nothing he could do about it.

Would things be different now that Lord Remnant was dead? Perhaps Clarissa would phone and ask him over for a drink. *She owed him a lot.* That was what she had told him the night Lord Remnant died.

What a night it had been . . .

The air had seemed full of electricity. They had stood about and stared . . . It was he and Sylvester-Sale who had eventually carried the body up the stairs – *not* to the master bedroom, Clarissa had said, but to Lord Remnant's dressing room next door. They had laid the body on some kind of couch.

He had watched Dr Sylvester-Sale take off Lord Remnant's cardboard nose, then his wig and the Gonzago beard. Lord Remnant's eyes had been darkened with kohl – his cheeks covered in rouge – his mouth painted with purplish lipstick. The whole episode had had a nightmarish quality about it. They had kept the velvet cushion from the chaise longue downstairs under Lord Remnant's head. The cushion had been damp with blood.

They had moved the body from the murder scene. They hadn't called the police. It seemed that different rules operated at La Sorcière. Clarissa's rules. Clarissa had taken charge of the situation.

He saw himself once more standing inside Lord Remnant's dressing room. Each detail remained seared on his mind. The couch was upholstered in dark brown leather. There was a door on the right leading to the bedroom and another, a green baize door, to the en-suite bathroom on the left. A picture hung on the wall above the couch, an Edwardian painting entitled *Cheating at Cards*. It showed four men in full evening dress sitting stiffly around a table, one of them pulling a card sneakily out of his pocket.

Underneath the picture, pushed against the wall, stood a washstand of the greatest elaboration, dating back to the 1890s, or so he imagined; a freak of fancy, really, decorated with silverwork and a series of rhomboid-shaped painted panels. In the centre of it, forming the climax of the design, there was a prominent, highly ornamental copper tap.

As he stood looking down at Lord Remnant's body, he had heard a sound. A laugh. A high-pitched giggle. He was sure he hadn't imagined it. It had given him – well, quite a jolt, really. He had caught his breath. His hair had stood on end. Sylvester-Sale had been there, beside the door, on his way out, but he said he had heard nothing.

In a moment of weakness Basil had told Louise about it. He shouldn't have. Louise had started speculating, wondering, propounding absurd theories . . . How could he *ever* have married her!

Basil Hunter stood still in his tracks and frowned. Though the window had been open, he didn't think the sound had come from outside. He didn't believe it had been made by a bird or an animal. It had been a human sound. *Someone had laughed*. Had there been someone hiding in the bathroom? But who? Who *could* it have been? Everybody had been downstairs – hadn't they?

12

The Giant Shadow

Their eyes were glued to the TV screen. Again they saw the french windows and the net curtains over them and once more the woman with the silver hair and the glasses – Clarissa's aunt – was walking briskly towards the windows, but before she managed to draw the silk curtains, Payne held out the remote control and pressed the Pause button.

'There it is.' Payne pointed at the frozen image. 'Do you see it?'

'See what, Hughie?'

'Do look carefully, darling.'

'I am looking,' Lady Grylls said a little peevishly. 'Though I have no idea what I am supposed to see. There's Roderick in the ghastly Gonzago beard lying on the divan – is that a divan?'

'A chaise longue. What do you see behind the chaise longue?'

'You make it sound like a game. What do I spy with my little eye? I see the french windows – the aunt – I have a feeling the aunt's pretending to be scattier than she is. Beware of emotionally volatile women of a certain age – I wouldn't trust the aunt.'

'Never mind the aunt. What else do you see?'

'I see a pedestal with what looks like a too perfect statuette of Pallas Athene. She has an annoyingly smug expression on her face. Am I the only one who finds classical figures forbidding?'

'We'll discuss art later,' said Payne. 'What else do you see?'

'Nothing else. Only the net curtains.'

'Concentrate on the net curtains . . . D'you notice anything?'

'What is there to notice?'

'Do you mean the shadow?' Felicity Remnant said quietly.

'I do mean the shadow. Eureka! You see it, Lady Remnant, don't you?'

'I do.'

'Goodness, yes. You are absolutely right. There is some sort of shadow outlined against the net curtain. Someone is standing outside.' Lady Grylls pushed her glasses up her nose. 'Doesn't look like a human shadow – too big. What are those things sticking out of it?'

'Are those – *ears*?' Felicity frowned.

'I believe so.'

Lady Grylls screwed up her eyes. 'What *is* it? Looks like a giant rabbit. Goodness, how gruesome.'

'It's a person dressed up as some kind of long-eared animal,' Felicity said.

Payne fast-forwarded and paused again. The silk curtains were now drawn across the french windows.

'Watch carefully,' he said. 'Do keep your eyes on the curtains. What do you see? *Now*.'

'The curtains move – they part – oh, there's someone standing there! Yes! Goodness!' Lady Grylls's hand was at her bosom. 'Something's protruding from between the curtains – oh, it's gone! It caught the light for a moment, but it's gone now. Something shiny. Something made of metal. There was a flash of sorts, but it happened awfully fast!'

'Yes. It happened very fast.' Payne leant back in his seat.

They watched the flailing Lord Remnant lift his head, gape and stare at the camera as though in tremendous surprise, then fall back and lie still.

There was a pause.

'I believe that was a gun,' Felicity said. 'Wasn't it?'

Payne nodded. 'It was a gun, no bigger than a toy.'

'So *that's* what killed him,' Lady Grylls said. 'A gunshot to the head.'

13

Two Go Adventuring Again

Two hours later Major Payne was back in Hampstead.

'Well, you will be pleased to know my copy-editing problem has been resolved,' Antonia said. 'My beloved Emmy has been persuaded not to hang up her pencil quite yet . . . Did the chest live up to your expectations?'

'What chest?'

'The chest you went to inspect, Hugh. Felicity Fenwick's chest. The Damascus chest. I thought your aunt was taking you to see Felicity Fenwick's Damascus chest.'

'She was. I saw it. It has a secret drawer. The chest is fine,' Payne said absently. 'One of the most beautiful objects that has ever been crafted by man. I found it quite remarkable. Definitely on my list of desiderata.'

There was a pause.

'What is it, Hugh? Has something happened?'

'Well, yes. You'd never believe it if I told you. The most extraordinary business. The devil of a business.'

'Surely not?'

'I am afraid so.' Payne produced his pipe portentously. 'The game, as they say, is afoot.'

Antonia remained unimpressed. 'You say that at least once every couple of days. You said it when Dupin disappeared and you said it when we were charged for phone calls we'd never made.'

Dupin was their cat. Dupin had eventually reappeared, but Payne was convinced that he had been lured away and held captive by one of their neighbours, a solitary eccentric spinster who had been trying to persuade them to sell her Dupin.

'This time it is much more serious than any cat or call we may or may not have made,' said Payne. '*Much* more serious, my love, and utterly fascinating. More intriguing than, say, the case of the assassins at Ospreys.'

'I don't suppose you are talking about murder, are you?'

'I *am* talking about murder. It happened on the privately owned Caribbean island of Grenadin. At a house called La Sorcière. No, I am not joking. The murder was committed with startling boldness in full view of at least five people, though none of them seemed to be aware that a shot had been fired.'

'You are making this up.'

'I am not. I saw it all with my very eyes.'

'You mean you were one of the five witnesses?'

'No. I saw a recording of it. The murder was captured on camera. That's what makes the whole thing so terribly extraordinary.'

'The island of Grenadin. Wasn't that where—? It's nothing to do with Lord Remnant, is it?'

'It's everything to do with Lord Remnant.'

Antonia stared back at him.

They had read Lord Remnant's *Times* obituary together only a couple of days before. Antonia had idly commented on Lord Remnant's photograph. She had said something to the effect that he looked arrogant and self-satisfied and she had taken particular exception to his wolfish smile.

'The *Times* obituary said he died of a heart attack.'

'That's the official version. The consensus of opinion is that Lord Remnant was murdered.'

'What consensus? Who are you talking about?'

'My aunt. Felicity Remnant. Yours truly. We all agreed he was murdered. The whole thing is quite incredible. It starts with Felicity Remnant's having her suspicions aroused at the crematorium,' Payne went on. 'She is struck by the conspiratorial behaviour of the people attending the cremation.'

'I assume they were the very same crowd who watched as Lord Remnant handed in his dinner pail?'

'The very same. Felicity thought they looked furtive. And then, as though in confirmation of her suspicions, she received an anonymous package containing a videotape showing Lord Remnant's last moments.'

Payne went on to tell the rest of the story.

There was a pause.

'Lord Remnant was shot through the back of the head by a giant rabbit,' Antonia said.

'Lord Remnant was shot by a person wearing a rabbit's head, though I doubt it was a rabbit. I don't think there are any rabbits in Shakespeare, are there?' Payne held up his pipe. 'Can you think of any animals at all in Shakespeare?'

'There is a dog – Balthasar in *Romeo and Juliet*,' said Antonia. 'No – Balthasar is not a dog, but Romeo's tragically precipitate friend. Sorry. How silly of me. I must be thinking of *The Forsyte Saga* – Old Jolyon and faithful Balthasar? Remember Balthasar's death and subsequent burial?'

'Vividly. The scene reduced me to tears. In which of Shakespeare's tragedies does a character exit pursued by a bear?'

'*The Winter's Tale*? What has Shakespeare to do with Lord Remnant's death?'

'Lord Remnant died during a private performance of *The Murder of Gonzago*.'

'I see. How fascinating . . . Hamlet's brainwave. Hamlet was playing the detective. The play within the play. Hamlet also called it *The Mousetrap* . . . That's where Agatha Christie got *her* idea.'

'They keep thinking of ingenious ways of making Shakespeare more accessible to the masses, but there seem to be more misses than hits . . . Do you remember the way they did Gonzago in the David Tennant *Hamlet?* You hated it, didn't you? The Player Queen! Remember the Player Queen?'

'I most certainly do. The whole thing was terrible.' Antonia shuddered squeamishly. 'A veritable freak show.'

The Player King had sported monkey ears, and shuffled on boots attached to his knees. The Player Queen was a bare-breasted transvestite. Once murdered, the Player King had been shrouded in a white sheet and winched into the air where he had hovered, ghost-like. The regicide Lucianus had strutted about, wearing a heart-shaped spangled codpiece.

'Lord Remnant's murderer appears to have been dressed up as some long-eared creature,' Payne said. 'If not a rabbit, then Bottom in *Midsummer Night's Dream* seems indicated, wouldn't you say? I can't think of any other ass in Shakespeare – can you?'

'No. Bottom is not *really* an ass . . . Am I the only one who doesn't find Shakespeare's comedies funny? Who videotaped the thing?' Antonia asked.

'A servant, but then the camera changed hands and it was Clarissa Remnant's aunt who took over.'

'You said there was no sound?'

'No, sadly. No subtitles either. It made me exercise my brains and eyes harder, which wasn't such a bad thing.'

'The package was addressed to Gerard Fenwick who is Lord Remnant's brother . . . Any idea as to who the sender might be?'

'Well, Clarissa's aunt was the last to handle the camera, so the logical assumption is that she had the best chance of monkeying about with the film. This is backed up by the postmark.' Payne frowned reflectively. 'Her name is Hortense Tilling. Felicity says she looked particularly hag-ridden at the funeral. Well, Aunt Hortense may turn out to be one of those lonely middle-aged sensationalists who specialize in stirring up trouble for trouble's sake – but it's also possible that she sent the tape out of noble if somewhat muddled motives. She may be itching to spill the beans.'

'Did you say postmark? What postmark?'

'The Jiffy bag in which the tape was despatched bears the postmark Kensington and Chelsea and Aunt Hortense is the only member of the fatal house party who lives in Kensington. Dr Sylvester-Sale lives in Knightsbridge, the Hunters at a farm not far from Remnant Castle in Hertfordshire. Clarissa resides at Remnant Castle . . . As a matter of fact, I have been instructed to go and interview Aunt Hortense as soon as possible.'

'What do you mean "instructed"? Who instructed you?'

'The new Countess Remnant. Felicity. She wants me to investigate the circumstances surrounding her brother-in-law's murder. She urged me to leave no stone unturned. She wants to know what exactly happened. She said that if I discovered the truth, the Damascus chest would be mine free of charge. She said she would tear up the cheque I gave her.'

'She would tear up the cheque? How very interesting. And you accepted her commission, just like that? No hesitation?'

He shrugged. 'One mustn't refuse the unusual if it is offered to one. That, perhaps, should be our motto. You agree of course?'

'It seems to me that the new Countess Remnant doesn't care much for the family she married into,' Antonia said. 'Or is that too fanciful?'

'Not too fanciful. I think she would be pleased if her husband's family were to be embroiled in some sort of scandal. My aunt suspects the settling of old scores.

Apparently, Gerard's late mama was beastly to Felicity when Gerard and Felicity first got married. Felicity doesn't seem to think much of Clarissa either . . . None of my business, but I can't help thinking there is something wrong with the Fenwick marriage. You should have seen the way her face hardened when her husband's club got a mention.'

'I don't suppose you've been able to obtain Aunt Hortense's address?'

'As it happens, I have. Felicity managed to get it for me.' Payne waved a piece of paper. 'Well, my love, I'm going to pay Aunt Hortense a visit tomorrow morning, at about eleven. Um . . . What do you think?'

'What does it matter what I think?'

He cleared his throat. 'I was wondering whether you'd care to join me.'

14

The Sphinx without a Secret

Sometimes my wife suffers from a fury of possession and she cannot bear me to be drawn to anyone but her, Gerard Fenwick wrote in his diary. *She may not look the kind of woman who falls prey to the emerald-eyed lizard, but the sad truth is she is jealous not only of pretty young things like Renée Glover, but of our Lithuanian maid, of my Davidoff Grand Cru cigars, of my books, of my silver-topped stylo and, indeed, of my writing.*

I am at my club at the moment. If I have to be honest, I prefer my club to my house. My rooms overlook St James's Park and they are rather splendid. I feel exceedingly comfortable and at peace here.

I am at my happiest when I am writing. Writing has the effect of a heavenly balm. Writing brings with it a sense of release, of assuagement, of profound contentment.

For some peculiar reason my penchant for a good cigar riles Felicity. Maybe because she associates it with my tête-à-têtes with Renée? Only the other day Felicity told me that I was the worst liar she had ever known, which, apart from being damned unfair, somehow manages to suggest she moves exclusively in the society of liars.

It is all rather tiresome, but, fortunately, I am of an equable temperament. I will not deny that sometimes Felicity taxes my patience, but I accept her acrimonious outbursts as an act of God

and no more think of rebelling against them than I would against
bad weather or a cold in the head . . .

Leaning back in his chair, he reached for his cigar case.
Shouldn't bother too much about Felicity, really. It would
be wrong to get fixated on Felicity. The broader picture was
not too bad at all. His shockingly unpopular elder brother
was dead and he, Gerard Fenwick, was rich. Rich at last.
Well, not yet, not technically speaking, but he would be
soon enough.

As it happened, the opening and reading of the will was
taking place later in the afternoon. He looked at his watch.
He must try not to be late. He expected no surprises. How
splendid it would be to be rich. He wouldn't dream of
actually articulating the sentiment, frightfully bad form, but
a multi-million-pound fortune was, well, a multi-million-
pound fortune. He would be so rich, he could buy the club
and make it his writing pad, if he felt like it. He smiled at
the idea.

Holding his cigar between his thumb and forefinger, he
glanced round. He liked what he saw. The room had been
recently repapered and hung with pleasing Piranesi prints
– there was a good fire – a revolving mahogany bookcase,
which he had filled with old favourites (Lord Berners's *A
Distant Prospect*, Salinger's *The Catcher in the Rye*, Saki's *Beasts
and Super-Beasts*, Donna Tartt's *The Secret History*) – a photo
of him winning a shooting competition – his humidor. The
ambience couldn't have been cosier or more bachelor-ish.

Where *had* his cigar cutter disappeared to? For some
reason he felt the stirrings of unease. Oh well, never mind,
he'd use the point of his paper knife – it should do the trick
– *voilà*. He clicked his lighter. Bliss. *A woman is only a woman
but a good cigar is a smoke*. He wished it was he and not old
Kipling who'd said that!

He regarded his lighter with some amusement. It was
made of silver and shaped like a gun. It had been a present

from his wife, dating back to their shooting – and happier – days.

Gerard could handle any kind of gun. Big or small. He was a first-class shot. He was better than his late brother had been. Roderick had always been awfully jealous of him on that count. Awfully jealous. Odd chap, Roderick. Dangerous. What was it he told him once when they were children? *I'll smash your big head like a pumpkin.* More than once, actually. Fancied himself as a ladies' man too. Mad, most probably. Like Papa and Uncle William before him. Like Aunt Margot and Cousin Lionel. Living in a hot climate couldn't have made things any better.

Oh well, Roderick was dead now. Dead and gone. He might never have existed. All that was left of him was little more than a handful of dust. I no longer have a brother, Gerard thought.

He had spent the previous night at his club. Felicity had phoned to ask where he was. *I am at my club, my dear, didn't I say? No, you didn't, Gerard. I am sure I did, my dear. No, you didn't.* All too tiresome for words. Felicity appeared to think his writing was a cover for something else. It was fascinating to speculate what she might be suspecting. Gerard puffed at his cigar.

Brothels? The criminal underworld? Strolling up and down Piccadilly in drag? While all he did was sit at his club overlooking St James's, in his shabbiest tweeds, leaning over a desk, scribbling away! Well, he was a sphinx without a secret, like the woman in the Oscar Wilde story. She was suspected of harbouring some extraordinary secret, of doing things no respectable woman should, whereas all she did was sit in a rented room and drink tea.

He found the idea of men in drag a jolly curious one. What was it that caused phenomena like that? Some chemical anomaly in the brain? Perhaps he could write a short story about it? There used to be a chap back in the nineteenth century, a politician or a philosopher, who was said to have dressed much better as a woman than as a man and was an inspiration to a whole generation of Englishmen . . .

He could write a story about a man who disguises himself as his wife, makes himself look *exactly* like her, then starts following her about and makes sure she sees him. She is persuaded she has a twin sister of whose existence she hadn't been aware – no – that she has a double – and she remembers the old wives' tale that if you have seen your double, you are about to die. The husband's intention is to drive her mad. Something on those lines.

Felicity had informed him that a videotape had arrived, which he needed to see. She said it was important. Apparently it showed Roderick's death. She had been dashed mysterious about it.

He thought about Roderick's phone call – the awful things Roderick had said – how it had made him feel – he'd seen red – his subsequent decision and the action he had taken—

He still couldn't quite believe what he had done! It felt like a dream now. *Quite* unlike him.

Once more he glanced at his watch. Time to go. Old Saunders wouldn't start without him, though it would be terribly bad form to make him wait. *Noblesse oblige* and all that kind of rot. The reading of Roderick's will was going to take place in exactly three-quarters of an hour. Saunders's office was in New Bond Street. He could walk. The weather seemed fine at the moment, though, to be on the safe side, he would take his faithful brolly with him.

People who didn't know him well thought him mild-mannered, slightly eccentric, not terribly practical, completely unremarkable. Nothing like his exhibitionistic late brother – or the elusive Lucan – or Wodehouse's master of misrule, the havoc-wreaking Ickenham – all of them unreliable earls! Not a controversialist like Spencer (*that* speech) or the late Longford (Myra Hindley!) either.

As he rose and stubbed out his cigar in the ashtray, Gerard thought about his cigar cutter once more. Such a pity if he'd lost it. He'd allowed himself to become attached to it. He believed he was emotionally starved. The cigar cutter was made of silver, fashioned like a guillotine, with his monogram engraved on one side and the Remnant coat of arms on the other, and it could fit into his waistcoat pocket.

When was the last time he'd used it?

15

Fear Eats the Soul

They walked along an interminable avenue of tall houses with elegant if faded façades, none of which seemed to show any sign of life. If one could imagine a terrace of tombs, Payne murmured. Several moments later, having arrived at their destination, he observed that the steps to Hortense Tilling's front door were as steep as the side of a pyramid; one would hesitate to knock on the door for fear of a mummy emerging, didn't Antonia think?

'No, I don't. Sometimes, Hugh, I do wonder if you say these silly things with the sole purpose of finding out if I'm listening.' Antonia grasped the door knocker resolutely.

'Well, murder will out! Old deceits claim their dues! They always say that, don't they? Thy sin will find thee. I have been dreading this moment. Absolutely dreading it.' Hortense Tilling shut her eyes. 'Someone turning up out of the blue. The moment of truth. Having to *explain*.' She was holding her hand at her throat. 'Perhaps I shouldn't have let you in, but it's too late for that now.'

'If you show us the door, we shall march back to it with complete submission,' Payne said gravely.

'Will you really?' She hesitated. 'No – I hate making scenes. I haven't got the strength. I am afraid I don't feel awfully well. I have this persistent, rather sickening sense of down-rushing ruin, as if I've been flung off a precipice . . . It's loneliness that's said to beget loquaciousness, though in my case it is nerves. I talk too much, don't I?'

'No, not at all,' Antonia said. They *wanted* her to talk.

'Would you like to sit down?'

'Thank you,' Payne said. 'Most kind.'

They had decided to call on Hortense Tilling without giving her any notice. Always more effective than trying to make arrangements over the phone. Didn't give her the chance to say no and put down the receiver.

'I might as well offer you tea,' Hortense said.

'Tea would be lovely,' Antonia said.

'I *must* give you scones too. With Devonshire cream and seedless raspberry jam? Though let me calm down first. My nerves are in a bad state, you see.'

'Perhaps you should sit down for a bit?'

'No, no, my dear. I'd rather stand. It induces in me the feeling of being in control. It's completely illusory. Could we pretend we have known each other for years and this is a social call?'

'I don't see why not,' Payne said.

'Perhaps we could talk about the weather first? It will make things easier, I think. I find talking about the weather relaxing, don't you?'

She was a thin, birdlike woman in her sixties, wearing a silk dress in what Antonia thought were strong dead colours: dark red and old gold and purple. Her face was pale pink and gently wrinkled, her silver hair parted in the middle, and she wore round horn-rimmed spectacles which seemed to accentuate her oddly pious expression and made her look rather like a nun.

'Isn't it cold today?' Antonia said.

'There was a chill drizzle from the north-east as we set out.' Payne glanced towards the window.

'It feels more like autumn than spring,' said Hortense.

'Spring is late this year,' Antonia said.

'It is, isn't it, my dear? *Terribly* late. I keep shivering, even with the central heating on. Well, that's England for you. One shouldn't wear silk. There! It's done the trick. I already feel better.' Hortense nodded. '*Thank* you.'

'I imagine you are feeling the cold more acutely than us,' Major Payne said. 'Having returned from the Caribbean not so long ago? Did the Caribbean agree with you?'

'It did, to start with.' She clasped her hands before her. 'Have you been to the Caribbean? No? Cobalt blue skies – cicadas – dragonflies with diamond wings. Fizzing hot days, as my father used to say. The endless susurrus of the sea. An easy life. *La dolce vita*. Used to be my idea of paradise. But then – then it all changed.'

'Because of Lord Remnant's death?'

'Well, yes. The morning after he died, I took a walk round the island and I was struck by the amazing absence of *meaningful ambulation*. The idea depressed me. Oh how it depressed me. I'd never thought in those terms before, you see. Suddenly I felt faint—'

'Was it very hot?'

'Well, yes, but up till then I hadn't minded the heat. It was the kind of heat that's been described as "swooning" . . . Everybody on the beach was in a horizontal position, limp and languorous, fanning themselves. I had the odd sense people were horizontal in their very *souls*. What a silly thing to say! Do forgive me. Why am I standing here? I was going to do something, wasn't I?'

'You were going to make us tea,' Antonia said brightly.

'Tea, yes! Let's have tea! The cup that cheereth!'

She disappeared into the kitchen.

The sofa was large and the colour of whipped cream. They sat among a proliferation of ancient tasselled cushions of petit-point. The wall above the sofa was covered with framed photographs, some of which had faded to so pale a brown that it was simply the pattern of the black rectangles of their frames on the pale cream walls that seemed to serve the purpose of decoration. But there were some good, clear ones . . .

It was the photograph of a stunningly beautiful dark-haired girl that drew their attention. The girl's hair was done in the style of the early sixties, her shoulders bare, one hand held clasped under her chin. Round her wrist she wore a striking bracelet in the shape of a coiled snake, most probably a cobra, made from what looked like black pearls.

Payne raised a quizzical eyebrow at Antonia. 'That our hostess? Can't be.'

'I think it's her . . . many summers ago. She's still got the same smile.'

'Golly, yes.'

'Isn't time cruel?'

'Merciless.' Payne's eyes had strayed towards the bookcase. 'Books on adoption . . . *Cuckoo in the Nest*. I can't help noticing people's books, can you?'

'I find myself instinctively disapproving of people who have no books in their houses. In a funny kind of way it puts me on guard,' Antonia said. 'I don't think I can be friends with people who don't read.'

'I can't be friends with people who read the wrong kind of books . . . Dan Brown, J. K. Rowling, Martina Cole, old McCall Smith, Jeffery Deaver – or is that unfair?'

'Do you think she's been considering adoption? A bit old for that,' Antonia whispered.

'The books are also old, which suggests she may have considered it when she was younger.'

'I am worried about her. She is in a febrile state . . . She seems scared out of her wits.'

Payne's eyes were back on the photograph. 'What a magnificent bracelet that is . . . Now where—?'

There was a tinkling sound as Hortense Tilling re-entered the room, a tea-tray in her hands. 'In case you are wondering, that's me, yes. You wouldn't think it, would you? *Vogue* offered me a modelling contract, but my mother made me turn it down. My mother disapproved of models. She feared for my virtue. It all seems like a dream now. I was an altogether different person then.' She hummed the tune of '*Where Is The Life That Late I Led*?' She set the tea-tray on the coffee table.

'I have been admiring your bracelet,' Payne said.

'Ah, the Keppel Clasp.'

'The Keppel Clasp? Is that what it's called? Exquisite craftsmanship. Is it Fabergé?'

'It is. You are a connoisseur, I see. As it happens, Mrs Keppel was a distant relation on my mother's side. The clasp was a present to her from you-know-who.' She picked up the silver pot and started pouring out tea.

'Edward VII?'

'Indeed. From Kingy. I believe that's what she called him. The stout sceptred satyr . . . Sugar? No?'

'It's in the form of a snake,' said Antonia.

'Yes. Are you squeamish about snakes? I don't blame you. Most people are. But snakes can be so beautiful . . . The snake's head and the tail form a knot, did you notice?'

'Yes. Most unusual. Exquisite craftsmanship,' Payne said again.

'The Keppel Clasp was quite unique.' Hortense sighed.

'Why the past tense? Haven't you still got it?' Antonia asked.

'I am afraid not. I'd love to be able to show it to you, my dear, but it is no longer in my possession. The Keppel Clasp was stolen from me. A long time ago. I hadn't even had it insured. Well, I believe I was punished for being a bad girl.' A shadow passed across her face.

There was a pause.

'Delicious scones,' Antonia said. 'I love raspberry jam.'

'It's home-made. I love making jam. Something comforting about jam-making.' Hortense perched on the arm of an armchair. 'How curious that you should have turned up. I was right. I mean I *knew* that sooner or later someone would ring my front door bell! I knew it was only a question of time, though of course I had no idea who it would be. The police? Private detectives? The intelligence service? Men in black? Anyhow, now that I have met you, the worst is over.'

'Fear of the unknown is the worst kind of fear,' Payne said amiably.

'Well, the heavens didn't fall and there wasn't a great bolt of lightning! You are not related to the Remnant family, are you?'

'Only in an exceedingly distant sort of way. My aunt tried to explain exactly how, but it all sounded too convoluted and far-fetched for words. I met Felicity Fenwick yesterday, for the first time. You are Clarissa's aunt, correct?'

'Correct. I am Clarissa's mother's sister. Clarissa's *late* mother. I am Clarissa's only living relation. Poor child. I care deeply about my daughter – I mean niece – Clarissa is like a daughter to me . . . I must admit I always had misgivings about Clarissa's marriage to Lord Remnant. I'd heard *stories*. I knew something would go wrong at some point. I felt it in my bones.'

'Was he really as awful as that?' Antonia asked.

For a moment or two, Hortense gazed at them, saying nothing. Then she leant forward slightly. '*I believe he was truly evil*. That marriage should never have taken place, never. I tried to warn Clarissa but she wouldn't listen to me. Marriage is a serious affair, to be entered into only after long deliberation and forethought, and suitability of tastes and inclinations should be considered very carefully indeed. I

98

don't think Clarissa had much in common with Remnant, apart from a penchant for theatricals.'

'He was older than her, wasn't he?'

'*Much* older. I suspect she was dazzled by his ancient title and – and by that island. How I hate that island!' Hortense cried. 'Almost as much as I hate St George's Church. At one time I felt like burning St George's Church to the ground. I really did.'

'St George's Church in Hanover Square?'

'Yes. That was where the wedding took place. That's where the accursed Remnant married her. Irrational of me, I know, but that's how I felt. Poor Clarissa. No daughter of mine should have had to endure—' Hortense broke off. 'I keep saying things I shouldn't be saying. Somehow you have succeeded in goading me into unguarded speech. I keep forgetting you are perfect strangers.'

'That's not such a bad thing, is it?' Antonia smiled.

'Did you say Felicity Fenwick showed you a tape? And perhaps you believe that it was I who sent it? What if I denied any knowledge of the tape?'

'Somehow I don't think you would.'

'You exude *such* certainty, Major Payne. It is reassuring somehow. It *is* Major Payne, isn't it? Of course you have nothing to do with the police?'

'Nothing at all.'

'I hope I never have to talk to the police, though heaven knows what the future holds . . . Do remind me of your name, my dear?'

'Antonia.'

'And you and Major Payne are—? Sorry! I have no business asking questions like that.'

'Husband and wife.'

'Husband and wife. I am so glad. Makes *such* a difference. You strike me as extremely nice people, if you don't mind my saying so. I am rarely wrong. I suppose I am old enough to be your mother?'

'I don't think so,' Antonia said. 'We are not as young as you seem to think.'

'I can never tell people's ages. I believe you to be of superior intelligence, but also sensitive, understanding, compassionate and, most importantly, *sympathetic*. I have the feeling I have known you a long time.'

'I am glad you don't find us threatening.'

'Murder is a terrible business. I keep thinking of those characters in Elizabethan tragedies, who burst into castle halls, shouting, "Murdered – he's been murdered!" . . . I can't get what happened out of my head . . . Didn't someone describe murder as a tangible expression of hysteria? No, I am fine, Antonia, just a touch of vertigo. I haven't been eating properly. Another cushion, yes, thank you, dear.'

'Have you taken anything?' Payne asked. 'Any medication?'

'I have been taking some tablets. I believe they are quite strong and they seem to have a number of side effects. In normal circumstances I am much more reticent. I was prescribed tablets for anxiety, you see. I was in *such* a bad state, I *had* to go to the doctor's.'

'You don't have to apologize,' Antonia said.

'I tend to regard going to the doctor's as an unnecessary indulgence. My mother was like that. My mother was terribly puritanical . . . Poor Clarissa told me she was taking something too. We are *so* alike. I have no idea about the Hunters' current state of mind. I don't know whether they are being gnawed at by their guilty conscience or whether they have managed to draw a veil over the whole shocking episode.'

'You know the Hunters well?'

'No, not at all well. We were fellow guests. I'd never met them before. She likes tea and he likes coffee. She is a big lumbering woman. He has a moustache. He is something of a Dismal Desmond. That's all I know about them. I don't think they communicate much. Communication is important in a marriage, isn't it?'

'*A sine qua non*,' Payne said solemnly.

Hortense took a sip of tea. 'Dr Valdemar wanted me to tell him what the trouble was, such a kind man, and I did want to tell him, but of course I couldn't. The same thing happened when a clergyman friend came to see me the other day. *Toute vérité n'est pas bonne à dire.* He said he would pray for me. I am not boring you, am I?'

'Not at all,' Antonia reassured her.

Sometimes she found herself telling the truth only *partially* – or with distortions, Hortense went on. 'Not the whole truth, if you know what I mean. I've managed to convince myself it makes me feel better. That it assuages the emotional chaos inside me. Who said, *Trust me not at all, or all in all*?'

'Tennyson, I think,' Payne said.

'Tennyson, yes. The Victorians knew all about trust, didn't they? You know the story of King Midas who had ass's ears? He kept trying to conceal them, poor wretch, couldn't live with the awful truth, so he dug a hole in the ground and jumped in and whispered, "King Midas has ass's ears!" Then he filled up the hole, but the earth, being a woman, spread the story and the reeds started whispering, "King Midas has donkey's ears!"'

'We promise to be more discreet than Mrs Earth,' Payne said. 'Ass's ears, eh? Why does this ring a bell? Oh yes. There was someone dressed up as an ungulate that night, wasn't there? Or rather, as Bottom after his transformation?'

'So you saw the shadow? I dreamt of it the other night. Well, we all knew he was there. I mean Stephan. He should have been kept in his room, under lock and key. We ought to have taken better care of him, then, perhaps, tragedy would have been averted.'

'Shall I pour you another cup of tea?'

'Yes, thank you, Antonia. Well, I must say this doesn't

feel like an inquisition at all. I assume it was Lord Remnant who asked you to look into the matter? I mean the *new* Lord Remnant. The thirteenth earl. The former Mr Fenwick.'

'We are actually acting on behalf of Lady Remnant,' Payne explained.

'Lady Remnant? You mean Clarissa asked you—? But that's impossible!' Hortense looked at him wildly. 'No. Clarissa is the *Dowager* Lady Remnant now. The Dowager Countess. Dear me. So confusing! You mean Felicity Fenwick of course. Poor Clarissa is far from well, but she said she didn't want me to feel sorry for her. She was a bit snappy with me. It causes me such pain – if only she knew!'

'You phoned her?'

'I did. I keep phoning her. I want to know how she is. I care about her deeply.' Hortense's eyes were fixed on the bookcase. 'If only I'd had the chance to bring her up myself, things might have been different . . . She seemed at first to think I was a man! My voice sounded terribly hoarse, I suppose. I only said, "That you, Clarissa?" She gasped. She sounded scared out of her wits, poor child. It really made me feel guilty.'

Payne frowned. 'Why was she so scared? Who did she think it was?'

'I have no idea. When she realized it was me, she got angry. Scolded me for having frightened her.'

'Shall I butter you a scone, Miss Tilling?' Antonia suggested.

'No, my dear. Nothing to eat. I couldn't possibly. You are too kind. But I'd like some more tea. My mouth feels dry. I am so terribly thirsty. It's those pills. One of the side effects. *Thank* you. None of what took place at La Sorcière was Clarissa's fault. Poor Clarissa is the victim of circumstance. I can't begin to tell you how much I worry about Clarissa.' Hortense's eyes filled with tears. 'Words can't express it. Each morning I wake up wondering if she is all right.'

'You are her mother, aren't you?' Antonia said gently.

16

Cards on the Table

'How perceptive of you,' Hortense Tilling said after a pause. 'I am hopeless at keeping secrets. *Hopeless*. All right. I am her aunt *and* her mother. None of this has anything to do with Lord Remnant's murder, mind. Nothing at all. I have been bottling things up for too long, that's the trouble. My story is not very edifying.'

'Does Clarissa know you are her mother?' Antonia asked.

'No. Clarissa has no idea. I was terribly young. I was a fool. I was seventeen. I went to a party. I met a Frenchman who asked me to dance – no, that's the wrong place to start – or rather the wrong story!' She turned deep red. She shook her head. 'Sorry! I need to collect my thoughts.'

She pressed the thumb and forefinger of her right hand on the bridge of her nose in a seeming effort to concentrate.

'I lived with my elder sister and brother-in-law. I was very pretty. My brother-in-law seduced me. He was terribly attractive, but quite an impossible character. The two often go together, have you noticed? I wouldn't call it an affair. The long and the short of it is that I became pregnant. I fell on my knees and confessed to my sister and she forgave me. She said she wanted the baby.'

'Your sister had no children?'

'No. She – she couldn't have any children, you see, but now she told people she was pregnant. She started strapping a cushion around her stomach. I kept out of the way. I went to Dieppe. I had the baby. It was a little girl. I then came back to England and my sister brought up Clarissa as her own daughter. She eventually split up with her husband who, as you may have gathered, was the worst of philanderers.'

'You never told Clarissa?'

'No. No. I decided not to. Perhaps I will, one day. I don't know.' Hortense paused. 'She doesn't like me much, I'm afraid. She finds me a nuisance. I tend to say and do things which annoy her. I love Clarissa, always have. I never married, you see, never had any other children. I keep worrying about Clarissa. She is so terribly unhappy. Her first marriage was quite hellish. Small wonder Stephan's turned out so badly. Her second – to Lord Remnant – was worse, far worse. And now of course it has all ended in disaster.'

'Stephan is Clarissa's son by her first marriage?'

'Yes. Poor boy. Clarissa used to be married to an awful man called Farrar. I am afraid Clarissa has shown a singular lack of judgement in her choice of soulmates.'

They seemed to be straying from the murder. Payne cleared his throat. 'Why was Stephan outside? Was he meant to be outside?'

'He'd been sent out. He was in disgrace for being rude to Lord Remnant. Well, it was Lord Remnant who insisted on our dressing up as characters out of Shakespeare. It was all his idea. Heaven knows why. He was neither a Shakespearean scholar nor a Shakespeare aficionado. He wasn't a great reader. The only books I ever saw him read were something called *The Youth Pill* and an ancient tome on resurrecting the dead.'

'Is that the sort of thing he believed in?'

'That was the *only* thing he seemed to believe in. He was

teaching himself how to raise the dead, he said. That was one of his less peculiar foibles. He described the book as a DIY manual. He was a godless man. He was mad about dressing up. Once they all dressed up as characters in *Winnie-the-Pooh*, apparently. I've seen a photo – perfectly absurd – Kanga, Piglet, Eeyore and Owl swigging cocktails . . . You recognized the play of course? The play on the tape?'

'*The Murder of Gonzago.*'

'Hamlet's ingenious and rather gruesome attempt to make his uncle give himself away. I have nightmares about it. A dumbshow. No talking, only mime. So macabre. There is something disconcerting about the absence of sound . . . Lord Remnant played Gonzago and, like Gonzago, he was killed . . . I can't describe the joy I felt when they told me he was dead. Did you ever meet Lord Remnant?'

'No, never.'

'He was quite horrible to me,' she said. 'On my first day at La Sorcière he hid my glasses under a sofa cushion. I spent *ages* looking for them. I am lost without my glasses. I didn't have a spare pair. He seemed to relish the spectacle of my taking an armchair for a fellow guest and apologizing after bumping into it,' Hortense rambled on. 'He made me look a fool. He referred to me by a nickname – Miss Baedeker – on account of the Baedeker he had seen on my bedside table. I don't suppose people use Baedekers any longer?'

'It's a bit dated now,' Payne said.

'Lord Remnant enjoyed humiliating people. He would do anything to be the centre of attention. For instance, he shot an enormous crocodile once; he then had it stuffed and encrusted with jewels and he put it in the bed in one of the guests' rooms!'

'Was he a hunter?'

'I believe he was. Most of his ideas were decidedly crackpot. Apparently, at one time he got it into his head that "Begin the Beguine" had such emotional power that it could destroy moral judgement and induce wantonness, so he played it all the time – now what do you think of *that*?'

'Decidedly crackpot,' Payne agreed.

'He was prey to the most disturbing urges. He wanted to box people's ears for interrupting him or for not getting the point of a joke!'

'Did he actually box anyone's ears?'

'He boxed Stephan's ears. He kept picking on the poor boy, even though he knew perfectly well he shouldn't. He kept provoking him. The boy is not well. Far from it.'

'What is wrong with Stephan?' Antonia asked.

'A lot of things. Drugs. General instability. Perhaps the two are connected? Bad heredity. Stephan is emotionally stunted. He can be extremely childish. Sucks his thumb. Uses baby language. He used to refer to Roderick as Daddy R. Louise Hunter was Auntie Lou. I was Aunt Tense. Stephan's been in and out of various private clinics and rehabs ever since he was fourteen.'

'How old is he now?'

'Eighteen and a half. Lord Remnant kept teasing him mercilessly, saying such awful things to him, driving him to rages. Stephan got his drugs from local suppliers, apparently. I mean West Indians. Lord Remnant knew all about it. I strongly suspect he actually *encouraged* Stephan to take drugs. I believe he enjoyed maintaining a hold over Stephan. Drugs are quite easy to get in the Caribbean, sadly.'

'So we have heard.'

'Lord Remnant upset everyone, but no one dared contradict him. People were afraid of him. I couldn't stand him. I thought the world would be a better place without him. I kept wishing him dead!'

'Isn't that a dangerous admission?' Payne said with a smile.

'Oh, it's one thing to wish people dead, a completely different thing to actually kill them,' Hortense said in dismissive tones. 'I am not brave enough. Besides – look at me – blind as a bat, even with my glasses on! I've never held a gun in my life. But I was telling you about *Gonzago*. Well, everyone went along with the idea. Clarissa made me watch their rehearsals. Lord Remnant put on such airs, you'd have thought he was the new Olivier! Clarissa kept asking me if she looked too ridiculous. I told her she looked marvellous.'

'Whose idea was it to record the performance with a video camera?'

'Clarissa's. Clarissa has a passion for home movies. Poor girl, she always wanted to be an actress. She is enormously talented. She's got a real flair for all things theatrical. It was Clarissa who chose the background music. "The Bilbao Song", and that was followed by "Le Roi d'Aquitaine". It's the kind of music that creates a peculiarly unsettling, high-camp sort of mood, which was precisely what she wanted.'

'So Lord Remnant was shot in the back of the head,' said Payne. 'How big was the revolver?'

'It was absurdly small. It looked like a toy. No one in the room heard the shot. The gun had a silencer. Louise said she heard a popping sound, but she imagined it was one of the sound effects in "The Bilbao Song", which had a kind of a drumbeat to it. No one saw the gun sticking out from between the window curtains either, or so they said.'

'You were not in the room when the shot was fired?' Payne tried to sound as casual as possible.

'I wasn't. I'd dashed to the loo. When I came back, it was all over. Lord Remnant lay dead. Everyone had frozen. They might have been stuffed with sawdust. I was beset by the kind of primeval panic that brings about mass hysteria, pogroms and stampedes, but that came later, much later, after I'd returned to England. At first they thought that he'd had a heart attack, he'd complained of chest pains earlier on, but then Dr Sylvester-Sale discovered the hole.'

'The hole in the back of Lord Remnant's head?'

'Yes. A very tiny hole, apparently. Later on we found the gun outside on the terrace. It was lying beside the head.'

'Bottom's head?'

'Yes. We'd seen the shadow outlined against the curtains earlier on . . . The shadow kept appearing and disappearing. We knew Stephan was lurking outside the windows. Perhaps we should have kept a closer eye on him, but we didn't.'

Antonia asked if anyone had seen the gun before.

'As a matter of fact we all had, my dear. It belonged to Lord Remnant. It was very small and beautifully crafted. Lord Remnant had kept several guns in the house since the trouble with the locals. He'd been receiving death threats because he'd had a lot of families evicted from his land. He'd had a lot of houses demolished and so on. He was very unpopular. He was universally loathed.'

'Death threats?' Payne echoed.

'Yes. Some gruesomely graphic ones. They were always pinned on the sundial in the garden, Clarissa said. It seems most of the locals had it in for Lord Remnant. They hated his guts . . . Clarissa kept finding voodoo dolls made in the likeness of Lord Remnant scattered about the estate – stuck with hundreds of needles! She thought at first they were baby porcupines! The irony is that in the end, it was the enemy within who killed Lord Remnant. His stepson.'

17

Unruly Son

'Such a sweet, gentle boy. So clever and he could be really funny.' Hortense sighed. 'But he became a demon when provoked . . . He is prey to the extremes of mood that seem to agonize all drug addicts. He had already tried to shoot his stepfather *with that very same gun.*'

'Really?'

'Yes! It happened earlier that day. Stephan detested his stepfather. Only the week before he'd stabbed Lord Remnant in the hand with a quill pen! It left a nasty red scar between his thumb and index finger.'

'Why did Stephan try to shoot Lord Remnant?' Antonia asked.

'Well, it seems the earl caught Stephan red-handed in his study, trying to steal an extremely valuable porcelain dragon of the Ming dynasty. Stephan said he needed money badly. He said he needed a fix. He was quite open about it. Stephan liked to talk about his addiction. When Lord Remnant took a step towards him, Stephan opened the top desk drawer and pulled out the gun.'

'He clearly knew it was there.'

'He did know it, Major Payne. He brandished the gun in Lord Remnant's face, then he aimed it at his head. The gun, as it happened, was empty, but Stephan kept pressing the trigger. Eventually, Lord Remnant and Augustine – that's the black major-domo – managed to disarm him. Lord Remnant told us the story himself, with great relish.'

'Where did Lord Remnant keep his ammunition?'

'In that same drawer. Several boxes of it. In some ways, he was a very stupid man – impetuous – careless – reckless – so you may say that he was to blame for his own death. He should have kept the ammunition under lock and key, only he didn't. It was almost as though he had a death wish!'

'Lord Remnant was shot only moments after the doctor pretended to pour poison in his ear,' said Payne thoughtfully.

'I believe that is so. It was SS – that's what we all called Dr Sylvester-Sale – who examined the body and told us Lord Remnant had been shot. We knew at once who had done it. We all knew it was Stephan.'

Antonia said, 'You didn't think it could have been someone else?'

'We didn't. At least no one offered any other theory. Who else could it have been? I personally don't believe it was one of the locals. Clarissa then asked SS and Basil Hunter to take Lord Remnant's body upstairs, to his dressing room.'

'No question of an ambulance and the police being called?'

'No. Clarissa said there would be no point in calling an ambulance since her husband was irreversibly dead. She said the local police were an absolute nightmare, a criminal bunch, a posse of desperadoes. She warned us we'd all be in big trouble if the police got involved. Lord Remnant had already managed to upset the local police chief in some way. Clarissa said we'd all be put in jail.'

'No one tried to argue with her?'

'Louise did, unsuccessfully. Clarissa managed to scare us off. She said she had a plan, which she described as foolproof. She assured us everything was going to be all right. She insisted her main concern was for Stephan's welfare. She said Stephan would die if he were to be locked away in a

Caribbean jail, which was the worst thing that could happen to anyone. I do believe she genuinely loves Stephan. So we never called the police.'

'All highly irregular.'

'We were perfectly aware it was all highly irregular, Major Payne, but we had no choice, really. Clarissa then told me to go and get Stephan. She wanted him inside the house.'

'I don't suppose you've told Stephan you are his grandmother?'

'No, of course not. He has no idea – but we get on. For some reason he has taken to me . . . Renée came with me. She is wonderful, simply wonderful, always so composed. We found him sitting calmly by the swimming pool, dropping pebbles. It was obvious he had been smoking pot. We could smell it. He came like a lamb. He could hardly walk. I took him to his room and put him to bed. Several minutes later Dr McLean arrived. Clarissa had called him.'

'A local doctor?'

'Yes. A black doctor, whom, it became clear, Clarissa knew very well indeed. She got both doctors – SS and McLean – together in Lord Remnant's study. The long and the short of it is that a death certificate was eventually produced giving the cause of death as 'heart attack'. It bore the signatures of the two doctors. Later that night Clarissa called us to the study—'

'All together?'

'No. One by one. When my turn came, she took my hand and said she relied on my discretion. She then gave me a cheque. She knew I had a passion for cruises, she said. She told me to treat myself to a cruise. The money she was giving me was enough for ten cruises.'

There was a pause. 'Did she give the others cheques as well?'

'I believe she did. I assume so. I never discussed it with anyone. Well, that's it, really. We all acted in cahoots. I am not in the least sorry Lord Remnant was killed. He was asking for it.' Hortense sounded defiant. 'But I am not as strong as I imagined I was. I have been suffering terrible pangs of conscience.'

'Didn't Lord Remnant employ any security guards?' Antonia asked.

'He did, but it was their night off. There were two of them – unreliable as they come. They returned about midnight, blind drunk. I don't think they quite took in what had happened. They held their hands to their foreheads in salute. I believe one of them tried to kiss Clarissa. She sacked them the very next day.'

'What did Stephan say? I mean when he recovered?' Payne asked. 'Did he actually admit killing his stepfather?'

'He said he didn't remember a thing. He said he must have done it. He actually got rather excited about it. He seemed pleased. He wanted to know every detail.'

'Where is Stephan now?'

'At an ultra-expensive place called Sans Souci. He's already been there a couple of times. Clarissa says they are used to Stephan and his hallucinations there. Which means that if he brags about killing his stepfather, they will think nothing of it.'

'Why did you send the tape to Gerard Fenwick?' Payne asked after a pause. 'You couldn't have wanted your grandson exposed as a murderer, surely?'

'No, of course not. That's the last thing I'd ever want.' Suddenly Hortense Tilling sat up. She took off her glasses. 'I have a confession to make. Please, don't be angry with me. *I never sent the tape.*'

'But you said—'

'I know I let you believe it was me. I did so because I was curious to know what's been happening. Who's been saying what and to whom. I've been sick with anxiety. I rather hoped you'd tell me more. I am sorry I misled you. I felt I needed to talk to someone. I rather liked your faces. I really did. That's God's truth.'

Payne stared back at her. 'But if you didn't send the tape, who did?'

'I left the camera on a side table. For several minutes there was general confusion. Augustine broke down and wept. Then the other two servants appeared – the two women. They also started weeping and wailing and tearing their hair . . . Then – then I saw—' Hortense broke off. 'Oh dear, it must have been her! Yes! I am sure it's her.'

'Who?'

'Louise. Louise Hunter. I saw Louise Hunter pick up the camera. She stood looking down at it. She has one of those big expressionless faces . . . She must have taken the film out. I don't think she likes Clarissa. Clarissa was a bit sharp with her . . . I didn't see her do it, but she must have done!'

'But the postmark on the padded envelope was Kensington and Chelsea,' Payne objected. 'You are the only one of the house party who lives in Kensington.'

'Louise comes to Kensington quite often. I have bumped into her several times. She goes to the V&A and other museums. There is also a tea place she goes to. Every Thursday afternoon, she told me. Belarus tearooms called Matroni. Actually,' Hortense said, 'I have seen her sitting at a table by the window, sipping tea out of a saucer and staring glassily at the samovar. I don't think she is a particularly contented woman.'

18

Sweet Bird of Youth

Stephan Farrar sat frowning down at his mobile phone. 'Mummy isn't answering. She's the busiest woman in the world. She hasn't got a moment to spare. That's why I'm here, I suppose?'

'That indeed is the reason, dear,' Nurse Highgrove said comfortably. She plumped the pillows and smoothed the bedspread.

'I must speak to her. I've remembered something. It's rather urgent, actually. Perhaps I could speak to someone else. Someone who was at La Sorcière when Daddy R. died? Let me see.' He looked down at his mobile once more. 'I've got Auntie Lou's number. And Gloves's. Now, shall I ring Gloves or shall I ring Auntie Lou?'

He was a slender youth who looked about fourteen, with hair the colour of pale butter, cut *en brosse*, a small nose, a wide mouth and startlingly bright blue eyes that burnt with a feverish flame. He was wearing dark blue silk pyjamas styled as some sort of uniform. He brought to mind Saint-Exupéry's *petit prince*.

'Why don't you phone both of them?' Nurse Highgrove suggested. 'I am sure they will be pleased to hear from you. What are friends for? But wait till you've had your tea first, why don't you?'

'I don't want any tea. What I want is a fix.'

'You know you can't do that sort of thing here, Stephan.'

'I can see you're brimming over with moral indignation, aren't you, Highgrove?'

'Not at all. I wouldn't know what moral indignation was if it hit me on the nose. I don't want you to make yourself sick, dear, that's all.'

'I won't make myself sick. I'm used to it.'

'You're sucking your thumb again, Stephan.'

'Am I? Sorry. Shall I tell you why I like having a fix, Highgrove? Shall I give you a highly rationalized explanation of my addiction? It's because I like being the subject *and* the object, the scientist *and* the experiment, all at the same time. When I have a fix, I'm setting the spirit free by enslaving the body.'

'That's clever talk, but I am not sure I approve of it,' Nurse Highgrove said briskly. 'Enslaving the body indeed. Doesn't sound at all nice. As a matter of fact, I'd rather you didn't say things like that ever again, Stephan.'

'I remember there was a dinner at Remnant once – a rather grand dinner party. As it happened I'd taken something earlier on, Diamond Skies, I think, while they were serving cocktails. As soon as we sat down, I removed my black tie and announced that I was in fact a rat, then I got under the table and proceeded to gnaw at the ankles of each guest in turn. I eventually passed out at Princess Michael of Kent's feet.' Stephan laughed. 'Everybody pretended nothing had happened, but I don't think Daddy R. was amused.'

'What's Diamond Skies? No, don't tell me. I don't want to know.'

'As in "Lucy in the Sky with Diamonds" – everybody knows what *that* means.' There was a pause. 'I've got something on my mind, Highgrove,' he said.

'What is it, dear?'

'You know that I said I killed Daddy R.?'

116

'Yes? What about it?' Nurse Highgrove had already heard the story of the killing of Daddy R. She was a stoutish, grey-haired woman in a neat uniform, with a robust no-nonsense air about her. She not only looked but sounded like an old-fashioned nanny of the tender ogress type. That, indeed, was one of the reasons she had got the job at the clinic.

'Well, I don't think I could actually have done it,' he said thoughtfully. 'It suddenly came to me.'

'Shall I tell you something? I never for a moment imagined you killed anyone, dear.' She patted his arm. 'A nice boy like you.'

'Could I have a smoke, do you think? It would help me to concentrate.'

'You know you can't, Stephan. It's not allowed.'

'I don't mean Mariá-Juana. I mean a cigarette.'

'Who is Mariá-Juana? Oh! I *see*. You are so naughty, Stephan!'

'I want a cigarette. I know you smoke. Give me one of your cigarettes, Highgrove. *Please*.'

'I am sorry, Stephan, but smoking is not allowed on the premises. Dr Mandrake would be furious. You don't want to make Dr Mandrake cross, do you?'

'No.' Stephan sighed.

'I might lose my job, you know . . . What was it you were saying about the murder? I thought it sounded very interesting.'

'Daddy R. was jolly rich and I always thought how good it would be if he were to die because then Mummy and Uncle Gerry would get everything. I hated Daddy R. because he was a bully and a madman. But I couldn't have killed him. I thought I did, but I was wrong.' Stephan frowned. 'I was at the right place, at the right time, as they say, but I couldn't have killed him.'

'A good thing you remembered, dear.'

'I *was* on the terrace and I remember wearing Bottom's head, but it was too hot, so I took the head off. It was very quiet. There was a full moon. It was the colour of blood oranges and it had taken its place, like something in a stage set, above and to the right of La Sorcière . . . I stood by the french window and peeped in. They were starting the play. Daddy R. was alive then. He and Mummy were wearing crowns and looked really silly. Daddy R. had a beard *and* a false nose.'

'A false nose! Fancy!'

'It was *too* hot, not a breath of wind, so I went to the pool. It is always cooler by the pool. I felt like having some Mariá-Juana, I really wanted some, so I rang Karen and told her to bring me some. I'd already had some cocoa, but that was earlier on, much earlier on.'

'Cocoa? Did you really? A nice hot cup of cocoa?'

'No, not that kind of cocoa, Highgrove. I mean *cocoa*.' He held up his pockmarked arm.

'Dear me! Please, don't do that, Stephan.' She covered her eyes with her hand. 'It gives me the heebie-jeebies.'

He laughed. 'I sat by the pool and waited. Then Karen came and we lit up.'

'Who was Karen? Do remind me.'

'My girlfriend. Sort of. Her skin is as black as the coal Tradewell puts in the fireplaces at Remnant. I like that. When it's dark, she is practically invisible. I don't like English girls. English girls are pink and they look like shrimps, or they are fat, and they can't kiss properly. Anyway, we kissed a bit, then we lit up. I don't remember what happened after that, but Karen stayed with me all the time and she only ran away when Aunt Tense and Gloves appeared, you see.'

'You remember them coming?'

'No – but Aunt Tense told me about it the next day. I phoned Karen earlier on, actually, because it bothered me. I mean the time factor. I asked her if I ever went somewhere and she said no. I then asked her if she ever left my side and she said, no, she didn't. Not till she'd heard footsteps.'

'You phoned Jamaica on your mobile? Isn't that expensive?'

'I phoned the Grenadin Island. That's *not* Jamaica. Mummy told me I could talk on my mobile as much as I pleased. We are awfully rich, you know. Daddy R. used to feed his dog with caviar. He loved his dog, but then one day he got angry with him and shot him. Anyway, Karen says she was with me all the time. She said I never went anywhere. She'd have known if I had. She wouldn't lie, why would she? There's also the gun.'

'What's so special about the gun?'

'It was the gun from Daddy R.'s desk, Highgrove. I mean Gloves said that. That's Renée. Now, I remember I *meant* to take the gun, I can't remember why exactly, but I sneaked up to Daddy R.'s study and opened the drawer and the gun wasn't there! That was *earlier on*. While everybody was getting into costume. Do you see what that means?'

'What, dear?'

'It means it couldn't have been me. I couldn't have shot Daddy R. It was somebody else. They thought it was me because I hated Daddy R., because I'd already tried to shoot him, but it wasn't.' Stephan frowned again. 'As a matter of fact, I think I know who killed him.'

'Who is it? Who killed Daddy R.?' Nurse Highgrove stood beside the door, looking at him. There was an odd expression in the boy's eyes. She knew it was all nonsense; the doctor had warned her to expect a lot of nonsense, yet she had to admit there was something in the way Stephan spoke, something about his wide staring eyes, that she found compelling.

'It's too scary. You'll probably think I'm making it all up. It's too scary,' he repeated. 'You'll get the heebie-jeebies,' he warned her.

'I won't.'

'You'd never believe it. You'll say I'm making it up. Would you let me have a smoke if I told you?'

'No. Smoking is not allowed.'

'*Please.*'

'Out of the question.'

He sighed. 'All right. It was the Grimaud. It was the Grimaud who killed Daddy R.'

19

Speak, Memory!

'Don't know what to make of Aunt Hortense,' Major Payne said. 'Would you say she was as cunning as the coiled cobra she used to wear round her wrist?'

'I am not sure. That would be overrating her, I think.'

He started the engine. *'Toute vérité n'est pas bonne à dire* indeed . . . Does she really believe that telling half-truths or distorted truths is better than telling no truth at all? It's pretty much the same thing, isn't it? No – it's worse!'

'She was quivering like a twig in a gale,' Antonia said thoughtfully. *'Could* she be the killer?'

'Technically speaking she could be. She wasn't in the room at the crucial time.'

'She said she'd gone to the loo . . . She'd watched their rehearsals. That means she must have been familiar with the exact position of the body on the chaise longue and so on,' Antonia mused. 'She knew Lord Remnant would be in a direct line to the french windows. She was actually caught on camera drawing the silk curtains across the windows just before the sketch started. Did you notice?'

'I most certainly did,' said Payne. 'You mean – she could have been making sure she wouldn't be seen?'

'Exactly. She could easily have popped out through a side

door, run across the terrace and shot Lord R. through the curtains, dropped the gun and run back into the room. It would have taken a minute, if that.'

'Yes. She might easily have got hold of the gun earlier on . . . She might have been hiding it in the folds of her dress, or inside her handbag.'

'Stephan was on the terrace, wearing the Bottom head, but he was probably too cranked up to make sense of what was going on . . .'

'Or he wasn't there at all,' said Payne. 'By the time Hortense appeared on the terrace, he might have taken off the head and removed himself. Perhaps it was Aunt Hortense who put on the Bottom head? A somewhat bizarre touch, but that's what she *would* do if she wanted to throw suspicion on Stephan.'

'Would she have wanted to throw suspicion on her grandson? Involve him in a murder case?'

'She might have instinctively assumed that the police would never be called, that Lord Remnant's murder would never become a *case*.'

'But what was her motive?'

'Well, she hated Lord Remnant. She made that abundantly clear. She thought the world would be a better place without him. Lord Remnant said and did infuriating things. He called her Miss Baedeker. He hid her glasses.'

'You wouldn't kill someone because they hid your glasses, would you?'

'He laughed when she said sorry to an armchair after bumping into it. Perhaps she couldn't bear to watch him humiliating Clarissa?'

'The mother love motive.' Antonia nodded. 'And what a powerful motive that can be . . . It's possible, I suppose. She kept saying how much she loved her daughter . . .'

'If this were a whodunnit, Miss Tilling would be the least likely suspect. The Addled Aunt. Bespectacled, garrulous, inconsequential and disarmingly scatty. Strictly for comic relief purposes.'

'Actually, Hugh, she is not such a typical aunt figure. She is the Aunt with a Past.'

'Yes. I keep wondering about her past . . . She looked damned attractive in that photo, with her come-hither smile and Keppel Clasp. Didn't look like an aunt at all. She was a bad girl. Giving birth out of wedlock and so on. Comes from a line of bad girls, if the Keppel link is anything to go by. Mrs Keppel, Violet Trefusis, the former Mrs Parker Bowles. All of them bad girls.'

Antonia said, 'I really doubt whether drug-riddled Stephan would have been able to focus well enough to plug his stepfather's nape.'

'The same objection could be raised about Hortense. If Hortense's eyesight is so bad that she apologizes to armchairs, could she have got Lord Remnant so accurately in the head? It would have been like the man in the fairy tale who manages to shoot a fly in one eye.'

'Unless she exaggerated her bad eyesight . . .'

There was a pause. 'Lord Remnant had been receiving death threats,' said Payne. 'It may have been one or more of the locals who killed him, though would they have been able to get hold of his gun?'

'The black major-domo might have given it to them.'

'Indeed he might . . . Still, the murder was committed with Lord Remnant's gun, which suggests it was an inside job.'

'Louise Hunter may be afraid of taking any direct action. Do you think she would talk to us?'

'She might. Let's try to beard her as she has tea at the Matroni tearooms in Kensington, shall we?' Payne suggested. 'Or you could do it by yourself – less threatening, perhaps?'

'I don't know what she looks like. I never saw that videotape,' Antonia reminded him.

'She wore a helmet. She looked preposterous. Far from prepossessing.'

'She is not very likely to be wearing a helmet when she has tea at Matroni, is she? I doubt a helmet is a permanent feature of her *toilette*.'

'You will recognize her, I am sure. A large lady with vague hair and big feet.'

'London is full of large ladies with big feet.'

'True. Gosh, how depressing.' Payne rubbed his chin. 'Well, I could come with you, point her out discreetly, then withdraw. How about that? She has tea at Matroni every Thursday afternoon . . . What day is it tomorrow?'

'Thursday.'

'Is it really? Now, isn't that lucky? We'll do it tomorrow,' said Payne. 'I don't think we should waste any time. We shall hunt down the Hunter! She is probably expecting someone to approach her anyhow.'

'There is something else that struck me as curious,' Antonia said thoughtfully. 'Why was Clarissa so frightened when she imagined it was a man who was phoning her? Is Clarissa expecting a call from someone? Is that in any way important?'

After Stephan rang off, Louise Hunter remained sitting very still. She told herself it was all nonsense. It was one of Stephan's drug-fuelled fantasies. He had been imagining things. Seeing things. He had been under the influence of heaven knew what lethal cocktail. The Grimaud was nothing but a preposterous superstition, a myth. The Grimaud didn't exist . . .

Despite herself, Louise felt disturbed. She felt – chilled. She had heard about the Grimaud. She believed she had seen a crude drawing of the Grimaud somewhere. A terrifying-looking creature . . . Of course it didn't exist. But Stephan had sounded so *positive*.

Should she have some ice-cream? She always had ice-cream when she was perplexed about something . . .

Three minutes later she resumed her seat, a tub of Häagen-Dazs in front of her. American ice-cream was the best. Yummy. Better than Italian ice-cream. Better than Belgian ice-cream. Louise was something of an expert on ice-cream. Midnight cookies was her favourite flavour.

Stephan claimed to have seen the Grimaud with his own eyes. And there was something else. Two things, in fact. Lord Remnant's hands. The laugh Basil had heard in Lord Remnant's dressing room. She couldn't say why, but she believed all three were connected somehow . . . Though how exactly were they connected?

No, Basil wouldn't listen to her. Basil found her annoying. Basil detested her. Through the binoculars she had seen him walk in the direction of Remnant Castle. She had caught a glimpse of his face. There had been a closed, cagey look about him – an air of – of suppressed yearning.

Basil was mad about Clarissa. That much was clear to her. Perhaps he was trying to engineer a meeting with Clarissa? How she hated Clarissa! Clarissa – with her sidling seductive walk – with that indescribably rampant look in her eyes—

Whore, Louise mouthed. Slut.

The tape. Had Gerard Fenwick received it? Had he watched it and, if he had, had he seen the gun showing through the window curtains? Most importantly, *what was he going to do about it?* Well, he would get in touch with Clarissa and ask her what it all meant. That would be the logical course of action, wouldn't it?

Louise rather liked the idea of Clarissa being pushed into a tight corner and asked awkward questions.

My brother was killed, wasn't he? You know who shot him, Clarissa, don't you? You must know. I am sure you are behind it. However did you manage to get a death certificate signed by two doctors?

The tape was not the only thing Louise had sent. There was also the anonymous letter to Clarissa. She had cut the letters out of *Country Life* and the *Field*. Well, the more harassed and harried Clarissa felt, the better. People, women in particular, aged prematurely when they were kept in a state of anxiety. Women lost their allure fast. What was it Lady Wishfort said? *Why, I am arrantly flayed; I look like an old peeled wall!*

Arrantly flayed. She would *love* to see Clarissa arrantly flayed!

Things between her and Basil hadn't always been as bad as they had become. Only a couple of months back they had *talked*. They had agreed there was nothing like the last days of summer – those beautiful hot days that had within them the seeds of their own fragility. She told him how much she enjoyed waking up to a mild pinkish dawn and watching the mist lifting from the garden. He said there was nothing like an autumn sun shining out of a cloudless blue sky, without glare and without brilliance—

Louise Hunter fumbled for her handkerchief. Odd thing, memories – rising at such unexpected moments, quite unsolicited – exploding on the surface like bubbles.

And then, without rhyme or reason, she remembered something else that had happened at La Sorcière.

It had been about an hour and a half after lunch. She and Hortense had happened to walk past the open door of Lord Remnant's study. Louise had been talking about the farm. Friends of Hortense's had apparently just bought a farm in South Africa.

They had caught sight of Lord Remnant sitting at his desk, a startlingly gleeful expression on his face. In his hands Lord Remnant had been holding—

20

The Conundrum of the Curious Codicil

Unlocking the front door, Gerard Fenwick let himself into the house. His nose twitched. How terribly peculiar, someone had been smoking a cigar – one of *his* cigars. His thoughts turned once more to his vanished cigar cutter.

'Felicity?' he called out. He went into the drawing room.

He looked at the TV. What was that rigmarole about a videotape showing his brother's death? His brother hadn't died naturally, Felicity had said. Well, he was perfectly aware of the fact—

He rang the bell. Their maid appeared.

'Ah, Goda. I would like a cup of tea.' He spoke slowly, making it sound like a sentence out of an English grammar book. 'And something to eat. A plate of sandwiches, perhaps? Have we got smoked salmon?'

'Sir?'

'People eat a lot of fish in Lithuania, don't they?' He tapped his forehead with a forefinger. 'Must be terribly brainy, Lithuanians.'

'Sir?'

'Awfully good for the brain, fish. Is my wife in?'

'My wife?'

'*My* wife.' He tapped his chest. 'Lady Remnant.'

'Lady Remnant is upstairs.'

'Upstairs? It's starting to rain again, now isn't that a bore? Does it rain a lot in Lithuania? I know it snows a lot, doesn't it? I understand parts of the Baltic freeze in winter, is that correct? I suppose skating parties are terribly popular in Lithuania? Skating's jolly graceful, if one does it properly. Do you miss Lithuania?'

'Everybody know Miss Lithuania, sir.' Goda beamed. 'Miss Lithuania is very beautiful girl. Her name Ugne Tautvydas. I see Miss Lithuania on television. My sister say to me, you look like Miss Lithuania!' Goda laughed. She shook her head vigorously. 'My sister joke.'

'Ah. *Miss* Lithuania. Beauty contests. Of course. Ha-ha. Most amusing. Jokes are so important. Life would be hellish without jokes. Ha-ha. Would you be kind enough to tell my wife I am back?'

Ten minutes later Gerard and Felicity sat in the drawing room drinking tea. I used to enjoy this, he thought. Perhaps we should get a divorce. She wanted to know about the will, so he told her.

'No real surprises, my dear, all as I expected, all terribly predictable, barring one curious codicil added not so long ago.' He took a sip of tea. 'Something of a mystery, though Clarissa didn't seem particularly surprised.'

'What curious codicil?' Felicity sounded impatient.

'Roderick left a largish sum of money to someone no one seems to have heard of. No, not a woman, my dear. Someone called Peter Quin.'

'Peter Quin? Who the devil is he?'

'No idea.'

'How large is the sum?'

He told her.

'You can't be serious.' She put her teacup down. 'That's a fortune.'

'Not really, my dear. What is five million pounds when

128

my brother left – um – I forget the exact figure, but you know perfectly well it's an awful lot. I mean – an awful lot. Indecent, almost.'

'Who *is* this Peter Quin?'

'Haven't the foggiest, I keep telling you. The fellow wasn't there. Saunders didn't know either, or maybe he's had instructions not to divulge anything. Didn't think it polite to press the point.'

'Didn't think it polite to press the point! Really, Gerard!'

'It's all being done through Quin's solicitors. Saunders had the details of Quin's bank account and so on. Oh, he also said that Quin was perfectly aware of the legacy. Apparently, Quin had done my brother some great favour or something.'

'Is there a chance of your being less vague, Gerard? What great favour? Peter Quin. I have a feeling I've seen the name somewhere. I may be imagining it.'

'*The Turn of the Screw*. If that's what you are thinking of. No, the name of the evil valet was Peter Quint. With a t, see? It's considered to be the greatest ghost story ever written, but, *entre nous*, the pacing is somewhat sluggish. And what exactly happens at the end, I would like to know?'

'I don't think I've read it.'

'*Did* it all take place in the governess's mind? But then who or what killed Miles? I may try my hand at a ghost story, actually. I would set it at a place like Remnant, which I remember one of my uncles describing as "magnificently macabre". Remnant would make the perfect setting for some bizarre melodrama that culminates in a *crime passionnel*.'

'What did Clarissa have to say about the codicil?'

'Not much. She's got awfully thin, you know. She wore black. Kept smoking. Egyptian cigarettes, I think. Had a haunted air about her. She didn't seem at all surprised about the Quin codicil, no.' He reached out for the teapot. 'She looked terrified, for some reason. More tea, my dear?'

'Terrified?'

'Yes. She clasped her hands, to prevent them from shaking. She didn't say much. She seemed oddly preoccupied. On a different planet altogether . . . Have you been smoking my cigars, Felicity?'

'Your cigars? What an extraordinary question. Of course I haven't been smoking your cigars.'

'Any idea where my cigar cutter might be?'

'No. You've already asked me. You probably dropped it somewhere. At your club, as likely as not. You are terribly absent-minded . . . I wonder if this Peter Quin had something to do with your brother's death,' she said in a thoughtful voice.

'An interesting if somewhat far-fetched notion.' Gerard raised the teacup to his lips. 'Liquidated by Quin. I must admit it's got quite a ring to it.'

'Your brother *was* killed, Gerard. It's all there, on the tape. I must show you the tape. I really must. After all, it was addressed to you.' Felicity rose. 'Hope you don't mind my opening the package?'

'No, of course not, my dear.' He found himself wondering what little Renée Glover was doing. 'I have no secrets from you, as I am sure you haven't any secrets from me.'

21

Les Amants

Should she tell him? No. Not yet.

Maybe never.

What difference would it make if he knew the truth? He wouldn't tell anyone, would he? Still, things were far from well between them, she was no longer sure of his loyalty.

She didn't think he loved her any more. Had he *ever* loved her? He seemed to have stopped finding her attractive. Earlier on his lips had only brushed her cheek. He seemed to be thinking of something else.

Clarissa and Dr Sylvester-Sale were having dinner at the Café Regal. It was he who had booked the table, but why had his phone been engaged for so long? Who had he been talking to? He said there was something wrong with his mobile. He sounded contrite, though she couldn't be sure it wasn't all an act. In her experience, good-looking men were invariably accomplished actors.

'You're not eating. Aren't you hungry?' Sylvester-Sale asked.

'No, not really.' She tried to smile.

As she raised her aperitif to her lips, her satin dress rustled. She wore pearls, round her neck and in her earlobes, offsetting the gold of her dress. She also had a tiny brooch, of diamonds and gold, on her left shoulder. When she had asked Syl how she looked, he said she reminded him of the famous usherettes at the Clermont Club. It was universally known that it was only the prettiest girls in London who became usherettes at the Clermont Club, but Clarissa didn't care much for the idea.

She was overdressed. She looked like a Christmas tree. She should have put on something more restrained – her Liberty smock in pale lavender would have been perfect.

'You seem thinner. You must eat,' he said. 'You will make yourself ill if you don't.'

'How nice of you to care about my health.'

'I am a doctor.'

'Of course you are, darling. I keep forgetting. Yours is the most humanitarian profession in the world.'

She had ordered sole Waleska. Sylvester-Sale had plumped for chargrilled quail breast and celeriac remoulade, with lots of French fries. Nothing wrong with *his* appetite, as far as she could see. He was being so annoyingly aloof. No one would have thought they were lovers, looking at them. White wine for her, red for him.

'Apparently,' he said, 'one should never refer to red wine as "red wine" but as "wine". Rosé, on the other hand, should be called "pink wine".'

'Is that so? What about white wine?'

'White wine can be called "white wine".'

'How fascinating.'

'The place is practically empty,' he said.

It was the kind of polite conversation a stranger would make.

'It is, isn't it?'

'Dining out is on the decline. The credit crunch has gnawed its way to the giddiest summits of high society.'

'My brother-in-law intends to write a book entitled *The Romance of Restaurants*. We met at Mr Saunders's office earlier on,' Clarissa explained. 'I told him I was having dinner at the Café Regal.'

'You didn't tell him you were having dinner with me, did you?'

'No. Don't worry, darling. Your secret is safe with me. Gerard said the Café Regal was going to feature prominently in his book. He is going to devote a whole chapter to it.' Clarissa glanced round. 'I wonder how many of the diners tonight are Freemasons. It seems the Café Regal is a haunt of Freemasons.'

'Really? They say Freemasons rule the world.' He didn't look particularly interested.

'Apparently there is a gilded room on the second floor. Gerard claims to have seen it. That's where they hold their hush-hush meetings and cook up various conspiracies. They masquerade as a culinary club of cheerful gourmets. They call themselves *Les Bons Frères*.'

'How many books has old Fenwick written?'

'I don't know. He's never been able to get anything published, I don't think. Well, now he's got Roderick's money, things may change. He seemed terribly excited about it.'

'Don't tell me he's contemplating vanity publishing?'

'I believe he is.'

'Waste of money.'

'Do you think so?'

'Yes. Utter waste of money.'

What an uninspiring conversation we are having, Clarissa thought. For the last five minutes she had been trying to will her lover to reach out and lay his hand over hers . . .

'Gerard is very keen on founding what he calls a small but exclusive press,' she said. 'He did try to get Roderick interested. He kept asking Roderick for funds. Roderick never said no; he strung Gerard along. He enjoyed teasing his brother. Poor Gerard kept writing to him – phoning him – kept leaving messages. I don't think Roderick ever answered his calls.'

Sylvester-Sale raised the wine glass to his lips. 'Actually he rang him the day before he died.'

'Roderick rang Gerard? Are you sure?'

'Yes. On his mobile.'

'How terribly peculiar.'

'We were on the terrace. Your late husband, Basil and I. Your late husband said, I am going to ring my brother now. He then said some truly awful things into the phone. It was terribly embarrassing for us, listening to his side of the conversation. Your late husband was showing off. He kept winking at us. He enjoyed having an audience.'

'My late husband was the worst exhibitionist who ever lived.'

'That night at dinner – the night he died. I still can't believe the things he said.' Sylvester-Sale shook his head. 'About the glorious sixties and his escapades – that story about the debs and their jewels! What a cad! Poor you.' He reached out and put his hand over hers. At long last!

'It was horrid.' She shut her eyes. '*Horrid*. In front of everybody! To be told that—' She broke off. 'I've never been so humiliated in my life. I felt debased. I didn't know where to look. I truly wished him dead at that moment.'

'Well, your wish was granted. He died an hour and a half later.' Sylvester-Sale removed his hand.

'Syl, there is something I . . . What if I told you . . .'

'If you told me what?'

'Nothing. Nothing!' If only I were sure he loved me, I would tell him the truth, she thought. 'What exactly did Roderick say to Gerard on the phone?'

'Some horribly personal things. Um. About Gerard's singular lack of talent and enterprise. He referred to some incident in their childhood. He also asked Gerard to come and murder him.'

134

'Murder him?'

'Yes!'

'What did he say exactly?'

Sylvester-Sale cleared his throat. '*Of course, dear boy, most of my earthly riches will be all yours to keep one day, no question about it, but you may have to wait some time – I may live to be a hundred, you know. Unless you kill me?*'

She laughed. 'How spooky! You sound exactly like him!'

'*That would be a solution, yes, most definitely a solution. Why don't you come over, dear boy? Hop on the next plane and pay us a visit, now why don't you? Have it out with me? Challenge me to a duel! Show that you are a real Remnant? Well, you know where to find me.*'

22

Nightmares and Dreamscapes

The hands were round her throat now and the ghastly grinning face was very close to hers. She had seen the hands first and, even before the face revealed itself to her, she knew it was Lord Remnant's.

The coffin stood beside her bed, parallel to it. It was a white coffin and it gleamed in the dull glow of the moon, which gave her bedroom an unearthly appearance. She had seen the lid sliding open, slowly and without a sound. Then the hands showed, lit by the moon—

Well, he knew how to do it. He had been reading about it; she had seen the ancient book on resurrecting the dead on his desk.

Lord Remnant had come back from the grave.

No, he hadn't. He couldn't have. He had never been inside a grave. He had been cremated. His ashes were in an urn somewhere at Remnant.

She had recognized the hands. That was how she had known at once it was him. There was the nasty red weal between the thumb and forefinger of his right hand, where Stephan had stabbed him.

But—

Louise Hunter woke up with a gasp. Her heart was racing.

A dream. It was only a dream, thank God. She had had a bad dream. It was very early in the morning, pitch dark, raindrops drumming against the window panes, wind whining in the chimney –

She got out of bed, making it creak horribly. She put on her dressing gown and then wrapped a blanket round her shoulders. Her teeth were chattering. She felt disoriented. Her ankles were swollen. *We are no sooner aloft than we begin to feel gravity's inevitable pull.* It occurred to her that she was much cleverer than anyone ever realized.

She stood beside the window. She thought she could just about distinguish the stunted trees writhing and struggling as if in agony.

Suddenly she knew what it was that had been bothering her all this time.

It had come back to her.

There hadn't been a weal on his hand when he died.

Gerard Fenwick, who had also woken up early, sat at his desk, writing in his diary.

A journey into the unknown, that's what a novel should be. There is pleasure to be derived from following a novelist on a voyage of exploration, one in which the style reflects uncertainties, a novel written as if it were in answer to the question, 'How do I know what I think till I see what I've said?'

There is equal pleasure, if of a different order, that comes from a novelist who uses events not to change characters, but to reveal them. If one style, hesitating, probing, mazy, is suited to one kind of novel, then a different style, lucid, terse and epigrammatic, fits another.

I have now tried everything, or almost everything. I have written in the plainest and most clichéd, weary man-of-the-world manner, such as Somerset Maugham's. I have attempted

Hemingway's short, simple sentences, clear as a mountain stream. I have written in the style of a vacuous viscount out of Wodehouse. I have produced writing that is impossible to understand because it is oblique without really being very suggestive. I also have had the temerity to try to write like Monsieur Proust – in long, stately sentences, magnificently tortuous and full of qualifications – a style like a lush if overgrown garden full of unexpected delights.

I have even started a modern version of one of those gloomy Greek dramas with the Eumenides lurking outside ready to make their entrance.

The only intolerable style is one that draws attention to itself and distracts from the matter.

For some reason I keep thinking of detective stories, maybe because of that bloody tape, though I don't really see myself actually starting to write one. I hate the idea of formulas, which are as predictable as they are banal. In my opinion, detective stories of the 'traditional' kind do little more than repetitively tread their own sorry clichés.

The setting: a cosy English village, a luxuriously exotic villa on a private island, or some decaying castle not unlike Remnant. A plot that depends on a certain person ordering scrambled eggs in the middle of the day, then slipping on discarded mandarin peel as a yellow Rolls roars by and certain other seemingly irrelevant accidents all aligning miraculously at the end.

A highly unsympathetic victim, someone like my late brother, so that no reader should be tempted to weep for him. Suspects stumbling across the chessboard strictly according to the 'rules of the game'. And finally the denouement in the library, which of course is a symbol of mankind's futile search for mysteries. Why the library? Why not the stables or the wine cellar, the butler's pantry or, for that matter, the bell tower?

Slowly welling from the point of his gold nib, dark blue ink dissolved the question mark, for there his pen had stuck.

'Bother,' Gerard Fenwick said mildly.

He had always found chronicles of cunningly contrived homicide disappointing, even when he was a boy. He remembered turning the last page of *The Hound of the Baskervilles*, thinking, what a rotten ending! The diabolical hound had been revealed as something little more diabolical than the original Dulux Dog. He had felt cheated!

He also recalled a novel by one of the so-called 'queens of crime', he'd forgotten which one. It had been short but ponderous beyond belief. He couldn't imagine anyone enjoying the experience of entering such a necropolis of 'fine' prose – unless one sought some kind of *extase par la souffrance*.

The over-complicated plot had moved at a crippling crawl. There had been too many descriptions of mental processes, the vagaries of the weather and suchlike. In the end he had been quite unmoved to discover it was the unlikely duo of the ne'er-do-well stepbrother and the gruesome girl in the wheelchair who had killed the ghastly detective-story writer and then cut off his hands at the wrists.

At Remnant Castle Clarissa was woken by the ringing of her mobile phone.

She turned on the bedside light and reached out for her mobile. Four thirty. Who the hell—? Suddenly she felt sick. Was this it? Was this the call she had been expecting?

No. It was Stephan. Why wasn't he asleep?

'Mummy?'

'What's the matter, darling?'

'Where have you been, Mummy? I've been trying to call you for a long time. I've been trying and trying. Where have you been?'

'I've been terribly busy. Can't we talk later on, darling? It's – it's some unearthly hour—'

'It's a question of life and death, Mummy.'

'You sound as though you haven't taken your medicine, Stephan.' Clarissa made an effort to appear calm. 'Dr Mandrake told me he would make sure your sleep is the sleep of angels. Don't they see to it that you take your pills and potions?' She did her best to keep the exasperation out of her voice.

He said he needed a smoke. *Badly*. He was desperate for a smoke. Couldn't she smuggle some Mariá-Juana into Sans Souci? *Please, Mummy*.

'It would be extremely difficult, darling.'

'Put some in your handbag. No one will search *you*.'

'Impossible, darling.'

'Please, Mummy.'

'No, darling. Out of the question.'

'Please.'

'Out of the question.'

'You sound like Highgrove. I hate her and I hate you. I will kill myself, see if I don't. Then you'll be sorry,' Stephan said.

'I want you to go to bed, darling,' she said. Why weren't they monitoring him? Why wasn't anyone with him? She was paying them a bloody fortune!

'If you don't bring me some Mariá-Juana, I will tell the police what I know,' he said. 'I'll tell them what I saw. I saw you talking to the coachman.'

'What coachman, darling?'

'The black coachman who brought the coffin. The coffin with the Grimaud!'

'Now listen to me, Stephan, I want you to go to bed—'

'I *am* in bed. *I saw you*. You kept looking at your watch. You were expecting the coffin. Which means you know about the Grimaud. You know what I think? I think you arranged for the Grimaud to come to La Sorcière, so that it could kill Daddy R. Everybody thinks I killed Daddy R., but I didn't. I've been remembering things, you see.'

She listened.

He had been in the garden. He had hidden in the bushes and watched from there. He told her what he had seen. He had seen the resplendent white hearse with the plumed horses carrying the white coffin with a surface as smooth as a mirror. The coffin had been lifted down by the coachman. A black giant, who handled the coffin single-handedly, with extreme care—

'I saw you speak to the coachman, Mummy. You looked nervous. You kept looking round. Everybody else was in the house. They were with Daddy R., watching those boring home movies. It was obvious you were expecting the coach. But you forgot about me! I was in the garden.'

'You seem to have got muddled up, darling,' she said. She couldn't think of anything else to say. 'I believe you dreamt it.'

But he was right. She had been expecting the coach. She would have preferred something unobtrusive, less conspicuous. The plumed horses and other theatrical flourishes had all been Roderick's idea.

She had instructed the coachman to leave the coffin inside the laundry room. The man had taken off his white topper. *My condolences, madam*. Quite absurd. She had given him a large tip. Perhaps the largest tip he had ever received in his entire life. She wasn't worried the coachman would ever question why the coffin had been brought to La Sorcière or wonder about the reason it was placed inside the laundry. Lord Remnant's eccentricities had been legendary.

No one else had witnessed the arrival of the coach but Stephan . . .

She had omitted to make sure Stephan was safely inside. One always tended to forget Stephan. Stephan so often moved in a zombified haze that one generally ignored him.

'You must have dreamt it, darling,' she said firmly. 'It was one of your nightmares.'

142

'I was curious, so I crept up to the laundry room and looked in through that tiny round window. I was curious about the coffin, you see. I wanted to take a proper look at it. The coach had left and you'd gone upstairs. I saw the coffin open and the Grimaud came out of it,' Stephan said.

As a rule Louise Hunter felt quite happy on Thursdays, more animated than on any other day of the week, because of London, but her broken night had left her listless, with an aching head and an instinctive shrinking from light. Familiar noises seemed amplified; the chirruping of birds outside the window, the ticking of the grandfather clock and the distant bleating of sheep all sounded distressingly piercing to her ears. She felt heavy and unwieldy; she might have been her own wax effigy – now wasn't that a curious concept?

'You are going to London, aren't you? Your usual haunts?' Basil had spoken from behind his *Telegraph*.

'I don't know. I am not sure,' she said hesitantly in the hope that he would try to persuade her not to go, that he might suggest they did something together, something simple like going for a walk or doing the crossword, but he didn't.

Recklessly, she started buttering her fourth piece of toast. So much for her intention to go on a diet!

'I am not sure,' she repeated.

'You love London,' he said firmly. 'Your week would be incomplete without your visit to London.'

He wants to be rid of me, she thought. 'Don't you like the marmalade?' She had seen him grimace.

'It tastes a little odd—'

'There is a sealed jar in the pantry.' She started to rise. 'I'll get it for you.'

'No, don't bother. Please. Don't fuss. I'll survive.' He gave a rueful smile. He poured himself a cup of coffee.

143

She saw him glance towards the window. A longing kind of gaze. A gaze of glazed devotion. On a bright day one could see the spires of Remnant Castle from here. That woman! She would tear her apart if she could!

'The coffee, on the other hand, is first class,' he said.

'I am so glad. I will order more of the same. It is a rather special kind of blend.'

'Not Harrods, is it?'

'No. Of course not.'

'That fellow mustn't be encouraged.'

'He mustn't. Though I believe he sold Harrods to someone else.'

'It's a matter of principle.'

'Of course it is. I completely agree,' she said. 'Shall I make you some more buttered soldiers?'

'No, thank you. Don't believe in gorging myself. Have you ever considered spending a day without eating?'

'Do you think I should go on a diet?' It was clear he found her fat. The thought plunged her into the depths of renewed depression and self-contempt.

'Do you good, I should think.' He rustled his paper. 'Wouldn't call it a diet. Not exactly.'

'What is it then?'

'One whole day without eating. Perhaps two. Or three. Why not four?' Basil Hunter went on, warming to his theme. 'Thinking of giving it a try myself. Apparently one wakes up the next day bright as a button. Mental faculties a great deal sharper. Starving encourages the flow of extra blood to the brain.'

'That's what happens when you stand on your head,' she said.

He shook his teaspoon at her. 'You will feel as though you are beginning to float away. And you find yourself laughing for no apparent reason.'

'Sounds marvellous,' Louise said. 'Absolutely enthralling.'

144

Two red spots had appeared on her cheeks and now she felt a surge of excitement. Why, this seemed like old times! They were having a *conversation*.

Her joy, however, was short-lived. Basil failed to answer her question about the new heifer he had bought. He didn't address her again and then she saw him gazing towards the window once more.

There was a silence.

Louise helped herself to a Danish pastry. She sighed. How she wished she had a narrower gullet, if not a supermodel's inhibited appetite. Her thoughts returned to her conversation with Stephan. Stephan claimed to have seen the Grimaud, the immaculately dressed homunculus that was said to turn up at the house of the doomed in a coffin.

The Grimaud was a malevolent spirit, some Caribbeans said the Devil himself. The Grimaud had sleek black hair, three rows of teeth and burning red eyes. The Grimaud was conjured up by a man's enemies and sent to his house to 'claim' him.

Nonsense. All nonsense, she told herself. Stephan had been under the influence of heaven knew what cocktail of drugs. Stephan had been hallucinating. Stephan had been seeing things that hadn't been there.

Still, the fact remained that strange things *had* happened at La Sorcière on the day Lord Remnant died . . .

How did one explain the hands? And how exactly did one account for the laughter?

23

Hands of a Stranger

'There she is, the big girl at the far end, the table on the right. The vanquished Valkyrie.' Payne pointed. 'Gosh, look at that turban of trumpeting vermilion!'

'Where? Oh yes. Goodness.'

'She's eating as though her life depends on it – what's that she's having? Blini? With dollops of what looks like blackcurrant jelly. I didn't think I'd ever live to see such an outrage.'

'*I am large, I contain multitudes* . . . Walt Whitman. Sorry. Perhaps she is terribly unhappy,' Antonia said. 'She's drinking tea out of a saucer.'

'I would be unhappy if I had to drink tea out of a saucer. Well, there you are, my love. The mighty Hunter is doing *exactly* what Hortense said she would be doing. It is clearly something of a ritual with her. This,' Major Payne said didactically, 'is what happens when people turn their backs on God.'

'You don't know if she's turned her back on God.'

'I am sure she has. You only have to take one look at her. This is actually quite exciting. The hunter becomes the hunted . . . *Make sure she doesn't eat you*,' Payne whispered in Antonia's ear. 'Don't forget to report back to base.'

'I won't.'

He kissed her. She watched him hold up his umbrella and hail a taxi.

Matroni clearly translated as 'matrons' and Antonia wondered if the Russian word held the same disparaging connotation as the English. What were matrons exactly? Motherly ladies? Respectable middle-aged women? Matrons were usually staid and stout. Was she a matron? She hoped not – not yet. Was Louise Hunter a matron? Most decidedly.

I will introduce myself as Antonia Rushton, she decided. She had been married to a Richard Rushton once.

A smiling young waiter with high Slav cheekbones, pale blue eyes and fair hair bowed disconcertingly low and asked where she would like to sit.

'Over there, perhaps?' Antonia waved towards an empty table alongside Louise Hunter's.

She bravely ordered a pot of Tibetan tea and a piece of gooseberry *pirog*. She was aware of Louise Hunter stealing a glance at her. The clothes Louise Hunter wore had presumably been constructed by a dressmaker of the better class, but it was hard to believe that she could have been adequately fitted out by anyone less spacious in his methods than Omar the Tent Maker.

As their eyes met, Antonia smiled at her. 'Excuse me – Mrs Hunter? It's Mrs Louise Hunter, isn't it?'

'Yes?' The fat woman in the red turban looked startled. 'Yes? I am sorry but I don't – have we met?'

'We haven't. My name is Antonia Rushton. I believe we have friends in common. The Fenwicks. Felicity and Gerard,' Antonia improvised. 'He is now the Earl Remnant.'

'Oh.' Louise Hunter suddenly looked frightened.

'Felicity and I were at school together. Gerard is awfully nice. Both of them are awfully nice,' Antonia prattled on. 'As it happens, I was at their place about an hour ago.'

'Actually, I don't know them awfully well . . . What – what did they say about me?'

'They pointed you out—'

'*Pointed me out?*'

'I am so sorry! That sounded *awful*. Do forgive me, Mrs Hunter. It's just that we were watching—' Antonia broke off. 'Sorry! I shouldn't have mentioned it at all.'

'What were you watching?'

'I was asked not to talk about it. It is an extremely delicate matter.'

'What delicate matter? What were you watching?' Louise's hand was at her heaving bosom.

'Well . . .'

'Please, tell me.'

'I am far from convinced I should.'

'You *must* tell me!'

Antonia pretended to hesitate. 'Felicity showed me something. She wanted my opinion, you see. She was a bit unsettled – out of her depth.'

'She showed you the tape. This is all about the tape, isn't it? I know it is.' Louise leant forward. 'She let you watch the tape.'

'All right. Yes. She let us watch the tape. I am sorry, Mrs Hunter. I shouldn't have referred to any of it at all. None of my business. It's just that Felicity wanted my advice. No, I don't work for the police. We – my husband and I – have what you might call a consultancy . . . Ah, here is my tea at last!'

'You are private detectives? You and your husband?'

'For fear of inviting ridicule we *never* call ourselves that . . . I have never had a *pirog* before, but I like trying new things.'

Louise Hunter seemed to reach a decision. 'Would you like to come over and sit at my table? I must talk to you.'

'Are you sure?'

'Positive!'

Antonia rose.

'It is true what they say, that in this life we never know what may be waiting for us around the next corner . . . So what did you make of it? You saw what happened, didn't you?' Louise asked in a low voice. Her lips were the colour of ripe German plums, Antonia noticed; her eyebrows perfect geometric arches. She really was a large lady.

'It is quite extraordinary, to have captured a murder live on camera,' said Antonia. 'Without intending to!'

'You saw the gun?'

'Yes. A murder that takes place within full view of everybody! Quite incredible . . . Why exactly did you send the tape?'

'What makes you think it was me?' There was a crafty glint in Louise Hunter's eye. I would have put it on YouTube if only I knew how, she was thinking. For the whole world to see.

'We worked it out. A process of elimination,' Antonia said slowly. She hoped Louise wouldn't urge her to explain. 'It was the boy who shot him, wasn't it? Lord Remnant's stepson. What was his name? Sacheverell?'

'Stephan.'

'We were told that he'd already made an attempt to kill Lord Remnant with that very same gun. It was hushed up, correct?' Antonia took a cautious sip of Tibetan tea.

'It was hushed up, yes. Clarissa orchestrated the whole thing . . . It's a very complicated story. We were *bribed*. I don't know where to begin . . . There are things which I don't understand at all,' Louise went on. 'Things that don't make any sense. It may be irrational of me, but I know that something somewhere is very, *very* wrong indeed.'

'What do you mean?'

'Stephan told me it couldn't have been him. He phoned me, you see. He's at some clinic. He'd been trying to call his mother, he said, but couldn't get through to her. I know

Stephan is far from trustworthy; I am aware he has serious problems with drugs, but I found myself wondering.'

'What did Stephan say?'

'He said he couldn't have shot his stepfather because he had been sitting beside the swimming pool at the time of the murder. He had been with his girlfriend, some local girl.' Louise Hunter ran her tongue across her lips. 'I believe something diabolical took place at La Sorcière that night, Mrs Rushton. Lord Remnant's bathroom adjoins his dressing room. Basil – my husband – believes there was someone in the bathroom. *He heard someone laugh*. They had just laid Lord Remnant's body on the bed. That's when Basil heard the laugh.'

'They?'

'Basil and SS – Dr Sylvester-Sale. Basil described the laugh as a "high-pitched giggle". He said it made him jump. SS on the other hand said he didn't hear a thing, so Basil persuaded himself he'd imagined it.'

'He is sure the sound came from the bathroom?'

'He believes so, yes. Everybody else was downstairs. He was startled – shocked – I mean, no one should laugh in the presence of the dead, should they?'

'No . . . How very curious,' said Antonia.

'And there's something else. It's been at the back of my mind all this time. It concerns Lord Remnant's hands. In fact I should have started with Lord Remnant's hands.'

Antonia urged her to continue.

'It was moments after Dr Sylvester-Sale discovered that Lord Remnant had been shot through the back of the head. I happened to look at Lord Remnant's hands—' Louise broke off. 'They shouldn't have moved him. That's a criminal offence! You don't cart around people who have died a violent death, do you?'

'No.'

'There should have been a proper investigation, but Clarissa wouldn't hear of it. She told me to shut up. She was appallingly rude to me. Clarissa managed to pass her husband's murder off as a natural death. She got the two doctors to sign the death certificate!'

'What exactly was wrong with Lord Remnant's hands?'

'Well, they were smooth, without a blemish, but they shouldn't have been. *The wound should have been there, but it wasn't.*'

'What wound?'

'The stabbing wound. Stephan stabbed him with a pen. In his right hand. Here—' Louise tapped the back of her hand, the space between her thumb and forefinger. 'It happened a couple of days earlier. Lord Remnant had it bandaged, but then he removed the bandage. He said it was nothing, though the red weal was there all right. A flaming kind of red.'

'But it wasn't there when you looked at his hands after he died?'

'No. It had disappeared! There was no wound. Not the slightest mark. The red scar was there all right at dinner! I was sitting next to Lord Remnant, you see.' Louise scowled. 'I don't know *how* the two things fit together, but I have an idea they do. I mean, the giggle and the wound that was not there – and in some mad way, it all ties up with the Grimaud.'

'Who or what is the Grimaud?' Antonia asked gravely.

Louise told her. 'Do you see? It doesn't exist, it's nothing but a superstition, yet Stephan insisted on having seen it arrive in a coffin! The Grimaud is believed to presage somebody's death, or rather to bring it about . . . Well, Lord Remnant did die that night,' she added thoughtfully.

'When did the coffin arrive at the house?'

'Some time in the afternoon, Stephan said. The coffin was brought by a hearse and was placed inside the laundry. Stephan went and looked through the window. He swears he saw the Grimaud crawl out of the coffin. Now, as a witness, Stephan is far from reliable, but he described the Grimaud in such vivid detail, it sent shivers down my spine!'

'What does the Grimaud look like?' This, Antonia decided, promises to become our most exotic case.

'Shiny papier-mâché head, like a ventriloquist's doll, nose so upturned as to resemble a pig's snout, and it has three rows of teeth. Quite nightmarish. It was dressed in white tails and Stephan believes he caught a glimpse of a white topper sticking out of the coffin as well.'

'Where were you at the time?'

'All of us – with the exception of Stephan and Clarissa – were inside the house. Lord Remnant insisted on showing us some of their home movies. Recordings of various amateur theatricals. So tedious. Everybody dressed up as dentists or minor émigré royalty or organic vegetables or Christmas tree decorations— Was that funny, Mrs Rushton?'

'No. Well, yes. Sorry.'

'The Remnants led a life of indolent futility – of effortless nullity – and seemed to expect to be admired for it!'

'Who do you think shot Lord Remnant? Do you have any ideas?'

'I am absolutely sure Clarissa is in some way involved. Perhaps it was one of her lovers, at her instigation? Clarissa was reputed to be running the most spectacular galaxy of lovers. That black doctor, for example, who later came and signed the death certificate?'

'You believe they were lovers?'

'Of course they were lovers. Oh, how she looked at him, how she smiled at him! A smile that would have melted Iceland. The slow rotten smile of a slut. She is that sort of woman, Mrs Rushton. You should have heard the sounds she made when there were men around! Soft and syrupy—'

153

'Am I right in thinking the gun came from Lord Remnant's study?'

'Yes. He kept it in the top drawer of his desk. The drawer was never locked. Everybody knew it was there . . . I saw him sitting at his desk, holding the gun, but that was in the morning, at about half past eleven. Hortense and I happened to be passing by the study – the door was open—'

Antonia frowned. 'You saw—?'

'He was smiling – he looked terribly pleased with himself. He was putting the silencer on the gun. At least I *think* it was a silencer. Hortense thought he was cleaning the gun, but I am sure she was wrong.'

Antonia couldn't believe her ears. She pushed the plate with the *pirog* to one side. 'Sorry – who was it you saw putting a silencer on the gun?'

'Oh, didn't I say? It was Lord Remnant.'

24

The Lost Symbol

The novel I propose to write falls into a genre often described by the cognoscenti as 'experimental' and by more conventional readers as 'puzzling', Gerard Fenwick, thirteenth Earl Remnant, wrote in his diary. *Its status as a novel will owe absolutely nothing to the traditional definition of the form. There will be no hero or heroine, but there will certainly be an anti-hero and an anti-heroine.*

At first sight my novel will seem more like a random collection of episodes, though the perceptive reader will soon become aware of interconnections at both a material and a thematic level: characters met in one story will pop up in another; a version of an event we heard of from one angle is later renarrated from another.

A tiny silver guillotine will make an intermittent symbolic appearance, a persistent reminder of the aristocracy's ultimate fate, until it eventually vanishes into thin air, only to reappear most amazingly in the hands of someone well versed in the gentle art of blackmail.

It will be a murder mystery of sorts.

The novel will start with the obituary in The Times *of an utterly impossible peer of the realm, the most peerless of asses, say, an earl. The obituary will give 'heart attack' as the cause of death, but in point of fact the unsavoury nobleman would have died as a result of a gun wound in the occiput.*

It has just occurred to me that modern-day murder holds as exact a state as a medieval monarch. The exits and entrances are all laid down according to the most formal of protocols. Investigating officer, surgeon, photographer, fingerprint experts, DNA experts and so on make their bow and play their appointed part. (Do readers like police procedurals? Terribly boring, surely?)

It's the dead man's brother who tells the story and one of the central themes of the book will be the difficulty, nay the impossibility, of telling of an honest story. The narrator, as the dear reader will discover soon enough, turns out to be dramatically unreliable.

It is the narrator who will be exposed as the killer at the end. Or has that been done before? The narrator is of a largely lunatic cast of mind, something of which he is only partially aware, but he contrives to write in a frighteningly lucid, pedantic sort of way, which imparts to his story the black comic feel of Nabokov's Pale Fire—

Gerard looked up. There had been a knock on the door.

It was the club steward. 'The young lady, sir. She said you were expecting her.'

The fellow had spoken in portentously hushed tones; it somehow suggested that his message might have a more sinister meaning than his words conveyed.

Gerard gave an amused smile. 'Am I expecting a young lady?'

'Yes, sir. A Miss Glover.'

'Oh yes, of course. Do let her in . . . Dear Renée!' Gerard took off his half-moon glasses and rose to his feet to greet the composed-looking young woman, whose dark hair was parted neatly in the middle and drawn back in two shining waves to form a knot.

'Hello, Gerard. Hope this is not frightfully inconvenient?'

'No, not at all, my dear.' He kissed her cheek. He stood beaming at her. 'How lovely to see you, Renée. A damsel with a dulcimer!'

'Is that how you see me, as an Abyssinian maid?'

'Only figuratively, my dear. I feel strangely inspired each time I see you. Inspiration is so terribly important to me. I am, after all, an artist, a writer. I do miss our tête-à-têtes, you know. You wouldn't believe this, but I am at the planning stages of a novel.'

'A new novel?'

'One of those postmodern thingummybobs. Shall I ring and ask them to bring us some tea? The grub here is awfully good. Better than anything I get at home. Infinitely better. Hope this doesn't sound too disloyal.'

'No, thank you. I don't want any tea.'

'Won't you sit down? That's a very comfortable chair by the fireplace.' He touched her elbow and pointed towards a high-backed chair, studded and covered in dark red leather. 'Like a papal throne, isn't it? Are you sure you don't want any tea? You look a little pale, my dear. Is everything all right?'

'Yes . . . I am fine, thank you, Gerard.'

'There are tiny dark smudges, like thumbprints, beneath your eyes, if you don't mind my saying so . . . Oddly becoming . . .'

'I didn't sleep very well last night, that's all.'

'I am so sorry. I don't want to appear curious or interfering, my dear, but it seems to me there's something you are keeping back – or is that my writer's imagination? How did you know I would be at the club?'

'Your maid told me. I rang your house first.'

'How clever of you! You were always an enterprising girl. Felicity made the biggest mistake in her life when she gave you the sack, don't you think?'

'It isn't for me to say. No doubt she thought she was doing the right thing.'

'Felicity can be a bore. I do hope you are profitably employed, my dear. You continue to do jobs for Clarissa, don't you?'

157

'No, not any longer. Not since Grenadin.'

'Really? That's some time ago now, isn't it? Shame. Any particular reason? You haven't fallen out with Clarissa, have you? I know she can be difficult. How are things at Remnant, I wonder? Are the servants happy?'

'I don't think they are. Clarissa doesn't want anyone at Remnant at the moment. She has dismissed all the servants. I bumped into Tradewell the other day. He was very upset about it. Practically in tears.'

'Dismissed *all* the servants?' Gerard stared at her. 'What an extraordinary thing to do. Did he say why?'

'She didn't give them any explanation.'

'You don't think it would help if I had a word with her? About reinstating you and so on?'

'No, thank you, Gerard.'

'Is there anything at all I can do for you, my dear? I could give you money, you know, as much as you want. That wouldn't be a problem.'

'You are extremely kind, but no, I am sure I can manage.'

'It's awfully sweet of you to come and see me, my dear. I was terribly fond of you, you know. Still am. I feared our paths might never cross again. I thought you were furious with us.'

'I am not. Not with you.'

'You won't mind my smoking one of my cigars, will you? It will bring back the good old times when we had our regular pow-wows.' He reached for his cigar case. 'A cigar can be as potently Proustian as the madeleine of memory. That sounds quite good, doesn't it?'

'Yes. You do say clever things, Gerard.'

'You strike me as a bit tense, Renée. What is it? A drink, perhaps? I've got some first-class malt. You were never averse to malt. Or would you like some brandy?'

'No, thank you, Gerard.'

'You keep saying, No, thank you, Gerard. Don't think I

like it . . . Hope you won't mind me biting off the end? Most uncouth, I know, but I happen to have lost— Good lord, that looks like my lost cigar cutter!' Gerard stared at the metal object that lay across the palm of Renée's outstretched hand. She had risen to her feet. 'I could swear that is my cigar cutter!'

'It *is* your cigar cutter.'

'Are you sure?'

'Yes. It's got your initials on it. GF.'

'How peculiar. Yes, you are perfectly correct. Thank you so much, my dear. I'm awfully glad to be reunited with it. I must confess I was absurdly attached to my cigar cutter.' He gave a rueful smile. 'It's emotionally starved people who get obsessed with trinkets and *objets*, isn't it?' He inserted the tip of his cigar inside the cutter. 'Wherever did you find the damned thing?'

She looked at him. 'Can't you remember where you lost it?'

'I can't. I'd been racking my brain, to no avail. Haven't the foggiest. Where was it?'

'I found it at La Sorcière. On the terrace outside the french windows.'

'At La Sorcière? That's my late brother's place on Grenadin. On the terrace, did you say?' He struck a match and put it to his cigar.

'Yes. I found it on the night your brother was killed. The cigar cutter was lying not far from the gun.' She paused. 'The gun your brother was shot with.'

'Shouldn't one say, the gun *with which* your brother was shot? Or am I being pedantic?'

'You came to Grenadin that night, didn't you?' Renée said quietly.

'You think I did?'

'I know you did. I smelt cigar smoke. Funnily enough I thought of you at once.'

'Is that so? What was that famous scene – it's in a book – now, what *was* it?' Gerard tapped his fingers across his forehead. 'No, don't tell me! *Jane Eyre*? Yes! Jane catches the whiff of Rochester's cigar and she says, *I know it well.* She is clearly thrilled. Well, Victorians knew how to convey eroticism.'

'Gerard—'

'Both Rochester and Jane are in the garden at Thornfield. The cigar smoke mingles with *sweet-briar and southern-wood, jasmine, pink, and rose.* With the heroine giddy on these scents, only one outcome is possible, Charlotte Brontë makes that abundantly clear. So you believe I was at La Sorcière on the fatal night, do you?'

'I do. At the crematorium I saw you scratch your hand. I remembered you saying once you'd never live somewhere like Grenadin because of the blood-sucking mosquitoes.'

He glanced down at his hand. 'Gone now. You think that was a mosquito bite? What if I told you I suffer from an allergy related to eggs? What if I told you that my wife filches my cigars and actually smokes them? Perhaps it was Felicity who was in Grenadin on the fatal night?'

'Where were you on the fatal night?'

'In Scotland. Fishing. Felicity was in London. Or so she said. We haven't got much in common, I fear. I used to be fond of her, but we've drifted apart. Happens often in marriages, or so I am told. Well, *either* of us could have gone to Grenadin, I suppose, without the other one knowing. It isn't as inconceivable as if, say, that stuffed mongoose over there' – he pointed with his cigar – 'should suddenly wag its tail and say hello, is it?'

'Why should Felicity want to kill your brother?'

'Same reason as me, my dear. *Money.* Felicity's awfully keen on expanding her antiques business. Besides, she's always found Roderick a trial, ever since he insisted on shooting an apple off her head . . . You don't really think it was me who plugged Roderick in the head, do you?'

'How do you know he was shot in the head?'

'I watched that videotape . . . One can actually see the gun protruding from between the window curtains!'

'What tape are you talking about?'

'Someone sent us a tape. A recording of the dumbshow you put on at La Sorcière . . . I knew what it was at once. *The Murder of Gonzago*. Fratricide is a jolly interesting subject. Old Hamlet was, by all accounts, a pussycat and he didn't really deserve the earful of poison he got.'

'Your brother phoned you the day before he died. Basil Hunter mentioned it to me. Your brother was quite horrible to you – he told you to go and kill him – he told you that was the only way to get hold of his money . . . You aren't going to deny that such a conversation took place, are you?'

'No, I am not. Perfectly true.' Gerard nodded. 'Roderick was frightfully rude to me. I'd been badgering him for money, but then Papa did say on his deathbed we must help each other. Roderick had an awful lot of money and yet he refused to finance the Dilettanti Droug Press, or rather he kept saying he would think about it. He was frightfully rude to me on the phone.'

'Were you upset?'

'Of course I was upset. I must admit I got angry too. *Furious*. I felt – well, I felt like killing him.' Gerard regarded the burning end of his cigar. There was a pause. 'They can't prove if someone's been to a foreign country, can they?'

'They can.'

'They'd have one's details at the airport, I suppose . . . It's all computers now, isn't it? Then there are the stamps in one's passport and so on. Unless one has used a *false* passport? Apparently an awful lot of people travel on false passports, I read somewhere.'

'You would have been caught on CCTV cameras,' Renée said a trifle wearily. 'They are everywhere.'

'Are they? Damn. No privacy these days. What if I'd changed my appearance?'

'Gerard, this could be serious—'

'I could have worn a false moustache . . . It's the kind of thing that happens in detective stories . . . As a matter of fact, detective stories could be vehicles for all kinds of ideas, so perhaps I shouldn't sneer at them,' he went on in a meditative voice. 'And nobody could stop me if I decided to write sentences like "His sleuthorial instincts were stimulated." I mean I could experiment in all kinds of ways . . . Incidentally, did you tell anyone where and when you came across my cigar cutter?'

'No. No one knows about it.'

'I am glad.' Suddenly he laughed. 'So if I were to kill you now, the secret, as they say, would die with you!'

'I feel so awful, I wouldn't mind dying,' Renée Glover whispered.

25

The Mysterious Mr Quin

'My memory's getting worse. What is a *meta*-documentary once again, not that it matters the tiniest bit, but do remind me?' Lady Grylls cupped her ear with her hand. 'I *see*. You are so terribly clever, Hughie, they must have hated you in the army, or did you contrive to keep a low profile?'

'I was clever enough not to let anyone suspect me of being clever at all. I believe I managed to blend in. Actually I was quite popular with my brother officers.'

'Were you? You mean you drank to excess, gambled for high stakes and talked about women and horses in a knowledgeable if highly irresponsible fashion? I am so proud of you.' Lady Grylls tapped the tape of the documentary. 'It's a real hoot, terribly funny. I am sure you will be amused. Is there any particular reason you are so keen on watching it?'

'We are curious to see what Lord Remnant was like,' Major Payne said. 'In any murder case the character of the victim is of paramount importance. Murder is frequently – though by no means invariably – a direct consequence of something the victim has done.'

'Roderick certainly managed to upset a great number of people and, from what I hear, he never quite knew when to stop. He called it "teasing". He seemed to have lacked the wisdom to be afraid. Well, the Grenadin locals had been threatening to carve him up and set La Sorcière aflame, so perhaps it was one of the locals who killed him after all? A case of raw revenge, what do you think?'

'You may be right, darling. Perhaps it was a case of raw revenge.'

Lady Grylls pushed her glasses up her nose. 'You don't sound too convinced. You think it's too simple. I imagine it's an addictive pursuit, the hunting down and ultimate unmasking of lethally inclined characters?'

'It is addictive, yes.'

'Who's your favourite suspect, Hughie?'

'I have no favourite suspect.'

'Not the stepson, surely?'

'The stepson seems to be the most obvious choice, but in a vague kind of way we are suspicious of Clarissa's aunt. As it happens, she is also Clarissa's mother. Well, Hortense Tilling is the only member of the house party, with the exception of Stephan, that is, who was *not* in the room at the time of the murder—' Payne broke off. 'What's the matter?'

'Mr Quin! I've been meaning to tell you about Mr Quin! The mysterious Mr Quin! Goodness, my memory's really bad these days. The Case of the Curious Codicil, that's how I think of it.'

'What are you talking about?'

'That would make a pretty decent title for a detective yarn. *The Conundrum of the Curious Codicil*. It's got a ring to it. Antonia might like it, what do you think?'

'It sounds like a short story title and you know Antonia doesn't write short stories, only novels.'

'How about *The Mysterious Mr Quin*?'

'I believe that's already been used.'

'Can't it be used again?'

'Not really, darling. What codicil and who or what is Mr Quin?'

'There's something peculiar about the whole business. I

164

mean, leaving a fortune to a fella no one's ever heard of. I *knew* there was something I needed to tell you, Hughie. You told me to keep my eyes and ears open for developments, didn't you?'

'I believe I did, darling, but perhaps you could try to present your facts in a slightly more linear fashion?'

'The other curious fact is that Clarissa has dismissed *all* the servants and is at Remnant on her own. Bobo believes she's gone bonkers. One of the Remnant maids is the sister of Bobo's gardener, you see. That's how he heard about it, from his gardener. The sister was terribly upset. They were given no notice. Clarissa just told them to go.'

'Clarissa is at Remnant on her own?'

'She is indeed. The mind boggles. Remnant is the size of a hippodrome, with high vaults, eccentrically hazardous staircases and endless corridors. A former abbey or something equally gruesome. For some reason Clarissa brings to mind the woman in the story who sits and waits for her demon lover.'

'Who *is* Mr Quin?' Something had started stirring in Major Payne's deep well of unconscious cerebration. He believed he was already in possession of a certain significant fact. What was it? Then it came to him. The Damascus chest in the Fenwicks' drawing room – the secret drawer – the letter from Marrakech signed 'Q' – Q for Quin?

'Quin is the enigmatic legatee. The fellow to whom Roderick left a fortune in his will. No one knows who he is. I was on the blower, talking to Felicity, just before you came and she told me all about it. She is puzzled and angry. Gerard had never heard Quin's name mentioned before, or so he says. Well, everybody seems to be puzzled. Only Clarissa, it appears, is not.'

Payne cocked an eyebrow. 'Clarissa is not puzzled?'

'No. At least, Gerard thought not. He was watching Clarissa while the will was being read, you see. She didn't seem to turn a hair. Didn't gasp. Didn't look round in dismay. Asked no questions. She seemed terrified – but that's a different thing altogether, isn't it?'

'Clarissa seemed terrified?'

'Yes. That's what Gerard said. He fancies himself as something of a writer, you know. He believes he has special insights into people's emotional states and all that sort of rot. Writers do like to put on a lot of airs, don't they?'

'Antonia doesn't.'

'The chap's full name is Peter Quin and he has been left a fortune in Lord Remnant's will. Five million pounds sterling, Felicity says, which does seem an exorbitant amount to leave to a stranger, doesn't it?'

'It does,' Payne agreed.

'Though of course it's nothing really, a trifling canapé *amuse-gueule* affair, considering Roderick was worth thirty million pounds, some such sum. Apparently Roderick used to boast about his wealth, so terribly vulgar, he behaved more like a baron than an earl. He said once that, if he felt like it, he could pay a great number of people to do nothing but paint his portrait for the rest of his life, even though he knew the value of the finished product would be negligible.'

'Was any reason given for the Quin legacy?'

'*For services rendered.* It appears Quin had done Roderick some great favour.'

'What kind of favour?'

'That was never specified. It's a mystery, I keep telling you. Felicity is annoyed with Gerard because Gerard doesn't seem to think it's such a big deal . . . She is also unhappy that he spends most of his time at his club. She said they had drifted apart . . . Perhaps this Quin saved Roderick's life?'

'Perhaps he did.' Payne spoke absently. 'Clarissa was not particularly surprised and she has dismissed all her servants, eh? Now I find *that* extremely curious.'

166

'It may turn out that it was Quin who killed Roderick after all. Five million is an awful lot of money. For some people, that is. Quin might have saved Roderick's life for that purpose alone. Quin might have engineered the life-threatening situation in the first place, so that he could save Lord Remnant from it. Do you see? Once he knows the legacy has been made in his name, as a token of Lord Remnant's gratitude, he kills Lord Remnant.'

'He saves his life, so that he can kill him later on?'

'Yes! I love paradoxes like that, don't you?'

'Terribly ingenious, darling. A beautiful example of what I believe they call "convoluted cerebration". Positively Chestertonian. Who was it you said Clarissa might be expecting at Remnant?'

'Her demon lover. But I never meant it seriously. Demon lovers don't exist. What is it, Hughie? Why are you looking like that?'

'I think you've just given me a very interesting idea,' Major Payne said.

'Lord Remnant was putting the silencer on his gun?' Antonia said slowly. 'You are sure it was a silencer?'

'Well, yes. The gun, when we found it, had a silencer screwed on it all right. A tubular thing. I thought, how odd, but then Lord Remnant was a very odd kind of person. He'd do *anything* to keep boredom at bay.'

'Was he a good shot?'

'I believe he was. The week before he was killed I saw him shoot a rabbit . . . May I have your *pirog*, if you're not going to eat it? It helps me to concentrate if I eat.'

'You are welcome to it. I haven't touched it. By all means.' Antonia pushed the plate towards her.

'I'd eat *anything* that's got jam in it . . . When I am tense, I tend to eat more than usual,' Louise confided. 'I love *pirog*. I'd sell my soul for a well-made *pirog*.'

'Did you say Lord Remnant shot a rabbit?'

'Yes. It happened the week before he died. I was in the garden next to La Sorcière – enormous botanical gardens, as large as a cricket pitch, stretching down to the sea. I saw Lord Remnant first, then I saw the rabbit. The silly thing was sitting on its haunches, still as a statue. It seemed to think that if it didn't move, it would remain unnoticed! Lord Remnant was wearing old corduroy trousers, a shabby tweed jacket and he had a pith helmet on his head. He looked terribly eccentric, quite ridiculous, really.'

'He had a gun with him?'

'Yes. He lifted the gun and took aim, but he didn't fire at once. I must have gasped – he glanced in my direction and smiled – as though to say, watch. *Then* he fired. The bullet hit the rabbit's hindquarters. The poor creature screamed – how it screamed! It started crawling towards the undergrowth—'

'Oh no.' Antonia couldn't help herself.

Louise stabbed her fork into the *pirog*. 'Lord Remnant fired again. This time the bullet hit the rabbit's head. But still it wasn't dead! It started twitching horribly. I thought he was going to grasp its hind legs and strike hard with his gun at the base of its neck, put it out of its misery. But he didn't. He stood gazing at the quivering, bleeding, mangled creature. He gave a little bow in my direction. It was only then that he bludgeoned it to death with the butt of his gun.'

'That wasn't the same gun he was killed with, was it?'

'Oh no, the gun he was killed with was much smaller. This was a four-ten gun. I am actually convinced he did it so very brutally because he knew I was watching. He then came up to me and said that shooting men and animals was the occupation of a gentleman, that it was the kind of thing that should be lauded and encouraged since it put a curb on effeminate impulses. Would you say that was funny? Or clever?'

'No, not particularly.'

'Lord Remnant took great pleasure in shocking and upsetting people. He had a real knack for it. He liked playing mind games – experimenting – goading people into doing things against their will – into compromising themselves. He liked setting people up. In my opinion, he displayed all the traits of a sociopath.'

There was a pause.

'Tell me about the lead-up to the murder,' Antonia said.

'Dinner that evening was superb. Cocktails, iced consommé, roast duckling with apple sauce, peas and new potatoes.' Louise sighed reminiscently. 'Pudding was a very special kind of ice-cream called Alaska Bombe. There were scented candles on the table. Augustine and his wives went round with silver bowls full of fragrant rosewater for the ladies to dip their fingers in. It was quite marvellous.'

'Was dinner on time or earlier than usual – because of the performance?'

'Much earlier. Well, Lord Remnant was in a highly excited state. He was wearing his snow-white robes and he kept making appalling jokes. He asked Basil how the pigs on the farm were shaping up and, as he did so, he looked at me fixedly. He pointed to the jewellery Clarissa was wearing – to her necklace, bracelet, rings, earrings – and informed us that it was he who had given it all to her. He reached out and raised Clarissa's hand to his lips. He then declared he hadn't actually paid a penny for any of Clarissa's jewels. He said he had pinched them.'

'Pinched them?'

'Yes. Every single piece of jewellery Clarissa was wearing that night had been stolen from the debs he had deflowered back in the sixties. There had been so many of them, he said, that sometimes, when he couldn't sleep, he counted deflowered debutantes the way other people count sheep.'

'He said that?'

'Yes! A very unusual brand of debs' delight, that's how he described himself. A sort of erotic Raffles. Plumbing the depths of bestial debauchery had been his favourite pastime, but then most of the girls had been more than willing to be seduced by him. It wasn't always plain sailing, though. Sometimes a girl struggled, which he found terribly irksome. He was not the kind of man who accepted no for an answer. Normally he was gentle and gracious, but he could also be pugnacious.' Louise raised the saucer to her lips.

'I hope he wasn't hinting at rape,' said Antonia.

'He *was* hinting at rape.'

'I don't suppose he used the word?'

'No. He had been firm, forceful and uncompromising, that's how he put it. He had been in the habit of collecting trophies, to remind himself of his conquests. It was mainly jewellery he stole, but he'd also taken scarves and gloves and, on one memorable occasion, a stiletto-heeled shoe. Well-born girls in those days were fond of bedecking themselves, he said, frequently wearing the family jewels, so there were always rich pickings.'

'You don't think he was making it up, do you? Perhaps he was just showing off? One of his appalling jokes?'

'Somehow I don't think he was . . . The girls were usually so scared or ashamed of what they had allowed him to do to them, he said, they never made any fuss afterwards. They never complained, never told anyone about it. But he took no chances. He was careful to make it hard for anyone to track him down.'

'How did he manage that?'

'He wore disguise. He described himself as an "inveterate masquerader". He had a talent for voices and accents. He would attend parties wearing a variety of beards, moustaches, wigs and so on, and each time he gave a false name. He said there was nothing like making love in disguise. He got a kick out of passing himself off as a

170

foreigner, French or Italian, sometimes Portuguese. He spoke French like a native. That made things easier, he said.'

'He chose nations he liked?'

'He chose nations he particularly *dis*liked. That was part of the joke. He'd pretended to be a sheikh and a maharaja several times, but maharajas, apparently, took ages to get right.'

'He was never recognized?'

'He said he wasn't. Afterwards no one would associate him with the character he had played. Some of his hosts and hostesses cooperated with him, though he was a notorious gatecrasher as well. He also admitted that on a number of occasions he resorted to spiking the girls' drinks.'

'He drugged them? Rohypnol? That's a notorious date drug,' Antonia murmured. 'I wonder if it was available in the sixties?'

'It was awful, sitting there listening to him. It was particularly awkward for Clarissa of course,' Louise said with ill-concealed relish. 'She pretended to treat the whole thing as a joke, as a ridiculous fantasy, but I could see she was upset. Poor old Hortense looked quite shaken too. I thought she might faint. In fact she got up and left the room. When she came back she looked sick as a parrot. Even Augustine seemed shocked – and he is rumoured to have slept with every single woman on Grenadin!'

'Did anyone say anything?'

'No. We all pretended that nothing untoward had been said. Basil praised the wine. SS asked if there was anything wrong with the air-conditioning. Renée, as usual, said nothing. Then suddenly Lord Remnant declared he was bored. He launched into one of his monologues. Why was it that most of the people he met were bores – conventional conformists, trivial-minded, insignificant little people with peanut-sized brains? Did anyone have an *explanation*? He invariably felt depressed and demoralized after a dinner party. Talking to bores was like prodding at particularly resilient mattresses. He could bear neither the sound nor the look of bores. He glanced round the table as he said that. He then said he felt an irresistible urge to have himself blindfolded. There was only one chap he knew who wasn't a bore. A chap called Quin.'

'Quin?'

'Yes. Peter Quin. Lord Remnant then said he intended to leave Quin something in his will, as a reward for not being a bore. He went on to describe Quin as one of the cleverest, most inventive, most stimulating men he had ever known. Hadn't we ever heard of Peter Quin, the man of the hundred faces? He seemed surprised and annoyed when we said we hadn't.'

'The man of the hundred faces,' Antonia said thoughtfully.

26

Contact

'Hello? Clarissa? It's Peter Quin speaking.'

There was silence on the line and he thought they had been cut off, but then he heard her catch her breath, so he smiled and said, '*Peter Quin*' again, with greater emphasis, then went on to greet her with courteous formality and ask after her health.

He wanted to know how things had been since the funeral. Had she been coping well with her widowed state? Was she feeling lonely? Was she feeling forlorn? She wouldn't go so far as to describe herself as 'inconsolable', would she?

At the sound of his voice Clarissa's hand had gone up to her mouth. 'Where – where are you?' Her voice sounded incredibly hoarse, as though she had suddenly developed a sore throat.

'Sharp, inquiring and purposeful as ever. No time for small talk, eh? You seem to have embraced the hyperactive spirit of the age, my dear . . . I don't suppose you have given the matter of the memorial service any serious consideration, have you?'

'What memorial service?'

'Lord Remnant's memorial service. The *éloges funèbres* are always the same and so tiresomely fulsome. If you've heard one sanctimonious, mock-sorrowful eulogy, you've heard them all. No one is likely to say what they really think, are they?'

'What – what do you mean?'

'No one is going to say that the late Lord Remnant will be remembered mainly for his monstrous manners, his terrible temper and his flair for inflicting discomfort. There won't be a single reference to the fact that when his death was announced, the whole island of Grenadin erupted in wildest jubilation, will there?'

'You aren't on Grenadin, are you?'

'No, of course not. On reflection, a memorial service may not be such a good idea. If you really miss someone,' he went on, 'you would be better off doing something you both enjoyed doing together, which is unlikely to mean, except in the most bizarre cases, standing around in a draughty church, wearing black and singing hymns.'

'Where *are* you?'

'In London. The Ritz is not, alas, as it used to be. London is not what it used to be. England is not what it used to be.' He sighed deeply. 'To think that once we had an empire, that we ruled the waves and so on, and now we have degenerated into a provincial, polyester sort of place.'

'Did you have a good flight?' She had secretly hoped the plane had crashed, that he had perished.

'A good flight? Are you trying to be clever, my darling? Wit has never been your strongest suit, you know. But do tell me, how are things? How is life at the castle? Does good old Remnant still stand? Smothered in mists, as usual? Are there daffodils and crocuses in the garden?'

'Everything's fine.'

'You don't consider yourself a prisoner of the vast ancestral barracks? I am prepared to bet you find cosiness unattainable? I want the truth – you *must* tell me the truth!'

'Everything's fine.'

'Remnant's cold, isn't it? I vividly remember how on one

174

memorable occasion you made the journey between your bedroom and the dining room wearing a fur coat, to escape pneumonia, you said, which I thought a perfectly charming kind of explanation. The feel of that fur coat drove me mad . . .'

'Everything's fine.'

'You sound as though you are in a state of narcosis.'

'I am not in a state of narcosis.'

'No need to be defensive, Clarissa. Your secret is safe with me. Safe as houses. You know it's not the kind of thing I disapprove of. Better ersatz happiness than no happiness, my darling. I *want* you to be happy . . . You did what I asked?'

'Yes.'

'You followed my instructions to the letter? You got rid of Tradewell and all the other flunkeys and lackeys?'

'Yes.'

'You are all alone at Remnant? Good girl. You know how much I value submission. I apportion you extra Brownie points. So no trouble of any sort? You haven't attracted the attention of agents provocateurs? Any police officers? Any snoopers – any well-meaning busybodies?'

'No. No one.'

'Splendid. You haven't had your fancy boy to stay yet? No? Splendid, absolutely splendid news. I suppose you've grown out of him, which doesn't surprise me at all. He was unworthy of you. That film now. I hope you destroyed it? I said burn it, didn't I? It shouldn't have been made in the first place. It was your idea, my darling. Your rather idiotic idea, I should say.'

'I am sorry.'

'Only the most conventional kind of brain would come up with an idea like that. It is almost as though you *wanted* me to be caught! . . . No, of course not. That was a joke. A little light relief. Oh well, too late to fuss and fret now. What is it they say? No day is so dead as the day before yesterday . . . You didn't forget to have the film destroyed, did you?'

'I didn't forget,' Clarissa lied after a moment's pause. 'The film's been destroyed.'

He would have been furious if she had told him she had no idea where the film was. The film had been the last thing on her mind that night. She had asked Aunt Hortense to put the camera away. She hadn't the foggiest what had become of the film.

'You burnt it? You let it be consumed by fire? Good girl,' she heard him say. 'I believe I have been misjudging you, my darling, for which I humbly apologize . . . I have a confession to make.'

'What confession?' She was filled with foreboding.

'It concerns our reunion,' he said solemnly. 'I find myself looking forward to our reunion with ardour and *tendresse*. You will indulge me, won't you, my darling? I want you to wear one of your fur coats. Mink . . . against . . . naked skin?'

27

Doctor's Dilemma

As Major Payne walked down Harley Street towards Dr Sylvester-Sale's surgery, he mulled over Louise Hunter's strange tale, which Antonia had recounted to him on her mobile phone some five minutes previously.

Well, there seemed to be only one explanation that covered all the facts: the dead man's hands, the high-pitched giggle in the bathroom, the arrival of the Grimaud, Lord Remnant putting a silencer on the gun, the mysterious Mr Quin, Clarissa dismissing all her servants . . . *Yes.*

Going up the couple of well-polished steps leading to Dr Sylvester-Sale's front door, Payne rang the bell.

A minute later he was ushered in. He wondered if he would be able to get the information he needed. It was a very tiny bit of the puzzle, but it was important to fit it in where Payne believed it belonged.

Late thirties or early forties, black hair smoothed back off a high forehead, sculpted nose and well-shaped mouth. Dr Sylvester-Sale possessed the dark and handsome, if somewhat conventional, looks of a matinée idol. Or what fifty years previously would have qualified as a matinée idol . . .

Dr Sylvester-Sale's consulting room did not look like a consulting room at all. The walls were covered in washed silk paper of an Oriental design, the parquet floor was the colour of burnt sugar. The mantelpiece was carved out of black marble and on it stood a very intricate-looking clock under a glass dome and two crystal candlesticks dripping with minute stalactites.

The fireplace was filled with oleander blossom placed in a copper bowl polished so that it shone like burnished red gold. The window curtains were made of light blue chenille and they were magnificently looped; the three tall windows looked out over the most decorous of inner-court gardens. The walnut desk was kidney-shaped and it was decorated with a delicate orchid in a vase made of Venetian glass.

Payne sat down in one of the two Chippendale chairs. He glanced at the comic triptych on the wall, eighteenth-century, at a guess, showing a bewigged medico in various difficult, surreally absurd situations.

'Doctor's dilemmas, eh?' He waved at them.

'That, I believe, is what the cycle is called.' Dr Sylvester-Sale glanced down at the card his visitor had handed him. 'It doesn't say here that you are a private detective . . . Are you really? Didn't think they existed any longer.'

Dr Sylvester-Sale wore a charcoal suit of a discreet stripe and a silk tie that hinted but only hinted at flamboyance.

'I am acting on behalf of Felicity Fenwick, who is now Lady Remnant. Lady Remnant asked me to look into the possibility that her brother-in-law might have been the victim of a local vendetta,' Payne said.

'You seem to have got hold of the wrong end of the stick.' Sylvester-Sale gave a superior smile. 'Lord Remnant died of natural causes. He had a heart attack. Whatever gave his sister-in-law the idea that he was killed?'

'Lady Remnant received a videotape showing Lord Remnant's death in the course of a playlet based on *The*

178

Murder of Gonzago,' Payne said smoothly. 'One can actually see Lord Remnant being shot in the back of the head.'

'I very much doubt that such a tape exists,' Dr Sylvester-Sale said.

'It does exist. As it happens, I watched it twice. You are in it. You take part in the playlet.'

'Impossible. You seem to be taking me for someone else.'

'You are one of the protagonists. You are the murderous beau. It is you who kills the King. At one point the camera shows you carrying a tumbler *upside down*. Am I likely to know such a detail if I hadn't actually seen it?'

The doctor's expression didn't change, but his face turned the colour of a guardsman's jacket. 'I am sorry, Major Payne, but I am going to ask you to leave, if you don't mind.' He glanced at his watch. 'I've remembered that I have a patient coming any moment now.'

Payne didn't stir. 'You are seen examining Lord Remnant's body. There is no sound, sadly, so it is impossible to ascertain what you are saying, but everybody looks quite shocked.'

'Didn't you hear what I said? *You must leave.*'

'The tape was sent to Lady Remnant by one of your fellow guests, who has subsequently talked to us about what happened. You were all involved in a cover-up,' Payne went on relentlessly. 'It was you and another doctor – a Dr McLean – who signed the death certificate, giving the cause of Lord Remnant's death as a heart attack.'

'If you don't leave my surgery within the next minute, I'll have no other option but to call the police,' Dr Sylvester-Sale said.

'By all means. I am sure they will be interested in hearing the story about the tape. And perhaps they will choose to follow it up.'

Sylvester-Sale passed a weary hand across his face. 'What is it you actually want from me?'

'A simple answer to a simple question – is the place safe? I mean Grenadin. Is Grenadin safe?'

There was a pause. 'You want me to tell you – if Grenadin is safe? Is that all you want to know? Is that why – why you came to see me?'

'That is all I want to know, yes.' Payne smiled pleasantly. 'Lady Remnant – Felicity Fenwick, as she once was – is anxious to ascertain exactly how safe the island of Grenadin is. She and her husband – the thirteenth earl – are considering building property on Grenadin.'

'I thought the Fenwicks couldn't stand the place. Not their kind of scene at all.'

Payne had prepared his answer.

'Neither Lady Remnant nor her husband proposes to live on Grenadin. Their intention is to have several holiday villas built and then to let them. Lady Remnant believes it was one or more of the locals who brought about her brother-in-law's death. She has heard about the death threats Lord Remnant had been receiving.'

There was another pause. 'Very well. It's true. Lord Remnant did receive a number of anonymous death threats. I am afraid his popularity ratings among the people of Grenadin were rather low . . . No, he wasn't perturbed, at least that was the impression he gave. He amused himself by sticking the death threats in a scrapbook.'

'Did he ever show them to you?'

'He did. He showed them to all of us one evening after dinner. He read aloud three or four of the more lurid ones. He put on an exaggerated Grenadin accent, which was actually quite funny . . . He was warned that he'd have his left arm chopped off, then his right, then his right ear, then his nose – you get the idea. There were some silly ones as well, like threatening to unleash the Grimaud on him.'

Payne feigned ignorance. 'What's that? A dog?'

'No. A demon. The Grimaud is conjured up by a curse. It

is one of the most popular superstitions on the island. Lord Remnant said he longed to meet the Grimaud.'

'He wasn't at all frightened?'

'I don't think he was. He said once emotionalism was for the lower orders and that he was bound by his blue blood code. In his own mad way he was quite brave. A rattlesnake appeared in his bathroom one night, but he managed to spear it with his swordstick and then carried it down to the incinerator in the basement. We saw him as he came down the stairs. He was holding the swordstick aloft, with the snake dangling from it, dripping blood. It made the women scream. That seemed to please him.'

'He liked striking attitudes?'

'Oh, very much so. He told us what happened in some detail. Apparently the snake went for him the moment he opened the bathroom door. It is my belief it had been injected with amphetamines – that would explain why it was so aggressive.'

'Are amphetamines easy to obtain on Grenadin?'

'I believe they are. Drugs, generally, are a big industry on Grenadin. According to some statistics, one in every three islanders is involved in the drug trade,' Sylvester-Sale drawled. He appeared to have regained his composure completely.

'When did the snake incident take place?'

'About a fortnight before he died, I think. Lord Remnant suspected it was one or more of the locals who'd doctored the snake and put it in his bathroom.'

'Do you have to be a doctor to be able to doctor a snake?'

'No, not necessarily. You need to have the stomach for it, though. Oh and a syringe . . . Lord Remnant said it was the work of his "enemies", but he refused to report the incident to the police. Guards? Yes, Lord Remnant had guards, but, as it happened, they were far from reliable.'

'I suppose Clarissa left the room in the immediate aftermath of her husband's murder?' Payne spoke casually.

'I don't see what that's got to do with anything. Why do you want to know?' Suddenly Sylvester-Sale looked extremely suspicious. 'You are wasting your time if you are trying to pin the murder on Clarissa.'

'That, I assure you, is not my intention.'

'Well, as it happens, she did leave the room,' Sylvester-Sale said. 'She needed to go to the bathroom. Nothing odd in that. I believe she needed to collect her thoughts.'

'How long was she out of the room?'

'No more than five or ten minutes.'

A consultation, thought Payne; Clarissa had needed an urgent consultation. It all fitted in. The situation had been extremely complicated. Clarissa had been out of her depth and unable to make a decision. She had needed to know what her next move should be . . .

'Did you like Lord Remnant, doctor?'

'You do ask some very strange questions, Major Payne.'

'Absolute monsters are rare, but the late Lord Remnant doesn't seem to have had a single redeeming feature. *Not a single one.* Is that possible? I find it very hard to believe.' Payne shook his head.

'Did I like Lord Remnant? No, not particularly. In fact, if you must know,' Dr Sylvester-Sale said, 'not at all. No one did.'

'No one? Not even Clarissa?'

'Least of all Clarissa. Sorry, I shouldn't have said that.'

'That's terribly sad,' said Payne. '*Can* one live without love?'

'Lord Remnant clearly could.'

'Mad, bad and dangerous to know . . . That's how he emerges from all the stories I've heard so far. I must admit this whole case exercises a peculiar fascination over me. The protagonists and their foibles have got me firmly in their grip.' Payne clenched his hand into a fist. 'I understand Clarissa's son has a serious drug problem?'

'That's been taken care of.'

'What's the likelihood of Lord Remnant having been involved in the drug trade on the island?'

'If, for argument's sake, he was involved, it couldn't have been for the money. At the time of his death he was an extremely rich man, you know.'

'Couldn't he have done it for the thrill of it? To escape boredom? Isn't that possible?'

Sylvester-Sale shrugged. 'I suppose it's possible. *Anything* was possible where Lord Remnant was concerned. He was prey to ennui. He referred to it as "my pathological condition". He would do *anything* to escape boredom, yes. He said that danger stimulated him . . . He did some very silly things. In many ways he was quite mad. I don't think he had a safety valve . . . So, yes, it's perfectly possible.'

'Was Lord Remnant a clever man, doctor?'

'Depends on how one defines "clever". He certainly thought of himself as clever, which is not quite the same thing. He considered himself a genius . . . I suppose he was clever – in a highly idiosyncratic kind of way. He seemed to identify with criminal masterminds like Dr No and Goldfinger.'

'Did he now?'

'Yes. He *loved* watching those awful James Bond films.'

'Would you say Lord Remnant was capable of planning and executing a murder?' Major Payne asked.

Dr Sylvester-Sale looked at him curiously. 'I would. Yes. Perfectly capable.'

It was only after his visitor had taken his leave that Dr Sylvester-Sale remembered that Grenadin had been left to Clarissa and that it was highly unlikely that the Fenwicks should be planning to have holiday villas built on the island. Clarissa would have told him had that indeed been the case. What exactly had Major Payne been after?

28

Call on the Dead

Renée broke down and dissolved into sobs. Gerard Fenwick put a slightly awkward avuncular arm around her shoulders.

'There, there. What is the matter? I knew there was something wrong.'

'Everything's wrong – everything!'

'That's not possible, my dear. Not *everything*. I don't believe the end of the world has come yet, has it?'

'No. No. I am sorry,' Renée said indistinctly, her face pressed against the lapel of his tweed jacket. 'I am so sorry.'

'Nothing to be sorry about,' he reassured her.

'I want to die. You can kill me if you like.'

'What a damned silly thing to say. Why should I want to kill you? I don't need to *silence* you. You don't really think I killed my brother, do you?'

'No. I know you didn't. It's just come to me. You couldn't have got hold of the gun. The gun was taken from Lord Remnant's study.' She pulled away slightly and sniffed. 'Unless someone handed it over to you.'

'Yes, I might have had an accomplice.' Gerard smiled. 'Only I didn't.'

'You were there that night – why were you there?'

He gave her his handkerchief and said gallantly, 'Won't you first tell me what's upset you so much? No, wait.' He crossed to his desk and produced a bottle of brandy and a tumbler. 'You *must* have some of this. It'll put some colour in your cheeks.'

She blew her nose, dabbed at her eyes and sat down. She held the glass of brandy, took a dutiful sip. She then blurted out the whole pathetic tale. She knew it was a doomed entanglement, she said; she had known it from the very start, yet she had allowed herself to become obsessed with Dr Sylvester-Sale.

They had had a secret affair at La Sorcière. Syl had told her he loved her. He had said that she was his only really solid and unseverable lien with the world—

'That's rather good, actually, do let me make a note of it.' Gerard reached for his notebook. '*Unseverable lien with the world*. Do chaps talk like that? Outside books, that is?'

'I've never heard anyone else say it,' she admitted.

'No, of course not. He said it to impress you. He never meant any of it. That should have put you on your guard, my dear. "Syl", did you say? How very interesting. It's an anagram of "sly". "Rain" now is an anagram of "Iran", though I don't think that's in any way important. *An anachronistic anagram annoyed by anonymity . . .*'

Dr Sylvester-Sale had made promises, Renée said, which she had believed, even though she had been perfectly aware of his affair with Clarissa. Her waking moments had been filled with thoughts of him. He was terribly good-looking, she hadn't been able to help herself.

They had planned their future together, but, after they had been back in England a couple of days, his phone calls had suddenly stopped. She had started stalking him, she was ashamed to admit. She had seen him in the company of a red-haired woman. She had seen them kiss. She had been distraught. She had thought of throwing herself under a passing car. She might have been a lovelorn schoolgirl.

186

Gerard leant back and, picking up his smouldering cigar, said, 'I must admit I am extremely surprised, Renée. I thought you were the epitome of cool and self-possession.'

'Well, I'm not.'

'Shall we have a game of demon patience, the way we used to? It might help you see things in perspective. I have a pack of cards somewhere.' He glanced vaguely round.

'No, thank you, Gerard. Not now. I'll be fine.' She blew her nose.

'Would you allow me to take you out to dinner somewhere later on?' I'd very much like to marry her, he thought. 'At about seven?'

'I am not sure.'

'Of course you are. I don't think you have a prior engagement, have you?'

'I am not sure. I haven't.'

'There you are! How about the Caprice?' He glanced at his watch. 'I am going to book a table. If you fancy eggs Benedict and steak tartare, that's the place to go.'

Over dinner, he told her *his* story. It was as pathetic as hers. He too had made a fool of himself. He had acted irrationally, out of character, without much thought as to what *exactly* he intended to do. He had been in Scotland, in the Highlands, fishing in the river Spey when he had received a call from Roderick. None of this would have happened if he hadn't had his mobile phone in his pocket. Weren't mobiles the scourge of the modern age? After his late brother had challenged him, Gerard had got exceedingly angry, he'd seen red, he'd felt like killing Roderick – quite unlike himself, really. He had changed, packed a small case and driven to the nearest airport, hopped on a plane and flown to Grenadin.

'I only had an overnight bag with me. I got a cab from the airport, but when we reached the estate, I decided to walk. I wanted to clear my head. There was a moon. Lovely weather – apart from the blasted mosquitoes.'

'So that *was* a mosquito bite!'

'Yes. That was most perspicacious of you, my dear. Well, I got to La Sorcière and went in through the gate at the back. I walked up the avenue. I no longer felt cross, only a little stupid. Still, I intended to discuss finance with Roderick. I thought it might make a difference if I confronted him, if I put him "on the spot", as the phrase goes.'

'You needed money . . .'

'Well, yes. He had so much money, it was ridiculous, keeping it all to himself. I needed money for my Dilettanti Droug idea. Well, I came up to the terrace – heard voices coming from behind the french windows – heard a splashing sound coming from the garden—'

'Stephan. That was Stephan. He was beside the pool.'

'Then I saw a movement – there was someone by the french windows. Couldn't tell if it was man or woman. Figure dressed in some light-coloured clothing. Put me in mind of the woman in white, though it might have been a man. My brother always wore white, didn't he? Sorry, that's neither here nor there. I saw the figure move away from the window and disappear down the side steps of the terrace.'

'Which way did the figure go?'

'Haven't the foggiest. I didn't think anything of it, though I instinctively knew there had been something excessively furtive about the way it had moved—'

'Furtive?'

'Yes . . . I threw away my cigar. I hadn't finished it, but I didn't want to attract attention, you know. I walked up the steps – and on to the terrace. I saw the french windows were ajar, but of course the curtains were drawn over them on the inside, so I couldn't see anything. I heard voices. A man said something – someone gasped – *did he really mean Lord Remnant had been murdered?* Something on those lines. I am sure it was a woman who said that.'

'Louise Hunter.'

'For a moment I thought it was all part of some silly charade or parlour game. The Murder Game, you know, or that you were putting on some kind of a play. Roderick was potty about theatricals, wasn't he?'

'He was. Liked nothing better.'

'I didn't really know what to make of it. Then I remembered the figure I'd seen earlier on and suddenly felt goosebumps down my spine. I stumbled over some bulky object – a monstrous head goggled up at me!'

'Bottom's head.'

'Made me jump out of my skin. That's when I must have dropped my cigar cutter, don't you think?' Gerard pulled at his lip. 'The next moment I saw the gun. It lay beside the head. Well, I knew then there was something very rotten indeed in the state of Denmark. I realized I'd made a mistake coming. It had been madness. If Roderick had really been killed, I'd be a prime suspect. After all I had a goodish motive for wanting my brother out of the way.'

'What did you do?'

'Well, I swung round and ran down the terrace steps and back on the avenue. I got out and hailed a cab, which took me back to the airport. I hopped on the next plane back to Scotland.'

There was a pause.

'You found yourself standing on the terrace *after* the murder was committed. I wonder if the figure you saw was the killer,' Renée Glover said. 'It couldn't have been Stephan. Stephan was sitting beside the pool – you heard him – he was dropping pebbles. That's where we found him later on . . . So you can't say if it was a man or a woman you saw outside the windows?'

'I am afraid not, my dear. It happened very fast. One moment the figure in white was there, the next moment it was gone. Was anyone out of the room at the time of the shooting?'

'Well, yes,' Renée answered promptly. 'Hortense. She said she was going to the loo.'

'It might have been her then. She might have run out and shot Roderick . . . Was she dressed in white that evening?'

'I believe she was.' Renée smiled. 'I don't think Hortense shot your brother. She is muddle-headed and scatty and not particularly practical. It took her *ages* to understand how a camera works. Besides, her eyesight's really bad. She couldn't even see the stripes on a zebra.'

'She may have been putting it on.'

'I don't think she was. She disliked Lord Remnant, but I very much doubt it was she who killed him.'

'Well, if Stephan didn't shoot Roderick and if Hortense didn't and if I didn't – who did?'

There was a pause.

'It was *such* a strange evening,' said Renée. 'Just before dinner I happened to go into the laundry room and what do you think I saw there? You'd never guess. *A brand new coffin painted white.*'

'A coffin in the laundry room? Odd place to leave a coffin. Couldn't it have been a prop of some kind? For a play my brother may have been contemplating?'

'When I mentioned the coffin to Clarissa, she said she had no idea where it had come from. She looked annoyed. With me – but I also had an idea she was annoyed with herself.'

'How terribly interesting. Annoyed with herself – for not being more careful? Suggests she was involved – um – in whatever was going on? Perhaps something was brought to La Sorcière in that coffin? Or *someone*? A coffin suggests transportation . . . Would you like a cigar, my dear?'

'No, thank you.'

'No, it wouldn't be quite your style. You do look awfully pretty in that dress, Renée. So terribly fresh and innocent. Perhaps we could take a holiday together some time, you and I? What do you think? Felicity smokes my cigars, did

I tell you? I wonder if that's good enough grounds for divorce?'

'I don't think so.'

'She says it isn't her. But it *must* be her. She keeps pinching my cigars and then denies it. Hate petty deceptions like that.'

'Something else happened later that night,' Renée said. 'Clarissa announced she wanted to spend some time alone with her husband's body. She told everybody to go to bed. As I didn't feel at all tired, I sneaked out and took a turn in the garden. When I eventually went up, I happened to pass Lord Remnant's dressing-room door. She was inside. I heard her voice. She was talking in an urgent whisper.'

'She may have been praying. Isn't that possible? For Roderick's soul and so on? Asking God to spare Roderick and not despatch him to hell? She may be a Catholic, you know. There was a time when no Remnant would touch a Catholic with a bargepole, but things have changed. We know nothing about Clarissa. Nothing at all.'

'It didn't sound like a prayer.' Renée shook her head. 'It sounded as though – as though she was arguing with someone.'

'She couldn't have been arguing with my brother because he was dead. Well, people living in the Balkans and suchlike countries tend to talk to their dead as they lie in the coffin. Part of a long-standing tradition, I imagine. I think it's called "lamentations", but lamenting is hardly what one would expect of Clarissa, is it?'

'Hardly.'

'Clarissa loathed my brother – or so Felicity says. Felicity insists Clarissa had lots of lovers . . . Did you say you thought Clarissa was arguing with someone? You didn't hear anyone answer her, did you?'

'No. I didn't dare go too near the door. I didn't stop for long. I was terribly nervous.'

'She may have been talking to herself. In my opinion Clarissa's gone mad. Getting rid of all the servants, staying at Remnant all by herself and so on.'

'I can't help feeling that there is some unknown factor at work . . .'

'Perhaps my brother's death is destined to go down the centuries as one of those unsolved mysteries – unless Payne and his detective-story-writing wife manage to crack it somehow, though that seems most unlikely. It is only in books that the zeal of amateurs is rewarded by success. I do believe, my dear, my next novel will be a whodunnit.'

'I thought you hated whodunnits.'

'Not any longer. I have every intention of experimenting with the form. Genre conventions could be subverted while still being decorously observed.' Gerard spoke dreamily. 'A mysterious death in an exotic locale. A murder committed during an amateur theatrical production. A small circle of suspects—'

'You intend to write an autobiographical whodunnit?'

'I don't see why novels shouldn't be rooted in experience. Not such a bad idea if a character's emotional concerns are in fact the author's emotional concerns, even if I do take exception to the concept of uninhibited autobiography. What I am drawn to is the novelist's freedom to blend, to compress, to conflate, to reframe. There's a phrase that sums it up awfully well. What was it? Transformative power. Being able to take things that were terribly puzzling and make them lucid, producing an entertainment out of what was horrifying and disturbing. Now *that* would be a whacking big achievement. Wouldn't you say?'

'I would.' She smiled. 'I see what you mean.'

'*Who eliminated the earl?* That will be the question in everybody's mind. Is it the drug-crazed stepson? The dotty aunt? The flighty chatelaine? The dashing doctor? The cigar-smoking sister-in-law? The actual solution will of course be something completely unexpected ... I rather like the idea of there being an unknown factor at work. Readers expect radical reversals, don't they?'

29

Bent Sinister

No blinding light on the road to Damascus! No, of course not. Cold and sharp as flint. It cut his face as soon as he walked out of the Ritz. His hand went up to check he was not bleeding.

He put on his gloves. *'Je reviens,'* he murmured.

He'd forgotten how perfectly foul the English weather could be.

He already missed the ambience of hedonistic freedom he had left behind, the glinting harmonies of sea, sky and golden sands. He missed his white pyjamas. And what a bore it was, having to wait for his 'inheritance'! He was not used to waiting, to not being able to spend as lavishly as he at some point might feel like.

There was shockingly little money in the account of the man renowned for his one hundred faces and one hundred and one voices, as he had discovered. (Had Quin been a gambler?) His own cards he could no longer use since they had all been cancelled the day after he had 'died'. Damned frustrating. What was it they said? Reasonable thrift is a virtue when practised by the rich, a dire necessity when practised by the poor. As it happened, he wasn't used to thrift of any kind, so there.

Neither by training nor by temperament was he fitted

to the rigours of everyday life. Never before had he found himself lashed to the masts of actuality. A good many things, mundane, rather banal things, which mere mortals did all the time, he had never done. He had been shielded by his immense wealth and position. He had never been on a double-decker bus, for example, never travelled by tube, never got up early in the morning because he had to, never had to wait to see a doctor or a dentist, never stood in a queue.

At one time, before he'd decided it constituted a gross intrusion into his privacy, he had never dressed in the mornings without the help of a personal valet.

But there was no question of him practising thrift. He was going to claim his legacy very soon now. Then he could do as he pleased. He would be able to satisfy his every whim.

He wouldn't stay in England, oh no. He hated England. So terribly dull and cold and shoddy and so full of foreigners. He would travel. He wouldn't stop in a place for more than five days because he would get bored.

Perhaps he would sell his soul to the Devil and achieve immortality. He'd been thinking about it. He had the spell written out on a slip of paper in his breast pocket; the voodoo doctor had assured him that it worked.

He was clad in an immense black cloak with a burgundy silk lining, which imparted to him the air of a stage magician, which in a way he was. (Now you see me, now you don't.) On his head he wore a homburg, on his eyes tinted glasses. His sideburns were reddish brown. Of course they were not *his* sideburns. Not strictly speaking. Thinking about his false whiskers cheered him up and he swung his silver-topped cane. He hummed an old-fashioned tune. *I am the pride of Piccadilly, the blasé roué.*

He rather enjoyed wearing disguise, always had. He found it liberating. Each time he wore disguise he felt like a butterfly that had broken from its chrysalis and taken wing. His disguise at the moment was of the minimal kind. He liked taking risks. He delighted in pushing his luck. It occurred to him that he possessed the full Byronic equipment of noble lineage, unorthodox imagination, a restless spirit and a daring soul.

He found staying at the Ritz irksome; he couldn't quite put his finger on the reason for it. He didn't relish walking up and down Piccadilly either. He thought he did, but he didn't. Too many people of little or no distinction, rather common-looking, in fact; a great stumbling mass; a herd of accursed *canaille* following their hackneyed inclinations.

He had never been in a crowd before. Nothing as intolerable as a crowd had ever been imposed on his person. He hated to be touched. He'd rather swim Lake Maracaibo than allow himself to be touched. Why did they keep touching him? He felt like raising his stick and hitting out left and right, then right and left. *Swish-swish*. It would be like topping nettles.

He looked foreign, he supposed, with his bleached eyebrows and polished mahogany complexion, but then most of the people who bumped into him also looked foreign, which wasn't something he approved of. Not in England, at any rate. It was all too disorienting for words. It gave him a headache.

England was going to the dogs, no doubt about it.

There was nothing like a walk round St James's, he found, to get his bile flowing. He had always been aware of a strong anti-Establishment streak in him.

He detested the 'distinguished' hatters, gunsmiths and boot-makers, the 'exclusive' shops selling unbelievably small, exorbitantly priced fiddly bits connected with fly-fishing, the whole area designed predominantly for a certain type of elderly pinstriped pillar of the Establishment. But most of all he hated the gentlemen's clubs, those middens of priggishness and betrayal.

It was only with great difficulty that he resisted the temptation to pay his old club a visit and wreak some kind of havoc inside. He would have enjoyed smashing a gilded mirror or two with his stick, knocking off old Rees-Mogg's glasses or punching a hole in that portrait of Baden-Powell. Oh, how his hands itched!

The management had blackballed him a couple of years back, the moralizing morons. He couldn't remember the reason for his expulsion. Well, he didn't think much of them either. Smug, small-minded nincompoops, mostly rather inept, quite absurd, leading puzzled, barren lives – like children standing at a grave, searching futilely for the secret of life. He had no patience with them. Not worth his wrath, really.

The moment you learnt to speak, you dedicated your new faculty to unsettling or outraging people. That was what a tedious old uncle of his, long dead, had once told him. His French governess had babbled about his *mauvaises habitudes.* He had been the proverbial demon child. He remembered Deirdre, his late wife, telling him that he was evil in a rather *old-fashioned* kind of way, whatever that might mean.

No, he mustn't do anything that would attract attention. They would most certainly try to arrest him if he did, which would be a bore. He mustn't let the police take a close look at him. Or, rather, at Peter Quin. Which of course was the same thing. He kept forgetting.

There is no difference between continued affectation and reality. It was Congreve or someone who wrote that.

Yes. Quite.

He sat on a bench in Green Park, yawned prodigiously and stared before him for what seemed an age. He pushed his underlip out petulantly, always an ominous sign to those who knew him. His scowl deepened. He was bored. A dark despondency had him in its grip and he could see no future for the human race. He'd been hurl'd from th'ethereal sky, down to this bottomless perdition, here to dwell. Not in adamantine chains and penal fire, true, though that afforded him little consolation.

He hated being at a loose end. He felt like a shark out of water. He had an acute sense of anticlimax. He didn't think anonymity suited his temperament. Despatching couriers with horns to clear the roads for his passage would have been more his style.

Gripping his silver-topped stick between his gloved hands, he thrashed at a pigeon. His mood then suddenly improved. He rose. Moments later he was back in Piccadilly, standing in front of a shop window, admiring his reflection. He reminded himself that he belonged to that stratospheric breed of men to whom the world was but a lump of clay, infinitely pliable to their wants and whims.

'What I want,' he mouthed at his reflection, 'is a pair of wings. *Black* wings. They've *got* to be black.'

He found exactly the kind of wings he wanted half an hour later at a little shop in Covent Garden, which specialized in different kinds of theatrical paraphernalia. Black wings, something funereal about them, rather sinister, exactly as he had envisaged them.

'Are these real feathers? I like the feel of feathers nearly as much as I like the feel of fur. I am going to wear 'em, you know,' he said as he watched the young man place the wings inside a rectangular tulip-red box. '*Soon.*'

The shop assistant, accustomed to eccentric customers, gave a polite smile.

Looking round at the grinning masks on the shelves, he thought of the Grimaud. He hadn't seen the arrival of the magnificent white hearse drawn by plumed horses, but the knowledge that it had been there was enough for him. He liked putting on a show even when he was not around to see it.

Purchasing the wings put him in a state of reckless

excitement. He attempted to trip up a barbaric blob of a woman with his stick and stuck out his tongue at a little boy, then had a Cuba Libre with gin at the Criterion, which further raised his spirits, though he intensely disliked the girl who served him.

The silly creature was plump and she seemed to find the sight of him comical, for some reason. The flaming cheek of it! She had clapped her hand over her mouth.

He eyed her with a glare of indescribable malignancy, which only seemed to provide her with further amusement. His face turned the colour of raspberry jam. The impudent hussy clearly had no idea who he was; she couldn't possibly know that his pedigree had been established in a direct line by genealogists from the year 65 of the Christian era and that he had been brought up in a house where most objects had at one time or other been owned or handled by a king or an emperor! He nearly complained to the management about her but decided against it. Fuss was *so* middle-class.

He would stay at Remnant a while. Not for too long, goodness, no. He would be bored. But he would stay long enough.

His thoughts turned to Clarissa. Clarissa was not plump. Far from it. Clarissa was imperially slender, with the delicious, delicate curves of a succubus fashioned in dreams . . .

I am a traveller in an arid desert, he thought, but there is an oasis in sight.

He would drive. He would rent a car. Apart from Clarissa, there would be no one else at Remnant. No servants. Not even Tradewell, who had always gazed at him with a rather pathetic expression of awed devotion on his face. He had instructed Clarissa to keep the place empty and she had done so.

He had felt an unaccustomed leaning towards caution. Was he getting old? He hated the idea of encroaching old age. The funny thing was that he didn't feel he was sliding into his dotage. He felt energized, rejuvenated. He had started experiencing the kind of desires that had troubled him as young man . . .

The powder. The powder seemed to be working. Freshly aborted human foetuses. That was what the voodoo doctor had told him. Strange-looking fellow, jet-black, with peculiar orange-yellow eyes, like a cat's, veined with purple, but he clearly knew what he was talking about.

He now felt drawn towards Remnant Castle as if by some magnetic force. He would start early tomorrow morning, some time after four.

The hour between the first lightening of the morning sky and sunrise was his most auspicious time, the voodoo fellow had told him. It was then that his energies were at their most vibrant and his aura most vividly coloured, apparently.

He rather liked the idea of arriving at a house submerged in murk, or as morning came to consciousness and light crept up between the shutters . . .

He would sneak in through a side door and go up the stairs, past the portraits of his savage, wily, fearless ancestors. He had no doubt his ancestors would have approved not only of what he had done, but also of what he was planning to do.

He was a true Remnant. His brother, on the other hand, was not. The fact that Gerard had turned up at La Sorcière on the night of the murder suggested little more than misguided bravado. A damned ineffectual chap, Gerard, like all bookish chaps. As a boy his brother had been potty about the Arthurian legend and perhaps he had seen himself as that flower of chivalry, Sir Lancelot, on a white warhorse, charging the Monster of Remnant, lance at the ready!

There had been a full moon that night and he had seen Gerard from his dressing-room window. Had Gerard travelled all the way to Grenadin intent on committing fratricide? Who could tell? If he had, he'd been too late!

Once more he looked into the near future and saw himself arriving at Remnant Castle, striding stealthily down the corridor towards Clarissa's bedroom. Clarissa would be in her bed. She would still be sleeping. He would open her bedroom door – he'd be able to hear her breathing, perhaps he'd see the rising and falling of her bosom . . .

He experienced another surge of youthful energy.

The once-familiar flame. He might have swallowed a dose of ethyl chloride . . . Why, he hadn't felt like that for *years*.

30

The Criminal Comedy of the Complicit Couple

Clarissa woke with a start. It was terribly early, she could tell. Her heart was thumping wildly in her chest. I am on my own, she thought.

As she further drifted into consciousness, she heard the wind outside, alternately moaning and howling, hurling itself against the window panes like some demented monster intent on breaking in and devouring her.

She had had a dream. She'd seen a mouse on the floor, obviously ill, huddled and shivering, so in order to give it a quick death, she picked it up by the tail and threw it into a puddle of water. She'd heard a voice. *Don't you see that the water is not deep enough? The wretched thing won't drown; it will just go on swimming about.* So she picked the mouse out of the puddle, but as she did so the mouse twisted round and bit her finger. She heard the voice again. *That mouse has a disease and now you will get it.*

Thinking about it, she felt nauseous, ill. She looked down at her fingers. The only too familiar feeling of impending disaster was upon her, the sense of being poised on the very edge of chaos, the conviction that she'd never·be free from the tentacles of her impossible predicament—

What time was it? Half past three? Christ.

Reaching out for the silver-plated radio on her bedside table, she turned it on. She liked listening to the BBC World Service. It soothed her . . .

But she found it hard to concentrate. Her ordeal, she reminded herself, was only just starting. Should she take one of her pills?

Clarissa began to pray to God. She spoke the words aloud.

She promised never to have another affair as long as she lived. She would never dine at the Ritz again. She was going to take proper care of Stephan. She would devote the rest of her life to Stephan. She wouldn't wear lipstick in the morning. She would never wear stilettos again. She would be nice to Aunt Hortense—

'*How to murder someone and get away with it . . . You see, in Keldorp I shared living quarters with a little man called Harrison—*'

What was that? Sounded like some creepy radio drama. Should she change the station? Quite interesting, actually—

She listened.

'*Harrison was one of the most boring people I have ever met. Except on one subject. Murder. I don't mean he killed anyone himself. He was fascinated by the theory of it. He must have read every book ever printed on the subject. One night he told me he'd worked out the perfect murder. It all depended on one thing. The murderer had to have an accomplice. Someone he could trust absolutely. Someone who wanted – who needed – to kill as much as he did—*'

Wanted to kill as much as he did . . . No, that didn't quite apply to her. She had aided and abetted the killer, true, but that was *after* the murder had been committed.

The fact was, she had had no idea there was going to be a murder. If she had known Stephan had got hold of Roderick's gun, she would have done something about it – she would have taken the gun away from him. Of course she would have.

An idea began advancing from the shadows of Clarissa's mind slowly, gradually, like a figure emerging from a dark cave . . .

The codicil. The five million pounds to Peter Quin. The codicil suggested that the murder might have been carefully thought through, premeditated, planned in detail. Why hadn't she thought of it before? It suggested that it wasn't Stephan, poor thing, who had committed the murder, but her monster of a husband . . .

Yes.

She gasped. She saw it very clearly now. Roderick had lured Peter Quin to La Sorcière with the sole intention of killing him. She had believed it was Stephan who killed Quin, mistaking him for Roderick, and Roderick had encouraged her to continue thinking it because it had suited his book . . .

That night she had agreed to everything he told her to do; she had nodded and said yes; she had been dazed, confused, in a state of shock. Roderick told her that the idea had just occurred to him as he stood looking down at Quin's dead body – but that had been a lie.

She had been blind – yes, blind!

Roderick had *meant* things to happen that way all along.

She heard the voice on the radio announce the end of the play and she rose, propping herself on her elbow. She reached out for her pale pink kimono. She put it on and sat up in bed. She was extremely cold. Her teeth chattered. The heating wasn't working properly – but it wasn't only the heating – she felt a chill – a particular kind of chill – there had been a sound as well—

The next moment she knew.

He was at Remnant.

She saw her bedroom door open. She had locked it, but he

clearly had a key. She should have barricaded herself in. Why did all the good ideas come when it was too late?

He removed his homburg with a flourish.

'Peter Quin at your service, m'lady,' he said with a courtly bow. 'I don't think I woke you up, did I? My dear Clarissa, you look *ravissante*. It is with such a delectable sight that the Devil must have tempted Our Saviour. I have lived in the grip of a deep obsessive frustration,' he went on. 'You are the only one who can bring me out of it. I have been thinking about you an awful lot, you know.'

Clarissa had pulled the sheets up to her chin. She was so terrified, she could hardly move.

'Aren't you glad to see me?'

'I need to dress,' she managed to say. 'It is very early.'

'It is the right time, my dear. I know this on the highest authority. You don't need to dress. *Au contraire.*'

'I need to dress. Would you leave the room for a bit?'

'I don't think so.'

'Please.'

'Your cheek is white, but I have every intention of changing that lily to a rose.'

'No – please—'

'*Arise battalions and conquer,*' he hummed. He took a step towards her.

'Don't – please—'

'*Don't – please,*' he mimicked. He laughed. 'Too many pleases please me not.' He felt exhilarated. He might have been given a shot of helium. The next moment he became serious. 'We've got unfinished business, Clarissa. You couldn't have forgotten? Women usually remember things like that.'

'What are you talking about? You're mad.'

He pouted. 'I do hope this will not turn into another mortification of vain regrets.'

'Go away!'

'I feel it my duty to make up for the lack of post-nuptial

euphoria. There was a problem then, but there's no problem now. The problem's been resolved. I've been taking something. Pretty powerful stuff, my dear.' He licked his lips. 'Take off those stupid clothes. Come on, be a good girl. I want you to do it with a slow, twisting movement. I want to see them in a tangle on the floor – *there*.' He pointed.

'No!'

'You are being discourteous to an inconceivable degree. Or are you afraid that, like a dewdrop, you might disintegrate at the slightest touch?'

'Get out of my room!'

'When you were with the good doctor, you were not in the least inhibited. *Thou hast committed fornication – but that was in another country.*'

'Go away!'

'I have seen you, you know. The two of you together. I had a camera installed in your boudoir. I have watched the two of you – together. You had no idea? I can't help thinking Freud got it all wrong somehow,' he went on thoughtfully. 'Those all-too-respectable bourgeois women of Vienna who lay on his couch and spouted tales of being seduced or raped by their fathers—'

'Don't come near me!'

'The presumptuous fellow told them they were fantasizing, expressing their suppressed desires, but what proof was there they were fantasies? What if the women were telling the truth? I can't quite tell what put fathers and daughters in my mind. Was it the disparity in our respective ages?'

'Get out! Leave me alone!'

He took another step towards the bed. 'I have the right to expect a submission of sorts. In fact, I would insist on it. I know I am old enough to be your father, my dear, but I also happen to be your husband.'

'My God, what's that on your shoulders?' Clarissa gasped.

'D'you mean my wings? Don't you like them? Real feathers, you know.' Lord Remnant hitched up his shoulders and the black wings opened and closed.

Clarissa screamed.

31

The Double

It was later that same morning.

'This is actually very funny,' Antonia said. 'He is so awful. He is too good to be true. He is a monster. He is not quite real.'

'It's outrageously funny,' Payne agreed. 'Why is bad behaviour so compulsively watchable?'

They had been sitting in front of their TV set, watching *The Grenadier of Grenadin*, the documentary about the twelfth Earl Remnant. The film-makers had been following Lord Remnant as he strutted about his island paradise and bragged of the terrible things he had done and the even more terrible things he intended to do.

Equal parts high comedy and shock theatre, Payne thought. The documentary showed Lord Remnant as an expert at stirring up old animosities and taking a perverse delight in the creation of new ones.

'He may be one man's argument for reviving the guillotine,' Antonia murmured. She took a sip of coffee. 'Extremely entertaining.'

'The late Lord Remnant manages to convey the most disturbing impression that he has truly lost his marbles. Though of course he is neither "the late" nor is he Lord Remnant. That makes the whole thing even more fascinating,' Major Payne said. 'Don't you think?'

The credits were rolling.

'I thought I saw something – pause, would you? Rewind a bit,' Antonia said. 'That's it. Look! *Dedicated to Peter Quin, for saving my life.* Well, that clinches it.'

'It does indeed. It confirms the connection between them.' Payne turned off the video. 'That was his little joke. Lord Remnant didn't initially want to make the documentary, that's what Felicity told us. Then he suddenly changed his mind. Well, he changed his mind when he saw a way of appearing and yet not appearing. He likes teasing people, remember?'

'He thought he was being terribly clever,' Antonia said. 'He asked for the film to be dedicated to the actor who impersonated him.'

'The note signed Q, which I found in the secret drawer, makes it clear they had reached an agreement.' Payne waved his hand in the direction of the Damascus chest, which now graced their drawing room.

'What was it Peter Quin wrote exactly?'

'*I accept. All I need to do is shave off my whiskers and go bald* . . . My guess is that Remnant saw Quin's photo somewhere, while idly surfing the net, or perhaps he happened to watch one of Quin's films. He was struck by the resemblance between them.'

'That's when he had his brainwave?'

'Yes. He managed to get in touch with Quin and probably sent him photos of himself. He asked if Quin would "do" him.'

'What was it you said about Quin's antecedents? Swedish and English?'

'Scottish, Norwegian and German. But he could "do" any nationality. He spoke five languages. He was a character actor who travelled the world, working on international film and television projects.'

'The man of the hundred faces and hundred and one voices,' Antonia murmured.

'That's the name of his site, yes.' Payne picked up the internet downloads. 'His last and, as it turned out, fatal role was that of our friend, the lunatic laird, but before that he was a Russian revolutionary, one of Hitler's henchmen, a Mexican matador, a Paris pimp, a Puerto Rican politician and so on.'

'Lord Remnant couldn't have been hard to "do", could he?'

'I should imagine not. Eccentric, larger-than-life characters are the easiest to do. What does Lord R. look like? Tall, slightly stooping, a supercilious, somewhat spooky smile, bald, complexion like polished mahogany, roller of eyes and thrower of hissy fits. A piece of cake, really. Besides he never for a moment took off that ludicrous sombrero or his dark shades, did you notice?'

Antonia nodded. 'His face remains in shadow throughout...'

'When Gerard Fenwick saw the documentary, he apparently found his brother changed, but it was years since they had actually met, so he didn't think anything of it. Lord R. rarely came to England; consequently people who once knew him were likely to attribute any changes in him to the passing of time and the Caribbean climate.'

'I wonder if the documentary-makers knew he was not the real one,' said Antonia.

'Perhaps they did know. They may have been complicit in the joke – all those references to it being a *meta*-documentary! On the other hand, they may not have been aware that a trick was being played on them.'

'All the negotiations may have been made by Lord Remnant via email or phone . . . Perhaps they never saw him in the flesh. Peter Quin may have stepped into his part from the very start.'

'I haven't been able to find any information about Peter Quin's personal life. Nothing about family or friends or emotional attachments. He never seemed to have stayed in one place for long. According to something I read his agent had met him only once. No one seems to have known him at all well on a personal level.'

'Which was perfect for Lord Remnant's plan . . .'

'Perfect is the word. Well, Remnants have the reputation for concocting schemes that are at once lunatic and logical. Shakespeare is said to have invented the phrase "method in his madness" with a Remnant in mind.'

Antonia picked up the coffee pot. 'Let's sum up, shall we? Lord Remnant manages to antagonize most of the population of Grenadin and in consequence starts receiving death threats. He finds a rattlesnake crazed by amphetamines in his bathroom. He pretends not to be affected, but the incident has left him shaken up. He thinks of a plan. *He will make his enemies believe he is dead.* He will stage his own death, after which he will disappear – or rather become somebody else.'

'*He will become Peter Quin.* It is Peter Quin who will die in his place.' Payne started filling his pipe with tobacco from his tobacco jar. 'The murder will be pinned on his stepson, who has already made his murderous intentions clear enough – in front of witnesses.'

'Lord Remnant makes all the necessary preparations for the takeover. He contacts his solicitors and adds a codicil to his will, leaving five million pounds to Peter Quin.' Antonia's eyes narrowed. 'Perhaps he lets Quin know about it, which makes it difficult for him to refuse the commission? He tells Quin he will need his services again. This time for a more intimate, more *domestic* kind of show.'

'He explains he intends to play a prank on his house guests. They are staging *The Murder of Gonzago* at his Grenadin retreat. It is going to be a dumbshow. He wants Quin to switch places with him—'

'Lord Remnant will take part in the rehearsals, but it is Quin who will appear in the performance itself . . . Lord

Remnant says he wants to see if his guests will be able to tell the difference, something on those lines.' Antonia frowned. 'Quin doesn't suspect a trap, does he?'

'Not for a moment. Why should he? He has already worked for Lord Remnant. He is used to Lord Remnant's eccentricities. Well, Quin accepts the commission and thus signs his death warrant.' Payne struck a match and put it to his pipe.

'The instructions are that he arrives at La Sorcière earlier in the afternoon *concealed inside a coffin.*'

'A rococo embellishment which, again, is entirely in keeping with Remnant's histrionic nature,' said Payne. 'No one will see Quin actually enter the Remnant estate. If something goes wrong, Quin will emerge and be greeted as the grisly Grimaud, with which Lord Remnant has already been threatened. The whole thing will then be laughed off as a joke.'

'But nothing goes wrong—'

'No. Quin is smuggled into the house. He hides in Lord Remnant's dressing room. Later in the evening he makes his appearance in the drawing room, disguised as Gonzago. Meanwhile—'

'Meanwhile Lord Remnant has his revolver ready,' said Antonia. 'He has fixed a silencer to it. The guards have been given the evening off. Stephan is the only one lurking outside the house, but he is already under the influence of some drug.'

'Lord Remnant stands on the terrace beside the french windows. He takes aim through the gap in the curtains. He pulls the trigger. He is a good shot. The bullet gets Quin in the back of the head. Lord Remnant wipes the gun clean of fingerprints, drops it and quickly re-enters the house through a side door.'

'He sneaks up to his dressing room—'

'He conceals himself in the bathroom. It was his laugh

that Basil Hunter heard later on. Lord Remnant seems to have suddenly found the whole thing irresistibly comical.'

'How much does Clarissa know?' Antonia asked after a pause.

'I think she knows about the switch but no more. Lord Remnant tells her he is planning a prank. He enrols her assistance. He must have done. *Without her he can't do it.* He doesn't tell her that he intends to kill Quin of course. Nor that he plans to assume Quin's identity. I am sure she knows nothing about his real plan.'

'He wants her to think it was her son who did the shooting . . .'

'Yes. Lord R. knows that it would help his cause if his wife were to be emotionally involved . . . Well, Dr Sylvester-Sale discovers the hole in the dead man's skull. There seems to be little doubt in everybody's mind that it was Stephan who committed the murder. They had seen him lurking outside the window disguised as Bottom.'

'And of course they remember the incident in Lord Remnant's study when Stephan tried to shoot his stepfather with that very same gun,' said Antonia.

'Clarissa is convinced Stephan is the culprit. She doesn't want her son to be arrested and interrogated by the police.'

'Perhaps there are drugs in the house. Perhaps she takes drugs too? No, she doesn't want the police inside the house, conducting an investigation. She decides on concealment. But she must talk to her husband first. You said that she went upstairs immediately after the murder?'

'That's what Sylvester-Sale told me, yes.' Payne held up his pipe. 'Well, I believe she went to see her husband and tell him what had happened. She needed to know what they should do next. After all, the whole thing had been Lord Remnant's idea.'

'It was quite an extraordinary situation . . .'

'You can say that again. Everybody believes the dead man

is Lord Remnant. Only Clarissa knows that it is Peter Quin. I can imagine her whispering frantically. *Do we tell them that the dead man is not you?* Well, the answer of course is, *No, we don't. We let them continue believing it is me.*'

'He pretends he has thought of something?'

Payne cleared his throat theatrically. '*I've got an idea. It isn't as outlandish as you may think, Clarissa. Let everybody continue thinking I am dead. You see, no one knows Quin's been here. I specifically asked him to keep mum about it. I will take Quin's place.*'

'*What do you mean, Roderick? Have you gone mad?*' Antonia asked.

'*Pas du tout. This is my chance to cheat death. Don't you see?*'

'*What about the death certificate?*'

'*Your medico chums will have to fix that. Have Quin cremated, not buried. No chance of complications that way.*'

'*It won't work!*'

'*Of course it will work, Clarissa. Lord Remnant is no more. He has passed into Higher Service. He was Gently Translated. He Fell Asleep. I want everybody on this bloody island to know that. Then there'll be no more death threats and so on. Let the whole bloody world believe I am no more. Natural causes, don't forget. That will also be the way out for Stephan. Stephan doesn't need to come into the picture at all.*'

Payne resumed his normal voice. 'Well, that's what she did. She let the world know her husband died of a heart attack . . . So you think Clarissa speaks in a breathless Marilyn Monroe voice?'

Antonia shrugged. 'That's how it came out.'

'Damned attractive. Is it possible for you to speak in that voice always?'

'Do you really want me to? Wouldn't it drive you mad, eventually? It's interesting that neither Dr Sylvester-Sale nor Basil Hunter realized the dead man was not their host . . . I mean they took him to his room, didn't they?'

'Well, Peter Quin was grotesquely made up. People always look different when they die anyhow – they shrink – the mouth goes slack – the nose gets sharper – the eyes glaze over . . . Besides, they were working under tremendous pressure, remember.'

'They knew very well they shouldn't be moving the body . . .'

'They knew there could be big trouble. They must have been anxious, frightened. People's faculties simply cease to operate at times of extreme tension. The whole thing must have seemed to them unreal – the most awful of nightmares.'

'Where is Lord Remnant now, do you think?' Antonia asked.

'I have an idea that he might be at Remnant Castle. No other reason for Clarissa to dismiss all her servants, is there? She's been expecting him to turn up. Well, my love, it seems we have been investigating the wrong murder. It is Peter Quin who is dead. Lord Remnant is the killer and he has now taken refuge at his country seat. I think we should go to Remnant Castle.' Payne glanced at his watch. 'Make sure we are right . . . What do you say?'

'Shouldn't we call the police?'

'No, not yet. I suggest we put our theory to the test first,' said Major Payne. 'At the moment it is only a theory. I would hate to be made to look a fool – wouldn't you?'

32

The Castle of Crossed Destinies

Clarissa sat huddled beside an inscrutable bronze Buddha, speaking haltingly into the phone. She was a little calmer now.

'It was awful . . . He came into my bedroom. He was wearing black wings. He ordered me to undress . . . He came at me with the steadiness of a travelling bullet.'

'My poor child!'

'I managed to hit him on the head with the bedside lamp – I ran out. It would have been comical if it hadn't been so – so terrifying! All right. I know what I did was very wrong. I don't mind you knowing, Aunt Hortense. I promised God I'd be nice to you if only He would help me. And He did! He helped me escape Roderick's clutches. I didn't mean to tell you, I never meant to tell *anyone*, but there you are. I don't know what to do!'

'You must call the police! At once!'

'No! I can't get the police involved because of my own involvement in the affair. Don't you see? What the papers will no doubt call the "despicable deadly deception". Well, it'll be nothing compared to the kind of trouble *he* may find himself in, though he doesn't seem to care.'

'What is it – drugs?'

Clarissa's eyes shifted towards the black-lacquered cabinet

and fixed on the colourful figures embossed on its surface. The nausea and the faintness were returning. The palanquin in which an important-looking mandarin lounged shifted forward, the parasol held above his servants in shallow straw hats acquired a thin luminous band around its edges. The parasol started to revolve, at first hesitatingly and then faster . . . and faster. And, as though that were not enough, she then saw the mandarin wink at her!

I am in a state of shock, she thought. I need a fix. I can't go on without a fix. No, it wouldn't do for her to faint. Not *now*.

'It was drugs, yes. Roderick was part of several trade missions and advisory organizations that are suspected of being a cover for smuggling drugs from the Caribbean,' she explained. 'A couple of local gangs were after him as well, either for queering their pitch or for not "fulfilling his duties". There were several very good reasons for him to want to fake his death.'

'I do think you should call the police, Clarissa. The sooner the better. Or I could do it, if you like?'

'No! It would be madness. What shall I say to the police? I don't want to sleep with my husband, please despatch a rescue squad? Then the whole thing would be out in the open. He's bound to tell them that I was his accomplice, that I aided and abetted him. He wouldn't have been able to do any of it without me!'

'He is a monster!'

'He reminded me we were meant to be "one flesh", that ours was an "indissoluble union". He says he has the legal right to demand a thousand little intimacies from me, including the ultimate, and it is a wife's duty to honour and obey her husband. We have been married in name only, it's been bothering him an awful lot, but now he intends to change the status quo. Oh, you should have heard him. He stood ranting outside my door.'

'So he never . . . you never . . . ?'

'*No.* It never happened. The marriage was never consummated.'

'Are you sure?'

'Of course I am sure.' Suddenly Clarissa laughed.

'Thank God,' Hortense said. '*Thank God.*'

'There were – difficulties. All I can say is that it suited me. I couldn't stand him. I should never have married him. Well, he let me have lovers. I don't want to talk about it. Sorry. All too sordid for words. After he killed Quin, he promised he would disappear.'

'You are sure it was he who killed that man?'

'Well, yes! He planned the whole thing. The codicil makes that abundantly clear. He said I'd have a lot of money and then I could do whatever I pleased, but here he is now, back at Remnant, suddenly keen on uniting his flesh with mine!'

'Where are you at the moment?'

'In the smallest of the four Chinese rooms. There are fifty-eight rooms at Remnant,' Clarissa said wearily. 'I thought I might have killed him, but he seems to have recovered. He was knocking on the door a minute ago, asking me to be kind. He is mad . . . He said I'd split his forehead and that he was bleeding, but he has forgiven me.'

'Where is he?'

'In his bathroom, I imagine. He said he would have a bath. Perhaps he will drown in it. Or is that too much to hope? He said he wanted to be clean for me. He is mad,' Clarissa repeated. 'Oh God. What an impossible situation. He is supposed to be dead – and he is a murderer!'

'You must leave Remnant at once!'

'I can't. He said I would regret it if I did leave. He means it. He said he'd send a letter to the police. Apparently he's written an account of my involvement in the drug trade on Grenadin.'

'Were you involved in the drug trade on Grenadin?'

'In a way. All right. I didn't do it for the money. There

219

was a man I was in love with. Stanley – that's Dr McLean – and I were lovers.' Clarissa sighed. 'Stanley was involved in drug peddling and he managed to get me interested. He persuaded me to invest capital in his venture. I wanted to help him. I was quite smitten with him . . . Are you sure you want to hear this?'

'Yes. Do go on.'

'That was before Syl came on the scene. Roderick was also involved with drugs, but, as it happened, with a rival gang. It sounds absurd, I know, but that's the way it was. I thought Roderick didn't know about me and Dr McLean but he does. He's got papers *and* a tape.'

'What tape?'

'An audiotape. It seems he recorded one of our conversations on tape . . . It's a damnably compromising kind of conversation. I said things I shouldn't have said and so did Stanley. I am afraid we weren't very careful.'

'What did you say?'

'We refer to various people and organizations, all of which can be checked. Roderick said he could have me sent to jail for some considerable time . . . He would love to punish me, but if I did my wifely duties by him, he wouldn't. He's blackmailing me . . . I don't know what to do, Aunt Hortense. I really don't. I am trapped – literally – *trapped*.'

Hurry, *hurry*, Hortense told herself. My daughter needs me!

She locked her front door. Her hand shook a little.

I must save her from the monster. I hope I am not too late.

Payne was driving. Antonia had a map spread across her knees.

A minute passed, then another . . .

He spoke, 'I hate it when my ideas overlap, but—'

'What ideas?'

'For some reason I can't get Louise Hunter's account of that last supper at La Sorcière out of my head. I keep thinking about Lord Remnant's story. About the deflowered debs and all those stolen pieces of jewellery.'

'What a coincidence,' said Antonia. 'I've been thinking about that too. Are we by any chance interested in one particular piece of jewellery?'

'We are.' Payne cast her a sidelong glance. 'I believe Clarissa was wearing the bracelet during *Gonzago*. For a moment or two the camera lingered on it. OK. Let's be absolutely sure about it. Perhaps you could ring your friend, the hungry Hunter, and check with her?'

'I was just about to suggest it.'

'Yet another instance of the near-telepathic link that exists between us.'

'How tediously weird that makes us sound.'

'No, not tediously weird – fascinating. You know exactly what question to put to Mrs Hunter?'

'I will ask her to describe the bracelet Clarissa wore at dinner at La Sorcière on the fatal night.'

She produced her mobile phone.

'Mrs Hunter? This is Antonia Rushton speaking . . .'

A moment later she put away her phone and said, 'Louise remembers the bracelet vividly. It had a particularly distinctive design, a coiled serpent made of black pearls. She said Lord Remnant shuddered theatrically as he pointed to it.'

Roderick, Lord Remnant, was enjoying what he thought of as his 'second coming'.

He was having a bath. It was an old-fashioned bath made of enamelled cast iron and painted an azure kind of blue, its rounded corners supported on black claw and ball feet that stood on chequered black and white marble slabs. The bath had big brass taps with porcelain insets that said 'Hot' and 'Cold'.

A minute or so earlier he had turned the taps on in the hope that the thundering water would drown the sounds of what he imagined was Clarissa sobbing. He liked the idea of her sobbing. It excited him. Suffering intrigued him immeasurably – though not while he was having a bath. There was a time and place for everything.

He sat with water up to his chest, delighting in the fragrance of aromatic oils and therapeutic salts. A haze of steam was hovering above his head, like a halo. He was sipping from a tall glass full of hock and seltzer. He gazed at the picture on the wall that showed a mermaid lying on a fishmonger's slab, a resigned expression on her greenish face. He imagined the mermaid looked a bit like Clarissa . . .

Balnea, vina, Venus – how did it go on? Ages since he'd learnt Latin. Baths, wine and sex may wreck us up, but they – um – make life worth living?

Lord Remnant's forehead was bandaged, but that didn't seem to bother him. He hummed a little tune under his breath, '*Said the don to his inamorata, won't you let me past your garter?*'

The night before he had had a dream. He'd seen himself standing beside a gravestone made of black Carrara marble, tugging at the ivy that bound it like string, only to reveal his name and the dates of his birth and death carefully chiselled in.

Ridiculous things, dreams. Some people thought dreams revealed the future. Well, he had nothing to fear. In a manner of speaking, he was already dead. He couldn't die twice, could he?

Laughing, Lord Remnant got out of the bath. He dried himself with the wonderfully soft towel, rubbed some sweet-smelling musk lotion into his body and put on his mulberry-coloured dressing gown with the frogged lapels.

He stood in front of his mirror, examining his forehead. It hurt a little. They said that pain was the key to possession while pleasure was more likely to be illusory. The way she had conked him with that lamp! Having screamed herring-gull fashion first. It was like something out of a Feydeau farce, though he couldn't say he found the episode particularly entertaining. Well, Clarissa was only postponing the inevitable.

He was confident his wound would heal soon enough. He didn't think he needed any stitches. What he needed was another drink. And of course he needed Clarissa.

In that order.

His jawline had lost some of its firmness, but otherwise he looked as youthful as ever. He held his head up like a guardsman on parade and attached the reddish-brown whiskers to his face with the help of the special glue that went with them. He then put on the reddish-brown wig.

Making love in disguise – it would be like old times.

Picking up the powder puff, which he had taken from Clarissa's dressing table, he pressed it to his cheekbones, then ran it with affected coyness over the bridge of his nose. How smooth his skin looked. He was pleased with the result. He felt like a bride checking her veil in the last mirror before the aisle.

Pouring himself a malt, he drank it neat.

Clarissa was born under a treacherous star into a world that brimmed over with base energies. She wouldn't try to run away, would she? He didn't think she would. Well, she knew what would happen if she did run away.

He licked his lips. That misbehaving forelock on Clarissa's forehead! It drove him mad, thinking about it.

His thoughts turned to more practical matters. He had already made enquiries, in his Quin persona and in an American accent, regarding the money left to him by the late Lord Remnant. He had called Saunders's office and spoken to Saunders's clerk, who had been most helpful. He had told him all he needed to know. *The money would be in Mr Quin's bank account some time next week.*

Did he have everything he needed? Quin's cards – driving licence – passport. A little black-leather notebook had provided him with the details of Quin's internet account. User name: Bitchbail. Password: Bully1. Memorable name: Meredith. Memorable place: Greenpeals.

He also had Quin's PIN. Obtaining the latter had been as easy as falling off your chair. At the time of the documentary, they had spent some time together. Quin had wanted to observe him; he had been anxious to get Lord Remnant's speech patterns, mannerisms and so on right.

Quin had had no idea that his host was observing him too. At one point, as Quin took money out of a cash machine, Lord Remnant stood behind him. He prided himself on his sharp eyesight as well as on his memory for figures. He'd seen and memorized Quin's PIN: 4421.

Quin hadn't been in the least cautious, certainly not suspicious. Well, no reason for Quin to have been suspicious. It wasn't as though he was consorting with the Artful Dodger, was it? His host was after all a noble lord.

As for Quin's email details, Lord Remnant had managed to get them in a similar manner, by simply sitting beside him at an internet café and, again, watching carefully as Quin logged on. The password had been rather prophetic: doppelganger2.

It was all meant to happen, Lord Remnant thought.

Since Quin's death, Lord Remnant had answered several emails from Quin's agent concerning offers for appearances in films. He had written back: *Suffering from a* crise de nerfs *brought about by my inability to cope with the Spirit of the World. Will let you know if and when I am well again, which, I fear, may not be soon.* In a subsequent message he had hinted at a more serious nervous breakdown.

So far there had been no emails of what could be described as a personal nature. Quin seemed to be one of those rare individuals who possessed no relatives, no lovers and no friends. Quin had been God-sent.

'To Quin.' Lord Remnant raised the malt to his lips. He'd started finding Remnant oppressive. In fact he'd come to regard Remnant as the absolute abomination of desolation. Gerard was welcome to it. How funny that there should be *two* Earl Remnants at the moment, the twelfth and the thirteenth. Terribly amusing.

He heard the creaking of a board outside his room, then he saw the door start opening slowly. What a pleasant surprise. Clarissa's citadel of defence seemed to have crumbled. Clarissa had reconsidered. Clarissa knew which side of her brioche was buttered. Wise girl! Well, all he wanted from her was pleasant and pliant cooperation—

The next moment his smile faded. He put down his glass.

It wasn't Clarissa who had entered his room.

'What the hell are *you* doing here?'

Then he saw the gun in her hand.

33

The Rescuers

The principal ground-floor state room at Remnant had an air of desiccated luxury about it. It was also a quintessentially English room on the grand scale. There was the eighteenth-century Carlton House desk designed by Hepplewhite, the Axminster carpets that matched the date of the desk, the extremely rare Wedgwood Etruria vases on top of the breakfront bookcase, the Sèvres porcelain lyre clock ticking on the mantelpiece, the fire-shield made of a stuffed Himalayan pheasant with outspread wings, iridescent breast and plumed tiara, and, above all, there was the view across the park.

Clarissa stood by the french windows, looking out. She was dressed in a beige twinset and pearls. On her wrist she wore the Keppel Clasp. That was what it was called, her mother had told her. Her mother, who was also her aunt. Clarissa frowned. She was finding the idea a little hard to swallow. Her left sleeve was rolled up to the elbow.

It wasn't raining but the skies were ominously overcast. Like all English springs, the one which had come to Remnant Regis seemed unable to make up its mind whether to be nice or nasty. Only half an hour earlier the sun had been shining with extravagant brilliance, but then a sudden darkness had descended and the temperature had plummeted dramatically.

Clarissa looked down at the drop of blood drying on her forearm. She'd given herself a shot. She had needed a fix. She was in an impossible situation. She wouldn't have been able to cope without a fix. She wouldn't have been able to live another minute.

She heard the sound of a car. *Another* car? The front door bell rang. Tradewell will get it, she told herself. No, he wouldn't. Tradewell wasn't there. She heard the bell again. She didn't move. She shrugged. I am not at home.

The door bell rang a third time. Go away, she murmured. You are wasting your time. When too much was happening and the future seemed uncertain, the best thing to do was to stay very still. She went on standing beside the windows, gazing at the sky.

She was a little startled when the door opened and a man and a woman entered.

'Lady Remnant?' The man looked military, it was the way he held his arms. Greenish tweeds, a regimental tie. Rather nice, actually.

She smiled. 'Have we met?' Her voice sounded as though it was coming from hundreds of miles away. She had to strain her ears.

'You don't know us. My name is Hugh Payne and this is my wife Antonia. The front door was open . . . Are you all right?'

'Am I all right? I am not sure. Sweet of you to ask.' Her hand touched the forelock on her forehead. They were staring at her bared forearm.

'Have you had an accident?' It was the woman who asked that. A very nice woman. Blue suited her. Maybe she should do her hair *slightly* differently. Kind eyes. Kind but sharp. *Clever.*

'No, not really. It was something which I *had* to do. I had a terrible experience earlier on, but I am all right – now I am. At least I think so. Yes.'

'Where is your husband?'

'My husband? Let me see.' Clarissa frowned. 'He is upstairs. No, he is not upstairs. He is dead.' She laughed. She covered her mouth. 'Sorry. I forgot.'

She believed that was a line in a play. *My husband is not dead, he is upstairs.* She laughed again. Everything seemed so unreal. She felt a bit confused. A bit woozy. She was perfectly aware of the existence of formulas to be employed in social situations, when dealing with people one had never met before, and she searched for them in vain. The right things to say seemed to dash round the corner and conceal themselves, rather cunningly, she thought, in the crowd of things which she knew she should *not* say. Well, it happened each time she had a fix, she'd noticed.

No one was supposed to know her husband was alive. That was a fiction she had agreed to maintain. Roderick had sworn her to secrecy. Roderick had bribed her. And he had ordered her to bribe all the others. To buy their silence.

As the Dowager Lady Remnant she would have pots of money in the bank, she would be the sole possessor of Grenadin and she would be able go out with any man she liked. All she needed to do in return was keep her mouth firmly shut, or zipped up, as he'd put it.

As arrangements went, it hadn't sounded bad at all. Roderick had promised to disappear under an assumed name, or rather under Peter Quin's name. But now he wanted something from her – something that had *not* been part of the deal – that was the reason she had cranked herself up—

Why were they staring at her? Who were these people? How light-headed she felt. Perhaps she should shake their hands. That was what hostesses did. The next moment she saw the military-looking man standing beside her. How terribly odd. She hadn't seen him move! She had only blinked her eyes. She laughed again. Suddenly she felt extremely tired.

They were on either side of her now, these kind, well-bred people: goodness, how undignified. She seemed to have slumped to the floor. Her legs had turned to jelly. Her visitors were helping her up, they were doing it very gently, propelling her towards the sofa. Sweet of them. How her feet dragged!

She wouldn't have been able to manage by herself. They seemed awfully nice people. It was good to have them here. They were the perfect guests. She wouldn't mind having them stay on Grenadin some time—

'Is the car outside Lord Remnant's?' she heard the captain – she was sure he was a captain – ask.

'No – his car is in the garage – a rented car – he's been extremely careful.'

'Whose is the Mini? Who else is here?' Now it was the woman who had spoken. Was she his wife? Why were all the nice men always married?

'No one else.' Clarissa shook her head. 'No, that's not true. The Mini is Mama's. Mama is here. At least she told me she was my mama. My *real* mama. It is all very confusing. Dear Aunt Hortense.'

'Is Hortense Tilling here?'

'She is here, yes. She arrived quite unexpectedly. She seemed extremely agitated. She was in a real state. She kept staring at the Keppel Clasp – that's what it is called, apparently.' Clarissa held up her hand, showing them the bracelet. 'The Keppel Clasp. It's exquisite, isn't it?'

'It certainly is,' the man agreed.

'You don't look the kind of man who steps outside the rules,' she said, looking at him fixedly.

He said something, she didn't quite hear what, but it made her giggle. 'Aunt Hortense – Mama – seemed determined *not* to allow Roderick to get me into bed with him. I hate the idea of it of course, but she – she behaved as though it were the end of the world.'

230

'Where is she?'

'She'd have none of it. She looked *furious*. She clenched her fists and raised them above her head and shook them, as if summoning to her all thunderbolts and lightnings . . . Well, if the worst had come to the worst, I'd have had to shut my eyes and think of – no, not of England – of Grenadin.' Clarissa pulled a funny face indicative of rueful acceptance of her predicament.

'Where is she?'

'Aunt Hortense? I believe Mama is upstairs – Aunt Hortense and Mama are the same person, you see. How silly it sounds. I *must* get used to calling her Mama. She really cares about me. I've pledged never to be horrid to her. Mama wanted to have a word with Roderick. She seemed cross, oh so cross— Where are you going?'

34

The Beast Must Die

'You don't know who I am, do you?'

'That looks like one of the guns from the gun room. You shouldn't mess around with guns, you know. Highly dangerous. What if it's loaded?'

'It is loaded. The ammunition was in the desk. You don't seem to change your habits. You never lock anything up. Same as at La Sorcière.'

'You made a big mistake at La Sorcière. You risk making another mistake now.'

'Let me be the judge of that.'

'You should get a new pair of glasses, perhaps?'

'I hate you,' she said.

'Those one hates live for ever.'

'So you don't know who I am?'

'You are my Anima. That's a psychological term denoting the denied female element of the male psyche. Denied but desired.' Lord Remnant picked up his glass. 'Of course I know who you are, you old fool. You are Miss Baedeker. You are Clarissa's dotty old aunt.'

'I am five years younger than you.'

'I'd never have thought it possible.' He shook his head. 'Well, men age differently from women. May I suggest you leave my room at once? In the next hour or so I shall be frightfully busy. I don't want to be discourteous, but I've got things to do. Unfinished business, you may say. It's all rather delicate. Not for your tender ears. It may shock you. You'd probably say I had a genius for defilement.'

Hortense Tilling didn't lower the gun. Her eyes behind the glasses looked at him steadily. 'I thought you guessed that night. I thought you recognized me.'

'Go away, Aunt Hortense.' He waved his hands. 'Shoo!' Definitely a few stamps short of the first-class rate, he thought. Wouldn't be able to tell a hawk from a handsaw, if one accepted that feat as an adequate criterion of sanity.

'Look at me.' She took off her glasses. There were tears in her eyes. 'We met – years ago.'

'No day is so dead as the day before yesterday,' he said.

'We met at the party at the Bruce-Daltons'. On the fifth of June.'

'As a matter of fact, I used to know some people called Bruce-Dalton. I wonder if they are the same Bruce-Daltons. Do you mean we met at the Bruce-Daltons'? My memory is not what it used to be. Place in Blenheim Mews?'

'Yes. You and I were at the party. I had no idea who you were. Who you *really* were. I believe you were wearing disguise. You pretended to be a foreigner. You introduced yourself as a Frenchman called Pierre La Russe.'

He took a gulp of malt. 'One of my sobriquets, I imagine. Long time ago. No recollection of it at all. I'll have to take your word for it.'

'You asked me to dance. Then you brought me a drink. I don't think I really liked you, but you were very persistent. I couldn't shake you off. Then something happened. The room and everybody in it went fuzzy. Then I found I was in a cab with you.'

'That seems to ring a bell, but only because that was the sort of thing that happened quite often at one time . . . You were a deb?'

'I remember nothing after the cab. You spiked my drink, didn't you?'

He shrugged. 'I might have done. What if I did? It was the kind of thing I did every now and then. It doesn't kill, you know. Just makes you soft and pliant. You must have been quite pretty. Pretty but obdurate. I wouldn't have done it otherwise.'

'You took me somewhere. I remember nothing. Nothing at all. I woke up late in the morning, feeling dreadful.'

'Dreadful? Really? I believe it was jolly powerful stuff. Or maybe I overdosed you. Can't remember the technical name now. *Aide d'amour*, that's what *I* called it,' Lord Remnant said thoughtfully. 'Cost me a pretty penny, I think. I didn't have that much money in those days, you know.'

'Bastard,' she said.

'Hard to come by stuff like that in the sixties. No internet shopping in those days. No websites offering naughty meds. Why, in the name of Beelzebub, are you looking at me like that? So what if we spent a night together? We were young and impulsive. Must you make a song and dance about it?'

'You stole my bracelet.'

'Well, that's the kind of thing I did. The action of a cad, I agree.' He was getting impatient.

'None of it was my fault,' Hortense said, 'but I have lived with a sense of guilt ever since. I have been blaming myself. The shame never left me.'

'I'd rather you didn't start expounding the complications of your psyche just now. I can't help you, you know. I am no specialist. Have you considered going into therapy? Find yourself a good shrink? You may discover it is all a false memory.'

'Monster,' she said. 'Beast.'

'*Get thee to a nunnery* . . . How about religion? Why don't you try religion?'

'You deserve to die.'

'You seem determined to utterly crush the optimistic streak in my nature.' He gave a sigh.

'You ruined my life. You ruined my daughter's life.'

'Don't be so damned melodramatic. I don't know your daughter.'

'You don't know what happened, do you?' She spoke in a choked voice.

'I must admit to being thoroughly fogged. It was all a long time ago. No day is so dead as the day before yesterday, I keep telling you.' His eyes were on the gun in her hand.

'I got pregnant,' she said. 'Nine months later I gave birth to a baby girl.'

'Really? You mean I had a child?'

'You *have* a child.'

'It is alive? You didn't have an abortion?'

'No.'

'Stupid and irresponsible.' He shook his head. 'Such compulsive urges to replicate are usually associated with cancer cells.'

'I couldn't bring myself to have an abortion. I was confused – frightened – I was at my wits' end – I cried a lot – I felt great affection for my unborn child – I discovered I had a strong maternal instinct—'

'I hate haranguing, Aunt Hortense, I really do, but self-analysis can actually cause an awful lot of damage to the psyche. I know Freud did it, but he had the advantage of, well, of being Freud.' Lord Remnant wondered if he could disarm her if he pounced on her. He wasn't as agile as he once was. 'So we have a child? That's a cause for celebration, don't you think?'

'No, it is not.' Tears were rolling down her face. 'It is not.'

'Oh? Why not?' The old fool wouldn't dare pull the trigger, would she? On the other hand, she might. He reminded himself that she'd done it once already. If only he could get a little bit closer, he would have no problem disarming her.

He could cosh her with the bottle, he supposed. Or blind her by splashing malt in her eyes. Stupid old fool.

'How about a drinkie? Do you good. Give you a cosy feeling. No? I need to replenish my glass—' He reached out for the bottle of malt.

'Don't move.'

'No? It's time for you to throw in the towel, don't you think?'

'*Don't move.*' She raised the gun. Heavens, she was aiming at his forehead!

He sighed again. 'If you only knew how ridiculous you look. A woman at your time of life should be in her garden, snipping off the heads of defunct roses, or sitting in her boudoir, making intricately shaped tea-cosies.'

Actually she presented a damned unnerving sight with her complexion the colour of weak lemonade and those round glasses gleaming in the morning light.

'The baby was born on the third of March 1965. It was a girl.'

'Does the exact date matter?'

'It does. The third of March 1965.'

'Actually, that rings a bell,' he said after a pause. 'Now why is that?'

'I gave her the name Clarissa.'

'Oh yes. That's Clarissa's birthday. Of course. Third of March 1965. Actually, I met Clarissa at the Bruce-Daltons'. How things come back to one. That was three and a half years ago. Clarissa is the daughter of the Vuillaumys.'

'No, she isn't. They didn't have any children. They adopted Clarissa.'

He stared at her. There was a pause. He put down his glass. 'What are you trying to say, you old witch? What are you insinuating?'

'*Clarissa is our daughter. You married your own daughter.*'

It took him a moment to recover his poise. 'So what if I

237

did? That kind of thing does happen. More often than one imagines, I am sure. The way you go on, one might be excused for thinking I'd strangled a whole litter of newborn babies or – or gone to a funeral, propped up the corpse in its coffin and performed a ventriloquist act. What was it the wag said? Vice is nice but incest is best—' He broke off, amazed at his audacity. 'Too late to make amends, anyhow.'

'It is too late, yes,' she said.

'I suggest you keep your mouth zipped up, Miss Baedeker. Better, put a muzzle on it. You don't want the world to know I married my daughter, do you? There's the family name to consider and so on. I don't want to give my sister-in-law the chance to indulge in schadenfreude. Still, Clarissa is my wife and, as it happens, I have started finding her madly attractive. In fact, I am going to her now—'

'No, you are not.'

'Yes, I am.'

'You are *not*.'

'Keep out of my way, you old loon—'

'Stay where you are.'

Suddenly Lord Remnant was possessed by a fury so intense that for a few seconds it paralysed speech and even thought. It swept through his body like a wave of physical nausea, leaving him white and shaking. No one ever opposed him! No one ever told him where to stay! He flared up.

'How dare you hold me up? Who do you think you are? Give me the gun at once or I'll break your bloody neck—'

As he took a step towards her, she pulled the trigger.

The bullet hit him between the eyes.

For a moment he stood extremely still, a surprised expression on his face, then he fell to the floor.

The next moment the door burst open and Antonia and Major Payne entered the room.

'This time I got the right one,' Hortense Tilling said.

35

The Clue of the Coiled Cobra

The walls and ceiling of the library at Remnant were painted with classical figures in colours that had succumbed to the draining power of the sun and were now faded to pastel. The Louis XIII chairs were upholstered in mauve velvet, which, Gerard Fenwick had pointed out with a slight grimace, was one of Clarissa's legacies. The faience lions either side of the Gothic fireplace had once belonged to Catherine the Great. A lot of the books bore the coat of arms of Henry VIII or Elizabeth I. There were books printed on *papier vélin pur fil Lafuma*.

'She recognized him at dinner that night as he started recounting his unsavoury escapades from the mid-sixties,' Major Payne was explaining. 'He boasted of deflowering debutantes and of stealing their jewellery and keeping trophies. He then said that all the jewels his wife was wearing at that very moment had belonged to his victims.'

'And then Hortense got her second and much greater shock, which probably unhinged her and led her to do what she did,' said Antonia. 'Lord Remnant had pointed to the bracelet Clarissa was wearing. Hortense recognized it instantly. It had belonged to her once. It was fashioned like a coiled cobra and was known as the Keppel Clasp.'

It was three weeks later and they were sitting in the library at Remnant Castle.

Gerard Fenwick, thirteenth Earl Remnant, looked up from the notes he had been making. 'She put two and two together? The truth came to her in a flash? This is awfully good. Awfully good.' He wore country tweeds, twills, fawn suede shoes and a red-and-white neck-square tied at a jaunty angle. He looked relaxed and happy. One wouldn't have thought that that very morning his solicitors had warned him the divorce he was contemplating might turn out to be protracted, expensive and, very possibly, acrimonious.

Payne drew a forefinger across his jaw. 'There was only one Keppel Clasp. Hortense told us it was quite unique. She also admitted it had been stolen from her. So we knew that there couldn't be any mistake.'

'You had your Eureka moment.' Gerard nodded. 'That sudden, exultant sense of revelation, when the detective sees with absolute certainty the answer to the puzzle. I've been wondering about it. The image is quite striking, you know.'

'What image?'

'The multicoloured pieces of a spherical puzzle whirling wildly, round and round, and then, piece by piece, clicking together into a perfect globe . . . *Is* that how it happens?'

'More or less,' Antonia said. It wasn't quite like that, but why disappoint him?

'How terribly exciting. I do disapprove of murder, mind, but this is terribly exciting. How did you work things out exactly?'

'Well, we saw a photograph of Hortense wearing the bracelet. Hugh then remembered spotting that same bracelet on Clarissa's wrist in the *Gonzago* video. And then Louise Hunter told me what Lord Remnant had said at dinner – and she confirmed that Clarissa had been wearing the Keppel Clasp. She also said Hortense had looked extremely shocked – sick as a parrot.'

'There was a book I read as a boy. Cannot remember what

240

it was about, but it had a bloody marvellous title. *The Clue of the Coiled Cobra.*' Gerard Fenwick glanced at the high Gothic bookshelves surmounted by niches containing the busts of Homer, Horace and other ancient men of letters. 'By someone called Bruce Campbell . . . There it is – I think that's the one – between *Bonjour Tristesse* and Burton's *Anatomy of Melancholy*. It shouldn't be there at all.'

'You haven't been trying to arrange the books thematically, have you?' Payne asked.

'No, of course not. Wouldn't dream of it. Tradewell has. A damned silly thing to do, but then Tradewell hasn't been himself. I've been humouring him.'

As though on cue, the door opened and Tradewell brought them coffee. The Remnant butler's expression was lugubrious. His eyes were bloodshot and his lower lip trembled. He wore black. His master – his *real* master this time – had been cremated only a couple of days earlier. At the funeral Tradewell had created something of a stir by falling on his knees and praying with his hands clasped above his head.

Antonia was intrigued by the coffee cups – round in shape, made of thin eighteenth-century china and decorated with blue and gold phoenixes floating up from the fires beneath them.

Needless to say, the coffee was excellent.

'Such things happen in bad dreams, from which one awakens in panic and terror,' Payne went on. 'At dinner that night Hortense found herself sitting opposite the man who had raped her forty-five years before, who had made her pregnant and – as though that were not enough – who, by a terrible trick of fate, had married her daughter.'

'Who was also his daughter,' said Antonia.

'My brother married his own daughter,' Gerard said meditatively. 'Well, that's the kind of thing Roderick *would* do. He was always a most peculiar fellow.'

'Hortense told us that it was her brother-in-law who fathered Clarissa,' Antonia said. 'That was a lie.'

'Clarissa is in the rather curious position of being an earl's daughter *and* an earl's relict,' said Payne. 'So she could be addressed as Lady Clarissa – as well as Lady Remnant.'

'You are absolutely right, Payne. How funny. D'you think someone should give the *Debrett*'s people a tinkle?'

'We believe the shock proved too great for Hortense.' Antonia took a sip of coffee. 'While we were waiting for the police, she told us what she felt. Horror – revulsion – outrage – an overpowering desire for revenge. She experienced a great sense of *urgency*, she said. Her daughter's marriage. It was all wrong. *Really* wrong. It mustn't be allowed to continue.'

'Earlier that same day Hortense had seen Lord Remnant put the silencer on the gun,' said Payne. 'She knew he kept the gun in his desk. The moment she realized who he was, she left the dinner table, went up to his study and took the gun. The best time to kill him, she decided, was during the dumbshow. She admitted she had no misgivings about framing Stephan. She knew Clarissa would never allow the police to get involved. Clarissa believed Stephan had killed Quin, mistaking him for his stepfather.'

'But it was Hortense who made that mistake,' said Antonia.

'We believe Lord Remnant guessed that Hortense was planning to kill him. He saw the look on her face at dinner. The shock and the dismay and the pure horror. He watched her dash out of the room like a bat out of hell. Later he discovered his gun had disappeared from his desk.'

'He didn't realize who she was?'

'No, Fenwick, he didn't. He never recognized her. He simply assumed she hated him because he had made her feel a fool. He thought her a mad old woman. He was not in the least perturbed. Well, your brother enjoyed playing games with people. He had a penchant for psychological experiments—'

'He decided to turn Hortense's hatred of him to his own advantage,' said Antonia.

'Let me get this thing clear. My brother had been planning to kill Peter Quin, but now he decided to step back and let her do his dirty work for him?'

'Yes. *He let her kill Peter Quin.*'

'That, I imagine, was the reason he felt so amused later on, as he lay doggo in his bathroom,' said Payne. 'The irony of the situation must have titillated him. It made him giggle.'

'Hortense told us some of the truth when we first talked to her,' Antonia said. 'She admitted to being out of the room at the crucial time, so we suspected her in a vague kind of way from the very start. She said she had gone to the loo.'

'What she in fact did was run out on the terrace, shoot the man she believed was Lord Remnant, drop the gun, then return to the drawing room,' said Payne.

'You are forgetting the Bottom head,' Antonia said. 'Before she did the shooting, she held up the Bottom head for a moment, hoping it would be seen by someone in the room. She admitted she wanted to make people believe Stephan was the killer. She knew the police would never be involved, she said.'

'She makes a jolly interesting psychological study, don't you think?' Gerard Fenwick glanced at Antonia, then at Payne.

'Absolutely fascinating,' said Antonia.

'I am sure Freud has written something about this sort of behaviour . . . We've got a book somewhere. There it is!' Gerard Fenwick pointed. '*The Loss of Reality in Neurosis and Psychosis* – next to *Diagnosing Depression in Donkeys.*'

'The second act of the drama took place here, at Remnant Castle. It was also the final act,' Payne said. 'Hortense phoned Clarissa to ask how she was and Clarissa blurted out the truth about the dead man not being really dead. Clarissa made it clear it was Peter Quin who had died.'

'She also revealed that her husband was at Remnant,' said Antonia. 'She told Hortense that her husband was blackmailing her.'

'Most importantly, Clarissa told Hortense that the marriage hadn't been consummated, but that Lord Remnant was eager to exercise his marital rights. This decided Hortense. She came to Remnant Castle determined not to allow your brother to go to bed with Clarissa. Incest was something she simply could *not* allow, she said.'

'Did you say you found the wretched woman with a smoking gun in her hand? But how the deuce did you know which room was my brother's? The place is a bloody labyrinth. Even I get confused sometimes.'

'It was the gunshot that sent us in the right direction.'

'What did she do when she saw you? She didn't try to shoot you, did she?'

'No. She handed over the gun, then sat down and chatted to us. She sat perched forward, knees together, head bowed, the palms of her hands flat together with the fingers pointing away from her, like a nun praying.'

'She was only too willing to fill in the gaps for us. I made her a cup of tea,' Antonia said. 'It was all rather cosy. When she had told us the whole story, she asked Hugh to call the police.'

Major Payne was looking out of the open window. The lawns were freshly mown, the shrubs clipped and a bevy of footmen could be seen rubbing away at the ancient statuary. Spring seemed to have come at last, with a vengeance, and little ripples of heat mist danced above the stone-flagged terrace.

'I see you have been busy, Fenwick,' he said.

'One must do one's bit. *Noblesse oblige* and all that kind of rot. This place used to be a veritable House of Usher, too macabre for words, but it all looks awfully pretty now, doesn't it, in an Arcadian kind of way?'

'Indeed it does . . . What are the advantages of being an earl, if you don't mind my asking?'

'The advantages, Payne? *Are* there advantages? Well, it's easier to get a table in a restaurant. Or a seat at the Coronation, I imagine. I'd enjoy that. Though heaven knows when that's going to be.'

'Are there any disadvantages?'

'Of course there are. Some people seem to think that if one's an earl, one is an absolute bloody fool. That's perhaps why I haven't been able to get any publisher interested in my stuff. They are all socialists, aren't they? The irony is that I am something of a socialist m'self.'

'No, not all of them,' Antonia said. 'Incidentally, those extracts you let me read earlier on show great promise. Only you should try to complete things, you know.'

'I am afraid I'm not frightfully disciplined.' Gerard Fenwick sighed. 'Well, my next effort will be something in your line, Antonia, and I have every intention of completing it. A detective story, which will also be a multi-layered psychodrama . . . I found your deductions frightfully stimulating. I say, would you like one of my cigars, Payne?'

'I would. Davidoff Grand Cru?'

'Yes, they are awfully good.'

'Thank you, Fenwick. I mean Remnant.'

The two men lit their cigars.

Gerard said dreamily, 'My story will be about a man who dies *twice*.'

The Murder of Gonzago (2)

It was a couple of days later.

Gerard Fenwick, thirteenth Earl Remnant, sat at his desk at Remnant, a brand new laptop before him.

'I see you mean business this time,' Renée Glover said with a smile. 'Beginnings are always difficult, aren't they?'

'No, not really,' Gerard said. 'Not this one.'

He was about to embark on a novel, which he had provisionally called *The Murder of Gonzago*.

Gerard knew exactly where to begin:

Three minutes passed before they realized he was dead and another two before it was established how he had died, though any suspicious observer might have argued that at least one of the five people in the room had been aware of both facts all along . . .

THE END